HOAX

HOAX

LEANNA SAIN

Lamplighter Mystery and Suspense is an imprint of LPCBooks
a division of Iron Stream Media
100 Missionary Ridge, Birmingham, AL 35242
ShopLPC.com

Cover design by Elaina Lee

Iron Stream Media serves its authors as they express their views, which may not express the views of the publisher.

This is a work of fiction. Names, characters, and incidents are all products of the author's imagination or are used for fictional purposes. Any mentioned brand names, places, and trademarks remain the property of their respective owners, bear no association with the author or the publisher, and are used for fictional purposes only.

Library of Congress Control Number: 2021943631

ISBN-13: 978-1-64526-327-2
E-book ISBN: 978-1-64526-328-9

PRAISE FOR *HOAX*

Filled with a good mix of tension and tenderness, Leanna Sain's fast-paced mystery, *Hoax,* hooked me from the start. Sain put together a cast of distinct, believable characters whose desires, delusions, fears, and hopes drive the action and intertwine to make for a richer story.

~Clarice G. James, Women's contemporary fiction author, including *The Least of These*

In *Hoax*, Leanna Sain guides unforgettable characters through a multi-faceted mystery to a thrilling climax and satisfying resolution. Well-crafted fiction, delightful reading.

~Donn Taylor, Author of *Rhapsody in Red*; *The Lazarus File*

"Wrapped in intrigue and gut-clenching suspense, *Hoax* mixes dreams with reality against the background of a fine art heist."

~Erin Hanson, Contemporary impressionist painter
www.erinhanson.com

From the moment Lacey discovers a mysterious birth certificate hidden in her parents' home you'll be hooked on *Hoax*. Leanna Sain has written a novel that's impossible to put down. The intriguing characters, crisp dialogue, and unexpected twists tempt you to turn page after page.

~Tina Boesch, Author of *Given*

Acknowledgments

There's an African proverb that a former First Lady made popular: "It takes a village to raise a child." Well, since I classify my books as being my "babies," I guess the same could be said for the birthing and growing of a novel. With that in mind, I have some people to thank.

A big thank you goes out to Trooper Robert Grayson for sharing his time and several of his more memorable law enforcement tales with me. The same goes for Christina Creasman. They say "truth is stranger than fiction," and boy, are they right. I can't make all this stuff up.

I'd like to thank my writer's groups: Weavers of Words (WOW), and Blue Ridge Writer's Group for helping me hone another story into a finished product.

Special thanks goes to my editor and superpower, Darla Crass, as well as the rest of the crowd at Lamplighter/Iron Stream. Thanks for being such an amazing team.

Another big thank you to Dr. Leisa Rundquist, art professor at UNC-Asheville (and Heidi Kelley for putting me in touch with her), as well as friends, Jill McLeod and Ashley Page. Your help was vital in the research part of writing this book. Since I knew next to nothing about the world of art forgery, I needed all the help I could get.

To painter-extraordinaire, Erin Hanson, whom I discovered while searching for a style of painting I wanted JD Campbell to have. Your wonderful paintings inspired me throughout the writing of this book. I want you to know I've fallen in love with your work and dream of owning a print of "Lilies on the Lake" someday.

For medical advice, I once again turned to my nurse friend, Lisa Gundersen. She's always there when I need to incapacitate someone in a book.

As always, I couldn't have written this book without the love and support of my husband, best friend, alpha reader/editor, and most enthusiastic cheerleader, Randy. Thank you for lifting me up.

And finally (but most importantly), I want to thank God for giving me this story and the ability to tell it well.

Dedicated to Lisa Dillon
Your Halloween party started it all.

hoax (hōks) *n.* 1. An act intended to deceive or trick. 2. Something that has been established or accepted by fraudulent means.

"We can only talk about the bad forgeries, the ones that have been detected. The good ones are still hanging on museum walls."

~Theodore Rousseau
Metropolitan Museum of Art

CHAPTER ONE

Lacey

The tented fold of worn, black leather, thick with someone's identity, lies face down on the packed sand. A lost wallet. I look up, squint into the distance, searching the deserted beach for the owner. A salted breeze whips ribbons of copper curls across my face and I run an impatient hand through the unruly mass, finger-combing it out of my eyes.

No one in sight. Oh, wait! There on the horizon. Little more than a smudge, but I know it's a man. I also know the wallet is his. Snatching it up, I sprint toward the stranger, calling out for him to stop. But he's too far away to hear me, and I soon yell myself hoarse.

It isn't long before my lack of athleticism has me bent over, clutching the stitch in my side and dragging air into my desperate lungs in painful gasps.

When I'm able to look again, there isn't a soul in sight. The man is gone.

Now what?

My eyes drop to the wallet I hold gingerly in my hand. I need to open it, find out if there's any contact information inside so I can get it back to its rightful owner, but now it feels threatening, as dangerous as a hand grenade with the pin already pulled.

Don't be silly, I chide myself. It's just a wallet. How can it hurt you?

I flip it open and freeze when I see the plastic-sleeved photograph.

My dad's eyes stare at me from a stranger's face.

***

I woke up with a gasp. The dream was already blurring at the edges, quickly fading away. It seemed important for me to remember the details, so I struggled to bring it back into focus.

The shoreline had been nondescript, definitely not Fernandina Beach on Amelia Island where I lived, and nowhere nearby, judging by the lack of crowds. Of course, it *was* a dream. That was the only way a Florida beach would be deserted. Maybe my subconscious longed for a coastline from the past—wide, white-sanded, and mostly uninhabited.

I compared the photograph in my dream to the one that had sat on my mother's side of my parents' dresser for as long as I could remember. Taken shortly after I was born, Dad still had a head full of curly, dark-brown hair. He'd been young, and very good looking— a dreamy-eyed artist.

Mmm. Make that a *wannabe* artist. Dad had never achieved the talent or acclaim celebrated by his own father, my granddad, but he was handsome. You had to give him that.

It was those arresting cerulean-blue eyes of his in the photograph—same as the ones in my dream, same as photos I'd seen of my granddad's. They seemed to have the ability to pierce through the hardest of hearts when he turned on his charm. I'd seen him do it many times. No doubt there'd been a whole line of girls dreaming of the day when he might glance their way, show them some small bit of attention. I'd often heard my mother say she felt lucky to be the wife of Daniel Campbell. Maybe she was trying to convince herself or maybe she really felt that way, but I had no way of knowing now.

Both of my parents were gone: Dad from cancer a few years back, and if Mom hadn't drowned two months ago—I swallowed the lump in my throat that formed at the thought—early onset Alzheimer's would have continued to chip away at her mind and body until there was nothing left. It had already stolen so much of the amazing, creative, intelligent woman she'd been.

Although I didn't know what the dream meant, I was pretty sure it was a result of stress, unlike the dreams I usually had. No, this one was more normal, a coherent whole, not the random flash of seemingly unrelated snapshots I usually got. Also, there wasn't a corpse, which was a dead giveaway. I groaned at the unintended pun.

I was sure some people thought having the ability to dream murders before they happened was good, but believe me, it wasn't. I usually only ever got flashes of the event, seldom more than bits and pieces of clues, and in no particular order, so I could never figure anything out quickly enough to actually *stop* the murders from happening. So what was the use in that?

It wasn't always murders. When I was younger, I was plagued with déjà vu—things I "remembered" already happening that hadn't occurred yet. When I realized I dreamed of things before they happened, it didn't occur to me that wasn't normal. I thought everyone dreamed that way.

Then my mother explained.

Apparently I had a "gift," something inherited from the women on her side of the family. All of them had it—at least six known generations of them—some more than others. It was strong in Mom in spite of the Alzheimer's, and I was thankful for that. I wouldn't still be alive otherwise. I believed this gift, or "sight," or whatever one chose to call it, had somehow struggled through the webs mucking up Mama's brain and told her to load that flare gun that day on Coop's yacht right before he tried to kill me—the same as he'd done with the rest of the Lullaby Murders victims. It was that action that saved my life. I was certain of it. There was no other way to explain how a gun that was supposedly empty was suddenly loaded.

Anyway, I was blessed with this *thing*, too. It was anything but normal, and it became my secret.

Things changed when I hit puberty. That's when I had the first "murder dream." A local child went missing, I dreamed pieces of the scene—which included the girl's dead body—and I realized I couldn't keep quiet about it any longer.

So I went to the police. And well, *that* didn't go as planned. Suffice it to say that's when the "crazy Campbell girl" label started circulating. I kept my mouth shut about it after that, hoping people would forget, but that only made it feel like a pot had been set to simmer. It bubbled quietly on a back burner, ready to boil over when I least expected it.

And it did, with more regularity than I would've liked. After all, Jacksonville was a big city—only forty minutes or so south of Amelia Island where Fernandina Beach was located—

and since my dreams seemed to deal only with killings that occurred within a fifty-mile radius, Jacksonville fell within that parameter. So I'd have a dream and then, more often than not, two or three days later, I'd hear about a murder on the news. Not every time though, so I had no way of knowing how many of these murders actually happened. But it was enough that it made me thankful that I didn't live close to a bigger, more crime-ridden city.

I dealt with a lot of guilt. I tried to ease that by reminding myself that I never dreamed enough clues to actually *stop* the murders from happening. But the only thing that helped even a little was when I'd hear that the police had actually caught the person responsible.

The fact that this wallet dream didn't include a body was a big relief.

I glanced at my alarm clock. Six twenty-nine? Shoot! I had hoped I could roll over and get another few minutes of sleep, but that was wishful thinking. I hurriedly fumbled for the off button before it reached the dreaded six-thirty mark and began its obnoxious shrieking tirade.

I rolled to my feet, stumbled to the bathroom. Shower first, then coffee.

Wiping the steam from the mirror a few minutes later, I grabbed a wide-toothed comb and began working it through my tangled curls, my mind already ticking off the list of things— wedding and otherwise—needing to be done that day before I headed to work.

"In hindsight, maybe you should've allowed yourself a bit more planning time," I spoke to my reflection. "You've been through more in the past two and a half months than most people experience in a lifetime. Being the target of a psychopathic serial killer and barely making it out alive"—I counted off on my first finger—"having a mother with Alzheimer's disease, losing her in a tragic accident, having to plan her funeral, and now planning a wedding." I stared at my thumb, which represented the fifth on my list of major things. "Even a simple ceremony is a huge undertaking. That's a lot of heavy lifting in a short amount of time."

My reflection made a face.

Thinking the word "funeral" caused a wave of sadness to wash over me. The woman who had been Eve Campbell—my mother—had been gone for much longer than the two months since her funeral. Alzheimer's had seen to that. But even with a brain resembling Swiss cheese, she still *looked* like my mother. Now she was gone, and I missed her. Terribly. Up to the time of her death, there'd been occasional moments when she was lucid, when we'd connected. I'd adopted a sort of Dickinsonian attitude about those instances, echoing the poet's sentiment that "Forever is composed of Nows." As those "Nows" with Mama got fewer and farther between, it only caused me to cherish them all the more when they did happen.

The cold, hard fact was: my wedding would happen without Mama. No mother of the bride—at least not in person, though I was sure she'd be there in spirit. But it wouldn't be the same. She was supposed to *be* there. To help me with my wedding. To share it all. That's the way it was *supposed* to be. It hurt to realize that couldn't happen, that it might not have happened even if she hadn't died. Alzheimer's stole that away from me. I hated that disease.

Tears glistened in the brown eyes of my reflection. I blinked them away and whispered Mama's oft-repeated words, "There's always, always, always something to be thankful for." Yes. There was.

Ford. My vision glazed over. Suddenly, I wasn't seeing my reflection in the mirror any more. Instead, I saw his sexy, sun-streaked hair, gorgeous sea-green eyes, tall, muscular frame, and a smile that made me go weak at the knees. The vision was so real I could even hear his sweet Southern drawl, the *g's* dropping like pennies in a wishing well. Ford Jamison. From high school crush, to hated enemy, to the man I'd be marrying in a week.

A week!

I still had to pinch myself to make sure it was real and that I wasn't dreaming.

I shook away the vision, refocusing on my reflection again, and reached for the hairdryer. Good thing I was good at multitasking. I could daydream about Ford and get ready at the same time.

***

"Take that!" I slammed the broom's bristles down on the huge and potentially lethal spider with a *thud*. My words sounded hollow, echo-y due to being in my parents' closet. Correction, *my* closet. I still lived in the home where I'd lived my whole life. And after Ford and I married, we'd live there together.

I'd been sifting through the last odds and ends on the shelves, in search of my mother's vintage sapphire hair combs, which I wanted to use in my wedding "'do" for both the "something old" and the "something blue." I'd just found the little box they were in when I saw the suspicious movement at the edge of my vision.

Those combs had been handed down to the oldest daughter in my mother's family for years. Mama just never got the chance to pass them on to me before it was too late. I couldn't help but wonder if they had some weird link to my dreaming ability, since it seemed every woman in the family who'd had possession of them also had the "gift," but I'd never taken the thought further. It was probably just a coincidence, but then again, maybe it wasn't.

Argh! No! The creepy spider was still alive. "We had an agreement," I hissed, a little breathless now that my heart was in hyperdrive. "Any place *outside* the house is yours. I don't bother you; you don't bother me. But *inside* this house is *mine*." I punctuated each sentence with a *whack*, getting harder each time. "You broke the bargain, encroached into my space. Now, you die!"

Uh-oh. That last wallop hit the wall and knocked one of the shiplap boards loose. Great. Something else to do. Oh well. Should be a simple fix. All I needed was a hammer and a nail.

I'd pound that sucker right back into place. I eyed the—now very dead—spider with grim satisfaction. I also needed a tissue.

After flushing the spider down the toilet, I grabbed my hammer, ready to make my repair. Squatting so I could reach the section of wall in the corner just above the baseboard, I realigned the board and, when I pressed it into place, I heard a *click.*

Huh?

Pressing it again made another *click,* and it popped out about an inch. I leaned closer for a better look.

A door? Why was there a door hiding away in the corner of the closet like this? I hooked a finger over the edge and pulled. The board swung open easily to reveal a large opening about a foot square. I thought I could see something at the bottom, but I wasn't about to put my hand in there to find out right after killing that spider. First things first. I needed some light.

One hand soon held my cell phone, aiming a beam of light into the dark, while my other hand held the broom ready just in case. Good. No signs of any other eight-legged wads of death. But I was right—there *was* something inside.

I reached a fearful hand in to retrieve a gray metal container, pulling it carefully out of the hole and into the light.

It looked like a firebox; the kind you put important papers in to protect them from flames. I frowned. Why? My parents already had a safe deposit box at the bank. I found that out when I'd had to access it after my dad's death to get papers I needed to care for Mom. So, why would they need this?

I stared in confusion at the hole in the wall again, reached out, and pushed the door closed. The hinges were tucked neatly into the corner, making it all but invisible. If I hadn't accidentally hit the wall with the broom, I never would've known it was there. It was so camouflaged that even knowing exactly where it was, it was hard to see. The secrecy of it made my stomach clench a little.

I gazed at the case I held in hands that began to tremble a little with sudden dread. The coldness of the metal caused an involuntary shiver to travel up my spine. No lock, I noticed.

Good thing. I'd have never found the key for it. What could it hold? The unforeseen troubles of Pandora's Box came to mind. Not a very comforting thought, but hidden away like this, I could only assume it held secrets and I was afraid they wouldn't be the good kind.

Taking a deep breath, I pressed the button to open the latch. Boldfaced words lined the top of the paper I held in trembling fingers:

State of Florida, Duval County, Certificate of Live Birth.

For a split second, I wondered why a copy of my birth certificate was hidden away in a closet instead of the safe deposit box at the bank where I knew the original to be. I had just retrieved it last week when Ford and I applied for our marriage license. Then my eyes went to the next line. In the blank where my name should be, it said "no name given."

What? That didn't make sense. Mama had known my name from the moment they'd laid me across her stomach. She'd loved to tell the story. I'd heard it many times. It was my hair—wisps of the damp red swirling across my tiny head that had given her the inspiration. She said it reminded her of delicate Irish lace. Hence my name: Lacey Elaine Campbell.

The next entry made me gasp. "Sex: male." *Male?*

This wasn't *my* birth certificate.

My gaze jumped to the next line. "Birthplace: Duval County. Birthdate: February 5, 1994."

I shook my head, confusion mushrooming. My birthday was March 6. This was a month *before* my birthday.

With growing dread, I scanned the next section. Father: Daniel Wade Campbell. Mother: Delilah Janine Edmunton. An address for each one; the beach house where I lived, and someplace in Jacksonville, respectively.

The certificate fluttered to the floor from my numb fingers. Questions, oh, so many questions whirled around and around in my brain like a never-ending vortex, but one trumped them all.

Who the heck was Delilah Edmunton?

CHAPTER TWO

Delilah

Twenty-eight years earlier
Everyone had dreams. Delilah Edmunton's was to paint like JD Campbell. She'd been trying to imitate his work for years, experimenting with depth of values, saturation of colors, studying techniques of the old masters whose work had somewhat similar characteristics. Degas' work had a luminescent quality, so did John Singer Sargent's, but those came from the use of many thin, translucent layers of paint, glazes over each one that allowed light to travel through the layers, bounce off the canvas, and reflect back. The viewer's eyes mixed those layers in order to see the final colors. That whole tedious process flew in the face of open impressionism's minimal brushstrokes and impasto application. So where did the luminescence come from?

She didn't know, but she wouldn't give up until she solved that mystery.

Out of breath, red-faced, and damp with perspiration, she slipped into the back of the auditorium where she'd see JD kick off the exhibition of his paintings at Jacksonville Museum of Contemporary Art, and eased into the first unoccupied seat she could find.

Made it, she thought as she surreptitiously used her sleeve to blot the sweat from her forehead when she couldn't find a tissue in her purse. She pulled her thick, dark hair up off her neck and into an untidy ponytail, securing it with the hair tie she always kept on her wrist.

Shoot! The program had already started. Her search for free parking had caused her to circle in an ever-widening loop, and by the time she'd finally located one, she was blocks away and had to run all the way back. But she was here now, and that's all that mattered.

She craned her neck to see around the man in front of her. Just her luck. The guy was freakishly tall and wide. He took up the equivalent of two entire seats—his and half of each of the ones on either side of him. Should she try to move? No, there was nothing closer, and since she'd come in late, she didn't want to draw attention to herself by changing places. She gave a frustrated sigh, and leaned as far to the left as she could without toppling into the aisle.

"Mr. Campbell?" The woman on the platform motioned toward a man on the front row. "Would you mind stepping up here with me?"

A shiver ran up Delilah's spine as she watched him join the woman on stage. There he was. JD Campbell. He looked bigger in life, even more amazing than any of the pictures she'd seen of him; prematurely silver hair, close-clipped goatee the same color, striking blue eyes. She could see their brilliance from here.

"I can't tell you folks how honored the Jacksonville Museum of Contemporary Art is to be exhibiting JD Campbell's latest work for the next month. We here at MOCA worked hard to get him, and I take a lot of pride in it. It's quite a coup." She gave a coquettish smile and continued her rambling, but Delilah barely heard her. Her fascinated eyes watched him fidget and sway from side to side. The restless movement gave her a sense of restrained strength, like a jaguar in a cage.

She could hardly believe she was actually seeing him in person. He'd been her idol and role model since she was nine years old, hooked from the moment she'd seen that photograph of one of his paintings in a magazine thirteen years ago. His art was her drug of choice.

The fact that he was here surprised her. Everything she'd read said he was a borderline hermit, hardly venturing from his little beach house, forty minutes north of here, in a little place called Fernandina Beach out on Amelia Island. She'd managed to track down his actual address. She considered it to be the most valuable piece of knowledge she'd gleaned from her frequent internet searches.

Armed with that information, she'd driven up there. The town itself was a charming place that practically oozed Victorian architecture and history. Cute, but not what she was looking for. He lived on the beach itself, which was a few miles east.

She'd never forget the first time she saw his house: two-story, plain white with black shutters, perched atop the familiar thick wooden stilts associated with beachfront property. A small vignette framed with the blue Atlantic Ocean on either side. It seemed both surprising and so right for him to live there. Surprising, because such an ordinary dwelling could be home to such an extraordinary man, and so right because it was such a contrast to the vibrancy he was capable of with his art.

Since that day, she'd driven up there numerous times, hoping—always hoping—for a glimpse of the man she practically worshipped.

It was because of his hermit tendencies that she'd been half afraid she'd read the announcement wrong or that he'd be a no-show at today's event. Just because he had an exhibition at MOCA, didn't mean he had to be here to speak to all these people. Her gaze swept across the auditorium. There must be three hundred or more people here. She nearly burst with pride. Look at him—holding it together in front of a crowd like this.

JD Campbell. She was in the same room as JD Campbell! Breathing the same air. She wanted to pinch herself to make sure it was real, but was afraid it might be a dream, and she didn't want to wake up.

The speaker went on about Campbell's minimal brush-strokes, his impasto application of paint. Open impression-ism—words coined to described his painting style. He used a limited palette of pure, unmuddied color, and with it he somehow captured the spontaneity of light and motion. It allowed him to bring the natural beauty of outdoors to his canvases. You could always tell whether a painting was a JD Campbell. They seemed to glow—from the inside out—with a sort of otherworldly light. Like he'd painted them around a candle.

Shut up and let *him* speak, she wanted to scream. We want to hear *him*, not you! But the annoying woman appeared to be in love with the sound of her own voice and seemed to be just getting warmed up. Delilah gave a disgusted sigh and while her eyes never strayed from the man on stage, her mind wandered.

Like he'd painted around a candle. Yes, that was a good description of his work. And if the woman ever gave him a chance to speak, maybe he'd hint at his secret. She knew it was some substance he added to his paint—something known only to him—that gave it that special essence of light. She knew he mixed his own oils. That had been mentioned in several of the articles she'd read. But so far, no one had been able to successfully copy his recipe. No one had even come close. Is was the art community's version of the "missing link." The secret to JD Campbell's amazing paintings remained a mystery.

The speaker finally stopped droning and Delilah felt her pulse quicken. This was it, her chance to hear whether his voice sounded any differently than it did in all the recordings she'd heard. Ms. Blabbermouth flung her arm out toward JD in a "ta-dah" gesture, following that with clapping. The audience erupted in applause.

All he did was smile and nod at them. After about a minute of this, he turned and followed the speaker out a side door. When it swung shut behind them, people began murmuring, gathering their things. The mountain-of-a-man in front of her lurched to his feet, lumbered out into the aisle.

She was stunned. That was it? He hadn't gotten a chance to say a word, and it was over? She drew a deep, disappointed breath before reluctantly standing. Try to look on the bright side, she thought, trying not to feel cheated. This will just allow you more time in the exhibition hall with his artwork—

the real thing, not photographs in a magazine or newspaper—time enough to get up close and personal with all those lovely paintings. Hurry now, so you can beat the crowd.

***

"Excuse me. Miss?"

Delilah reluctantly pulled her attention away from the painting of the exquisite sunset over a salt marsh at high tide. The artist's point of view was below eye level, up through the marsh grasses, making the sky resemble bits of mosaic, the stems acting as the lead of stained glass. The colors sang. She could swear she heard them. Their glow was so bright and intense it made her feel like she should be wearing sunglasses. Dazed, she turned toward the immaculately dressed young man who wore a badge bearing the MOCA insignia with the name Marc Lawter engraved in the shiny brass. "Yes?"

"The museum is closing for the day."

She glanced in surprise at her watch. Four fifty-seven? Already? "Yes. I'm so sorry. I lost track of time. One more minute?"

His smile seemed plastic. She could feel his impatience, his anxiousness to clock out and leave. He finally gave her a reluctant nod and walked away. Alone once more, she turned back to the painting, fighting the urge to squint. She wanted to absorb all that light and color and amazingness one last time. After a minute, she leaned forward until her nose almost touched the painting and inhaled deeply, filling her lungs. Was there still a hint of linseed oil?

She drew another deep breath, then stepped back. It was time to go. Better to leave on her own than to be escorted out by the guard. She turned and stepped around the corner, directly into the long strides of someone hurrying toward the front doors. The unexpected blow made her ears ring and caused her to stumble backward. She would have fallen if a strong hand hadn't grabbed her arm to steady her.

"Oh! I'm so sorry. Are you all right?" a deep voice asked. "I didn't know there was anybody left in here. I thought they'd already run everybody out."

She shook away the daze, looked up, and gasped when her eyes met a pair of very concerned, piercing blue ones. Silver hair gleamed in the gallery lights. "You're . . . you're—"

"JD Campbell, and so sorry for bulldozing you."

She waved away his concern with a trembling hand. "I'm fine," she answered in a shaky voice. "Just shocked. I thought you'd left right after the program."

He scoffed. "Well, that was my intent, but when Ms. Ballenger found out I hadn't had lunch, she insisted I join her and, well—"

She cocked an eyebrow. "If you're trying to tell me she's in love with the sound of her own voice, I already picked up on that."

The surprised look he gave her was almost comical, then he burst out laughing. He stuck out his hand. "You know my name. What's yours?"

She slipped her hand into his, thrilling at the strength and vitality she felt running through it. "Delilah Edmunton. I've been waiting most of my life to meet you."

His brow lifted. "Well, Delilah, you look pretty young, so most of your life can't have been very long."

She raised her chin in a prim way. "I'll have you know I'm twenty-two, and that's more than enough time."

"Twenty-two, huh?" Merriment sparkled in his eyes like sunshine on the ocean. "Well, I'm glad your long wait is over."

CHAPTER THREE

Ford

I'd just refilled my coffee mug for the third time since arriving at work that morning and was heading back to my office when raised voices coming down the hallway caught my attention. As the new chief of police, I felt I needed to keep abreast of what was going on in my department. I altered my course, veering toward the noise.

It didn't take much to draw a crowd here at the Fernandina Beach Police Department. So different from fast-paced Tallahassee where I'd been working for the last five years with the State Bureau of Investigation. Since Fernandina Beach was a small town, there usually wasn't a great deal to keep us busy. Our violent crime rate was low: forty-six percent lower than the rest of Florida and forty-two percent lower than the national average. Granted, those numbers didn't yet reflect what happened a couple of months previously when a crazy man used the words of a lullaby as his plan for a rash of murders. That one was personal since one of the intended victims was Lacey, my fiancée. Once they figured in those stats, our averages might never recover.

As a whole, though, other than the occasional vandalism, a few breaking and entering and shoplifting cases, and a car theft or two, this was a great place to live. I grew up here, was employed at this very station fresh out of the police academy. But when the opportunity to work for the Florida SBI fell into my lap, I felt like I'd hit the lottery. It was hardly that, but it initiated me into the unspeakable atrocities human beings do to one another. If that wasn't bad enough, add in the *miles* of bureaucratic red tape. It worked more in favor of the "bad guys" because of how it tied law enforcement's hands. Yes,

I knew there was protocol and I knew rules were necessary, but it seemed to me that the system was broken when law enforcement got treated like criminals for doing their job.

A buddy of mine had been involved in a shoot-out that resulted in a suspected murderer being killed, and Internal Affairs treated it just like a homicide— took his gun, car, and cell phone, drug-tested him, read him his rights, and put him on administrative leave. For doing his job.

They cleared him in the end—determined it "self-defense," but he retired early, so we lost a good agent. I blamed it on all the crap they put him through. I guess that's when my disenchantment with working for the "big guys" began. It made me long for a simpler existence, which is why I'd jumped at the opportunity when offered the police chief's position here. My experience with the SBI made me appreciate the slower, quieter, small-town life. But a little bit of excitement was okay, and from the sizeable number of people gathering around the booking desk, I wasn't the only one who felt that way. I eased into the fringes at the back of the crowd.

"Now, sir," Officer Dee Phillips said with a forced smile, "since you wouldn't cooperate with the arresting officer earlier, I'm going to ask you again to blow right here into this opening. Right here." She pointed, holding the Breathalyzer toward the young man's face. Poor Phillips. Trying to keep her cool in front of a growing audience took a toll. Clownish red circles of irritation bloomed under each of her eyes. It made me think of a boyhood outing to the circus.

"Naw, lady. I'm good," the man answered, shaking his head with a mellow smile. He swatted at the proffered mouthpiece, missing it entirely. "That machine's got bad mojo. Ain't drunk anyway. Just kinda sleepy. You got anything to eat? Some 'tater chips would be awesome, and I'd kill for a Pepsi. I'm 'bout to die of thirst."

I grunted, eyeing my watch. Ten 'til ten *a.m.* He'd either made an early start of it, or been at it all night. Probably the latter. The guy was in his early twenties, blond hair bunched into a scraggly ponytail, tattered blue jeans dangling from narrow hips. He was shirtless, sunburnt, and so thin I could count every one of his ribs. Well past the just-watching-my-carbs stage, this guy was borderline Holocaust survivor, with eyes so red he looked like he'd used Texas Pete hot sauce for eye drops. The smell of sweat, suntan lotion, and the unmistakable sweet/sour hint of burnt rope had wafted to the back of the room where I stood. No. He wasn't drunk. He was so high he was practically orbiting the earth. Forget about the Breathalyzer, they needed a urine specimen. I caught Officer Phillips' eye, miming the act of smoking a joint.

She nodded once. "On second thought, sir," Phillips tried again, "I'm going to need to get a urine sample from you. Take this cup and this officer will escort you down the hall to the—"

He frowned at the hand grasping his arm. "I ain't drunk, I tell ya—"

Something flickered, just below eye level, letting me know my assessment of his status was correct. I shouldered through the crowd. "I believe you," I said, gaining the attention of everyone present.

The guy's head swiveled around, red eyes trying to focus on me. He wore a bemused smile. "You do?"

"Absolutely. You are definitely not drunk."

His smile stretched wide and he swayed like a tall pine in a stiff breeze. "Does that mean I'm free to go?"

"Nope," I shook my head. "'Fraid not."

"Why not?" He tried to scowl, but he couldn't get his face to cooperate. "You just said—"

"I agreed that you weren't *drunk*. I didn't, however, agree that you weren't *high*." I could hear whispers and soft laughter behind me as others saw what I'd already seen.

"High?" His expression was comically outraged. "On what?"

"Oh, I don't know. Possibly— marijuana?"

He flushed. "I don't know what you're talking about."

Hmmm. That statement just proved the Pinocchio theory false. "Okay, possibly you know it as another name, but that doesn't change the fact."

"You can't prove that."

"Oh, but I can."

"How?"

"Well, you've heard the saying, 'Where there's smoke, there's fire'?"

"Smoke?"

I leaned forward until my nose almost touched his. "Next time you shove a joint in your pocket to save it for later, make sure it's not lit." I paused, waiting for him to try to make sense of my words. No luck there. Looked like I needed to spell it out. "Your pants are on fire."

It took a few seconds for my words to register, but when they did, he shrieked like a little girl, slapping frantically at the side of his jeans, swaying and stumbling, barely able to stay on his feet. The room erupted with laughter.

I turned to Officer Phillips. "You remember, as a kid, being secretly disappointed when someone said, 'Liar, liar, pants on fire' and it never really happened?" I asked her with a grin. "Well, today, that all changed right before our eyes. Book 'em, Danno. Uh, I mean, Phillips."

Her brow arched, amusement sparkled in her eyes.

I shrugged. "Sorry. I loved *Hawaii Five-O* as a kid, and I've always wanted to say that. You don't need the urine test. Just use the joint in his pocket for evidence, but try to get it before his pants burst into flame, will you?" I turned back toward my office. "Okay, everybody. Show's over. Back to work."

Laughter followed me down the hallway. My phone buzzed, indicating a text message. I turned it over, saw Lacey's name, and smiled before reading it. "Call me asap."

Uh-oh. My smile faded. I hit her number on speed dial and leaned back in my chair. I'd probably have to leave her a voice mail and we'd play phone tag for most of the day. We'd been doing a lot of that lately.

She surprised me by answering before it finished the first ring. "Ford!"

Her voice was frantic. I sat up straighter in my chair, suddenly all business. "What's up, sweetheart?"

"I was looking for Mom's hair clips and there was a huge spider and I broke the wall, or I thought I broke it, but it was really a hidey-hole and I found a birth certificate and I wonder if it had something to do with my dream—"

"Whoa, whoa, whoa. Hair clips, spider, hidey-hole, birth certificate, dream? You have too many subjects in that sentence. You're gonna need to whittle some of those down. Are you hurt?"

"No, but—"

"Is anybody around you bleedin'?"

"No—"

"Okay. Take a deep breath and *slowly* tell me what happened. One subject per sentence."

I heard her impatient sigh. "Is there any way you could get away for a few minutes and come over here?"

"Where's 'here'?"

"Home."

I glanced at the papers scattered across my desk. They could wait. "I'm leavin' now. I'll be there in ten minutes."

***

Lacey was waiting just outside her front door when I bounded up the stairs. I leaned forward to kiss her, but she grabbed my arm, dragged me into the house, and down the hallway. A woman on a mission. I wisely kept my mouth shut and allowed myself to be towed along behind her.

"There!" she pointed dramatically into the back corner of the empty closet. "That's where I found it."

I entered the closet, squatted for a better look. There was a hole in the wall, but not by accident. No, this was there on purpose, a sort of wall safe without the combination lock. It fit into the corner where it was all but invisible. Pretty clever. I glanced up at Lacey, who stood there, twisting her fingers, gnawing her lip. "What was in it?"

She hurried to the bed, and was back in a flash, shoving a gray metal box at me. "This."

I stood up, took it from her, and walked over to the dresser where I set it down. The lid popped open when I pressed the release.

It was empty.

"Oh!" she exclaimed. "Sorry. Here. This is what I found inside." She shoved a paper into my hand.

I scanned it, noting the embossed stamp at the bottom corner. Looked official. "Wow," I remarked, when finished.

"Wow?" she exploded. "That's all you can say? I find what amounts to a nuclear warhead, capable of blowing my world apart, and all you can say is, 'wow'?"

"Lace, I know findin' out your dad had an affair that resulted in a baby is upsettin', and findin' out like this." I gestured at the box, including the closet in the sweep of my hand. "Especially after almost being killed and losin' your mom a couple of months ago is bad, but 'blowin' your world apart'?"

"Is there a *good* way to find out one's dad cheated on one's mom?" Her big brown eyes filled with tears. "It's not even that I'm that surprised he had the affair. He always had a roving eye. I always hated it when he'd make his little comments about what other women were 'almost' wearing—right in front of me and Mom. She never said anything, but I could tell it upset her."

"Do you think she knew about this?" I waved the certificate.

She shrugged. "I don't know. She never said anything to me about it. If she did, I guess Alzheimer's was a blessing, in a horrible kind of way. A beautiful tragedy. She lost her memories of the bad things too.

"Dad started acting better after Mom was diagnosed," she continued. "I think it was sort of a wake-up call to him. I guess you could say it caused him to grow up, be the husband he was supposed to be. We helped each other with her care, at least until the cancer took him. That's not what I'm so upset about. It's the *timing* of it." She nodded to the certificate in my hand. "Look at the birthdate. He was born a month before I was. That makes him older."

"Yeah," I nodded in mock seriousness. "That usually happens when Person A has a birthday before Person B. Person

A tends to be older." I hoped she wouldn't get mad. I was trying to ease the tension.

"Don't think I don't know what you're doing." She gave an exasperated snort. "You're not getting it. This means Dad was involved with this woman right at the beginning of his and Mom's marriage. How could he do that? Newlyweds are usually so sickeningly in love with each other it's hard for other people to be in the same room with them. And he had an affair *then*?" Her voice broke on the last word, and tears welled up in her eyes. "Why did he even marry Mama if he was involved with someone else?" she wailed.

I tossed the birth certificate on the dresser beside the metal box before I gathered her into my arms, held her close, trying to absorb some of her pain and confusion. I wanted to lessen it for her if I could. "Listen, Lacey. I hate this happened, but we can't undo it. It's done. All we can do is to keep movin' forward." I waited for her sobs to calm, smoothing my hand down the length of her spine, slow and repetitive.

Once she'd quieted to an occasional snuffle, I ventured, "You mentioned a dream. You want to tell me about it?"

I was quiet when she finished, thinking about what it might mean. "Well, at least there's not a dead body this time," I said, trying to lighten things again, hoping it would work this time. "Different from your other dreams."

She let out a sound that was half sob and half giggle. "Yeah," she whispered. "At least there's that." After a moment of contemplative silence, she looked up. "I've always considered myself a bit of a visionary, so I guess it's true what Mama said. "'Little girls who dream grow up to be women with vision.'"

"I think I've seen that on a T-shirt," I quipped.

She rolled her eyes. "I'm glad Mama was a visionary too, in spite of her Alzheimer's. I wouldn't be here if she wasn't. I'm certain of that."

I swallowed hard, held her close, not wanting to remember that awful morning when I'd come so close to losing her, but unable to push the images from my mind. *Something* had warned Lacey's mother, told her what to do. There was no other way to explain how a flare gun that was supposed to be empty had somehow gotten loaded.

After a long moment, I cleared my throat, loosened my hold slightly. "Your dream probably has everything to do with this." I jerked my chin toward the dresser where the birth certificate lay. "You said your father's eyes looked at you from a stranger's face. I think it might be the half-brother you just found out about. It fits. Now, that doesn't mean I know what to do with the information yet, but we'll figure it out. I promise."

"I know," she replied, giving me a crooked smile. "That's why I told you. I couldn't handle this alone, not with everything else."

I tipped her head up with my finger so I could meet her eyes, then smoothed her rambunctious curls away from her face, sifting my fingers through the loose locks. "I'm sorry all this is happening, pilin' up on you, especially now with the weddin' and everything, but we'll get through it, together. I'm not so naïve as to think that everything will be perfect once we're married. We'll have hard times, times when we're sick, times when we're mad at each other; maybe even times when we don't like each other very much, but we'll get through those together too. I've decided to love you through it all, even when I might not like you."

She laughed softly and drew a quivering breath, her eyes deep pools of melted dark chocolate. "Chief Jamison, I believe you're a keeper."

"Don't look at me like that." I caressed the edge of her jaw with the backs of my fingers. "It makes me want to kiss you, and if I start, I won't stop."

She curved her hand against my cheek, then raised on her tiptoes, kissed the end of my nose, and whispered, "One more week."

"Right." I stepped back, when what I really wanted to do was pull her closer. Each point of contact—places our bodies had touched during our embrace—felt scorched and feverish. I breathed deep, expanded my lungs to their maximum capacity, and blew out in a rush, hoping to douse the fire a bit. "Okay, I'll take this with me"—I reached toward the dresser for the birth certificate—"do a little diggin' on Delilah Edmunton, see what I can find out. What do you have on tap for this morning?" I asked, heading for the door.

"I need to go by Liv's before going to work. We have to go through today's wedding stuff," she said, following me.

I slid her a sideways look. "You know, it would be a lot less stressful if we eloped. Sure you won't reconsider that option?"

"The answer is no," she laughed. "One, Miss Olivia Hale would never forgive me if I did that. We've been best friends since we were toddlers and we made a promise back when we were in elementary school that we'd be each other's maid of honor. You think I'm going to break that promise? I wouldn't be able to pull this thing together without her. Her, and her daily checklists, are what's getting me through this. She's in her element."

"Just kiddin', sweetheart. I want you to have the weddin' you want, but I have to say, since I'm next to useless with stuff like that, I'm glad Liv is helping you, even if she is a little kooky."

"Liv's not kooky! She's a genius businesswoman. I don't know where in the world she finds the things she stocks in her store, but she manages to sleuth out the most unique, educational items I've ever seen. I mean, she found 'superfood' teething toys made from kale, avocado, and broccoli, for heaven's sake. And you should see the giant lighted building blocks she just got in, and the glow-in-the-dark Play-Doh. The items she finds are perfect for what she's trying to do, which is not just entertain a child, but to grow his or her imagination."

"Wait. I wasn't tryin'—"

"She named the store too," Lacey went on, too intent on defending her friend to stop. "Par-a-dux—like *paradox*. Toys that aren't just toys. And her store sign—which she designed, by the way—ties in with that too. A pair of ducklings sporting rain boots and an umbrella. Ducks who don't like to get wet is a paradox, or in this case—a Par-a-dux."

I tilted my head and gave her a look. "Honey, I'm just sayin' she wears a pink tutu and sequined wings while riding a bike to work."

"Okay," she admitted a little grudgingly. "Maybe she's a little kooky, but there's method to her madness. It's the perfect marketing ploy. People follow her in droves right to her store."

"You're right about that," I chuckled. "I've seen it." Stopping at the door, I turned and stooped down a little so I could be eye level with her. "Listen, I need to get back to the station. You okay now?"

"Yes." She stepped forward, linked her hands around my neck. "Thank you for dropping everything and coming when I needed you. That's what I call love in action."

"Anytime, ma'am," I replied, brushing her lips with a quick kiss so as not to get heated up again. "I'll see you later, sweetheart."

***

As soon as I got back in my car, I dialed Myron, FBPD's computer geek who was such a help to me in the Lullaby* case.

"*Yell*-ow."

His telephone response made me roll my eyes as it usually did when I got it, but he was so invaluable at his job, I had to overlook it. Everybody had idiosyncrasies.

"Jamison here. Got something for you."

"Shoot."

"I need you to find out all you can about a Delilah Edmunton. Possible connection to Daniel Campbell."

"Lacey's dad?"

"Yeah." I could already hear his fingers tappity-tapping on his keyboard.

"You got it, boss."

I tossed my phone into the console and headed back to town. If there was anything to be found, Myron would find it.

*See Book 1-*Hush*

CHAPTER FOUR

Nick

Nick Bradford tested the library door to make sure it was locked before turning and heading for his truck.

Whew! He swiped at the sweat beading on his forehead. The sun was low in the sky, having long since dipped below the tall buildings to the west of the Jacksonville Public Library. Now it was rolling toward twilight, and *still* unbearably hot. The air felt weighted with the lingering heat of the day, practically shimmering with it. He groaned at the thought of what the rest of the summer would hold. Only early June and already it felt like the devil was funneling half the heat from hell through the city streets. Summer in Florida—definitely not for wimps.

This was what turned all those northern transplants into "halfbacks." They spent their whole adult lives dreaming of the day they'd retire and trade winter's snow and cold for Florida's warmth and sunshine. The reality of that decision hit them in the face like a sledgehammer by the time the calendar flipped to summer solstice. The shock of it sent many of them fleeing back north, usually stopping somewhere in the Carolinas or Virginia. They'd spend the brutal summer months in the cool mountains, then return in the fall once the temps inched down to a more bearable level.

This would be his twenty-ninth summer in Florida. He'd been born here. Well … not *here*, but a little less than an hour north and east of here in the little coastal town of Fernandina Beach. He wouldn't have thought there'd be that much difference in temperatures between the two places so close in proximity, but he didn't remember this kind of heat there. Of course, downtown Jacksonville didn't get the ocean breeze like

Fernandina Beach did, being on an island and all. Plus he'd been a kid then, and high temps didn't seem to bother them as much as it did adults. Either, or both, of them could be the reason.

He had a date tonight. That thought should fill him with anticipation, but considering his not-so-great track record in the dating realm of late, anticipation wasn't his dominant emotion.

Almost thirty and still single. That wasn't unusual, was it? The average age of people getting married nowadays was between twenty-five and thirty, with men even slightly older. That's what he'd read. Nothing to worry about, really, except that he was tired of dating and was ready to settle down. Problem was, he hadn't found anyone he'd like to settle down *with*. Of course, any woman fell woefully short when compared to—He stopped himself, and sighed. No use reliving that again. Hopefully, tonight's date with Marilee would be different.

He'd met Marilee at work. She was a grad student at Jacksonville University, doing research for her project, so she practically lived at the library. Packaging Science? He'd laughed when she told him what she was studying, thinking it was a joke. He hadn't known that was something one could major in, much less get a master's degree. Somehow they'd managed to maneuver past his *faux pas*, and here they were.

He had the evening all planned. She was really into modern art, and had mentioned an exhibit she was dying to see. When he'd looked up the details, he'd been surprised to learn that the gallery was in Fernandina Beach, on Amelia Island. Perfect. That should earn him points. After that, he'd made reservations at a little restaurant he'd heard some of his co-workers talking about. Black Pearl. New owner was Lacey Campbell, who happened to be the daughter of his second-grade teacher. He'd read a nice write-up about it in one of the food magazines. Or maybe in *Southern Living*.

Fernandina Beach. Thinking the name brought to mind his visit up there two months ago. He hadn't been back there since his parents had moved the family down to Ocala, when he was a boy. But when he'd spotted Eve Campbell's obituary in the paper, he knew he had to pay his respects to the woman who'd made such a difference in his life.

He'd been a struggling reader in first grade, spending the majority of that year stuck in something his teacher had dubbed "The Thinking Line." To this day he couldn't remember what it had been, exactly—his mind must've blocked all memories of it for protection—but the terror of being put in that stupid line was all he could think about. He'd passed, but that was probably only because the teacher hadn't wanted him in her class again. He'd spent the entire following summer dreading the thought of returning to school. Then he'd stepped into Mrs. Campbell's second-grade classroom and everything had changed.

Eve Campbell loved books. It was obvious to anyone who knew her. Her goal was to instill that same love into each and every one of her students, so she read to them. *A lot.* She acted out the story, spoke in different voices for each of the characters, brought them to life, and in so doing, pulled each of her students right into the stories with her. Second grade in her classroom changed his whole attitude toward reading. Thanks to Mrs. Campbell, he developed a love of books, which ultimately determined the course of his life. It was because of her that he chose library science as a career. So when he saw that a celebration of life was planned for her, he wanted to be a part of it. She deserved it.

He'd gone to the funeral, having no idea how his life was about to change.

***

The service at St. Peter's Episcopal Church had already begun by the time he got there—stupid interstate road construction. He felt like kicking himself for not allowing more time. Slipping into the first empty seat he could find, he scanned the assembly. Good. The sanctuary was packed. Nice for the family to see how much she meant to everybody.

His eyes roamed familiarly around the interior. Nothing had changed. He'd come here occasionally as a child—whenever his parents determined the family needed some "straightening out"—and even though those times weren't often, he remembered loving everything about this church. Most of that was probably due to Mrs. Campbell being a member. She was always the first person he'd look for when he walked in the door. As soon as she saw him, she'd hurry over, smiling that special smile, before wrapping him in a big hug, which made him feel like a million bucks.

The bell tower had always reminded him of a turret in a medieval castle. It made him feel like one of King Arthur's Knights of the Round Table. The bell was sure to still be there, *bonging* an invitation to anyone who could hear it every Sunday morning. The stained glass windows were just as beautiful as they'd always been. In his youthful mind, he'd been convinced that the rainbow stripes of warm light were flavored; cherry and orange and lime, blueberry and lemon. He remembered gulping them in great lungsful, nearly hyperventilating in his efforts to taste them. The memories took him back to a time he'd all but forgotten.

His gaze traveled over the sea of faces. Solemn music, solemn faces—exactly what one would expect at a funeral. He stared at the front row. The young woman with long auburn curls had to be Mrs. Campbell's daughter. From her profile, she looked just like her mother. Until that moment, he'd forgotten about Mrs. Campbell having a daughter, but seeing her now brought back the memory of a miniature Eve Campbell skipping along the first-grade hallway the year before he and his family moved. That was the summer before he'd gone into sixth grade. So she'd be four or five years younger than him.

The pastor sat down and then, one by one, several individuals stepped up onto the platform to tell what made Eve Campbell special to them. Each story was a glowing tribute to a remarkable woman. Then a woman with gleaming blonde curls who had been sitting beside Mrs. Campbell's daughter rose and took her place on the stage. When she turned toward the crowd, Nick felt as if someone had punched him squarely in the solar plexus. His mouth dropped open. All the air seemed to suck out of the sanctuary. The world turned upside down. Though her mouth moved, any words she'd spoken were drowned out by the pounding of his heart. Marilyn Monroe incarnate! No woman had a right to be that curvy. It wasn't fair to anyone; not to the women, because she'd give even Victoria Secret models inferiority complexes, and certainly not to the men, who needed to somehow keep functioning as civilized human beings while not tripping over their tongues.

At one point during her presentation, their eyes caught and locked across the crowd. For the briefest of moments he was drowning in their deep blue depths. A spark arced between them, long and bold. The image was so vivid, he was certain he smelled smoke and the soles of his feet grew warm. Seconds—that was all the time it had taken—and suddenly it felt like the earth had spun off its axis. The visual encounter left him shredded inside.

The rest of the service was a blur in which he tried—and failed—to concentrate on what the pastor was saying while trying not to stare a hole in the back of the woman's head. It was as if everything in his field of vision narrowed down to a single point of light—a headful of big blonde curls at the front of the church.

He was afraid if he stayed until the service was over, he'd do something crazy like drop to his knee and propose to her. At the very least he'd drool, and since that would be embarrassing, he'd slipped out as soon as the pastor instructed the congregation to bow in prayer. Love at first sight wasn't real. It was something one read about in cheesy romance novels. It didn't exist in real life, but it was better to be safe than sorry.

And for two months he'd tried to put her out of his mind, stepping up his game in the dating scene with an enthusiasm he didn't really feel. In his heart of hearts he knew the reason he was taking Marilee to Fernandina was in hopes that he'd see that girl again, but he pushed the thought away. Tonight was another chance to forget. Maybe Marilee was the one who would finally banish the beautiful blonde from his dreams. Anything was possible, right?

***

He arrived right on time. At his knock, Marilee swung open the door of her apartment, and a wave of sickly sweet perfume hit him in the face with the force of a sledgehammer. He actually took a step back. Whew! He could taste it. Had she spilled it on herself? His gaze flickered down, then back up. No telltale damp blotches, so that wasn't it. Gah! They had nearly an hour's drive ahead of them. How would he survive being cooped up in the truck with that smell?

"Ready to go?" Marilee trilled nervously.

He cleared his throat and hoped his smile didn't look as forced as it felt. "After you." He gestured ahead of him. Following in her wake was like being dragged through a viscous gel that burned his eyes and seemed to seep into his pores. Thankfully, since he was following her, he could breathe through his mouth undetected, but he was afraid his taste buds were being cauterized as a result. Would his sense of taste survive the evening? He was sure he'd have to crack the truck windows in order to get some cross-ventilation once they got on their way to keep from asphyxiating. Hopefully, the wind wouldn't blow her hair too badly.

He glanced in his rearview mirror before pulling away from the curb and noticed the headlights from a car two lengths back flick on. It pulled out at the same time as he did, driving a bit closer to his bumper than he'd like. Well, the road widened ahead at the traffic light. Whoever it was could go around him then.

But they didn't. Nick frowned and slowed down, hoping to encourage the tailgater to pass him.

The only thing that accomplished was for the driver to pull even closer to his truck. So he sped up, switched lanes, wove in and out of traffic the way he hated to see other people do. The car moved in perfect tandem with him, like a dance partner, always right on his bumper.

He narrowed his eyes. Okay, buddy, you want to play games. Let's play.

Moving over into the right-hand turn lane, he watched the car behind him do the same. The light turned green for the opposing traffic. He waited until the mass of cars began moving forward. At the last second, he zipped out in front of the lead vehicle, eliciting an angry blare of its horn, and a startled shriek from Marilee.

"What are you doing?" she exclaimed.

Before answering, he checked his mirror, nodding in grim satisfaction when the car behind him had to slam on its brakes as the mass of traffic moved forward, blocking its way. He sent her an apologetic smile. "Sorry. Trying to get rid of a tailgater."

Her eyes went wide and she twisted around to look. "Oh. Sorry about that."

Huh? "Sorry about what? You don't have anything to apologize for."

Her smile looked brittle and she smoothed her skirt with nervous hands. Uh-oh. Maybe she did.

"Mmm. That tailgater? Well, uh, that was probably my dad."

"Your dad."

"Yes, well, he's, uh . . ." From the pained expression she wore when she swallowed, it looked like she was choking down bits of glass. "He likes to tag along on my dates. He's a little overprotective." She twisted around to look again.

"A little?" His voice dripped sarcasm.

He couldn't tell whether the sound she made was a laugh or a sob. She faced forward again, fingers twisting anxiously in her lap. "Maybe you lost him." Another swallow. "For now," she tacked on in a whisper.

With a sudden feeling of dread, he asked, "You didn't happen to tell him where we're going, did you?"

She winced and gave a nearly imperceptible nod.

He drew a deep breath and slowly let it out. "Great."

Well, he thought in resignation, at least he wasn't thinking about Marilee's perfume now.

CHAPTER FIVE

Lacey

When I arrived at Jeb Billing's seafood market to place my daily order for what I'd need for the night's menu, I could see through the screen door that he was busy with another customer. The woman was red-faced, with perm-fried blonde hair that sprang straight out from her scalp, ends quivering in agitation. Her voice was strident and her finger jabbed emphatically at a sheet of paper lying atop the counter.

When the hinges screeched the news of my arrival, Jeb's dark eyes lifted to meet mine, and his expression practically screamed, *"Help me! Please!"* I bit my lip to keep from laughing and waved my own list at him. After placing it on the counter beside the antique cash register, I set the defunct counter bell on top of it to act as a paperweight. When I looked up again, Jeb's dark eyes were still on me. My eyebrows rose in silent question, and he nodded. He'd make sure I'd get what I needed.

Our silent transaction complete, he reluctantly turned his attention back to the frizzle-haired woman. It was impossible not to overhear her yammer about what she needed for her husband's surprise birthday party. She made sure to stress the word "surprise" about twenty times in case he missed it. Poor Jeb.

To anyone who didn't know him, the man-bun, bushy, unkempt beard, and heavy tats on all visible skin from the neck down would be enough to scare them away, but I'd known him since childhood and he was harmless. His dream of getting a boat and becoming a fisherman worked hand-in-hand with my seafood needs at Black Pearl. It was my responsibility to plan the daily menus and make sure we had all the necessary ingredients. Jeb had been my supplier for years and except for his short stint in jail on suspicion of murder a couple of months ago—a completely false charge, by the way—I'd never gone anywhere else. Simply put, Billing's Seafood provided the best product money could buy, and since Black Pearl was now mine, using the best ingredients was even more important to me.

I own a restaurant. The screech and slam of the screen door followed me out, acting as an exclamation point for the thought. A business owner. *Me!* I still had a hard time wrapping my head around it. What I'd always thought was an unattainable dream was now a reality. Finding my granddad's valuable paintings had been a double blessing. Not only did I have the beautiful artwork he'd created with his own hands, those canvases had made it financially feasible for me to approach my former boss, Pearl, with an offer to buy the restaurant. Tired of Florida's heat, she'd taken the money and run. Last I heard she'd bought a cabin somewhere in the mountains of western North Carolina in some sleepy little town whose claim to fame was that it had lots of apple orchards.

Black Pearl was mine.

The only glitch in the scenario was Raine Fairbanks, who'd been my nemesis since grade school. She'd been trying to buy the restaurant at the time and I'd embarrassed her when I'd swooped in and bought the business right out from under her. But if Raine had bought Black Pearl, she would've been my boss—something that made me shudder to even think about. So now, if there was a color blacker than black, *that* would be the color of the list I was on in Raine's mind. Though I felt a little guilty about it, I considered my action a smart move. It achieved two things: it made my dream a reality, and kept Raine from being my employer, which would've been an unbearable nightmare.

***

After running the rest of my errands, I headed over to Liv's toyshop. Her face lit up when she saw me enter and she fluttered over to greet me. I say "fluttered" because as she walked, the nylon-covered, glittery-pink wings she wore sort of waved back and forth as air passed around them, giving her a flying-fairy appearance.

"I hoped you'd have time to stop in today," she whispered excitedly after kissing the air beside both of my cheeks. "I have wedding stuff to go over with you and I wanted to show you something weird that I got this morn—"

"That can wait. What I have to tell you is more important."

Her eyebrows shot up, disappearing under her mop of blonde Betty Boop-type curls. "More important than your wedding?"

At my nod, her blue eyes widened even more. "Oh, dear. Monica?" She motioned to the young woman wearing a pink Par-a-dux vest, busily arranging a puzzle display. "Can you cover for me? I'll be in my office." Then she grabbed my arm, and practically dragged me through the curtain that separated the front of the store from the back, which acted as both storage for extra stock, and Liv's tiny office.

After pushing me down onto a chair opposite her desk, she hurried around and plopped into her own. "Wait!" She held up a hand when I started to speak. Opening one of the deep bottom drawers, she withdrew two napkins and a plastic container. Setting the napkins on her desktop, she popped off the container's lid and selected two cookies. Their rectangular shape, and the fact that they were red, white, and blue hinted at their supposed design. "I have some Meaux Jeaux 'rejects,'" she said as she placed them on the napkins. "Don't you just love the name Jo picked for her bakery? Exceptionally clever! Not only did she succeed in naming it after herself, she turned the word 'mojo' into something that sounds all posh and refined."

"Very French," I grinned.

"Anyway, these are compliments of the new girl Jo just hired. From the looks of them, she hasn't quite got the swing of

things yet. But taste buds don't have eyes, right?" She handed
me a mutated version of the American flag and winked as she
held hers up. "Happy Flag Day."

I eyed mine doubtfully before holding it up, mimicking her
mock toast. "This is supposed to be a flag? Uh, Jo may have to
change the name of her bakery if this new girl stays on. People
won't be buying 'meaux' of anything. And she better not let
the new girl anywhere near my wedding cake. Okay. Here
goes nothing." I took a tentative bite and my eyes grew round
as the wonderful buttery almond flavor melted in my mouth.
"Mmmm. I take it back. Who cares what they look like? This is
delicious! Thank you, new girl!"

"I know, right?" Liv responded. "I'll have to give half of
these to you, or I won't fit into my bridesmaid's dress by the
end of the week."

Once I finished my cookie, I dampened my fingertip,
dabbed at the crumbs, not wanting to waste a single bit. When I
looked up, Liv's eyes were sparkling and her lips trembled with
her effort not to laugh at me. I made a face at her and shrugged
away her mirth. "I skipped lunch, and I'm hungry. So sue me."

"I'm glad you enjoyed it. Need another?" She held the
container out to me.

After a moment of hesitation, I shook my head. "No. I need
to fit in my dress too."

Liv shoved the container back into her desk drawer and
leaned forward in anticipation. "Now, what's more important
than discussing your wedding?"

I drew a deep breath before beginning. "Okay, first off, I
had another dream."

Liv's mouth dropped open and her pink cheeks paled. "Not
again."

"No, don't worry. It was different this time."

"What do you mean, 'different'?"

"It . . ."—I struggled to explain—". . . *flowed*, I guess you
could say."

"Flowed?"

"Yeah, you know how my other dreams—the prophetic ones—were always kind of like a slideshow on LSD. Flashes of color and light, and no order or explanation? Well, this one was more like a trailer for a movie or something. It flowed. That's the best word I can come up with. It told a story from beginning to end."

"You mean like dreams *normal* people have?" she asked.

Her tone of voice sounded so dry it would have felt right at home in the Sahara Desert. I grimaced. "Well, you don't have to put it exactly like *that*."

She waved my comment away. "Tell me."

"I was on the beach, but it was empty. No people. And I found this wallet lying there in the sand like someone had dropped it. I looked up and saw a man far ahead of me, and somehow knew the wallet was his. So I tried to catch up with him to give it back, but I'm not a runner, even in my dreams, apparently. As fast as I ran, I got no closer to him and he was too far away to hear me yelling. I had to stop to catch my breath and when I looked up again, he was gone. That's when I opened the wallet. Inside was a picture. It was of a stranger, but one with my dad's eyes."

Liv was silent a whole minute, her blue eyes round and intense, apprehensive. Then she blinked. "Well?"

"What do you mean, 'well'?"

"That's it? You mean *that's* more important than your wedding?" she scoffed. "You need to get your priorities—"

"No! That's not all. Well, that's all of the dream, but when I put the dream with what happened later, it makes more sense."

"So what happened later?"

I took another deep breath. "I was looking in my parents' closet for my mom's sapphire combs, you know the ones you wanted me to find?"

"Did you find them?"

"Ugh. Yes! But that's not the point. Now, stop interrupting."

"Sor-*ree*. Geez. Touchy much?"

I gave her a glare. Sometimes Liv reverted back to teenager mode and I needed her to be an adult right now. "There was a spider, so I grabbed a broom and it hit the wall."

"The spider?"

"No, the *broom*. And a hidden door popped open."

"In the broom?"

Gah! Was she *trying* to be the punch line to a blonde joke? "No! In the closet wall, in the corner. A hidden compartment with a fireproof box inside. And when I opened it, there was a birth certificate of a boy. My dad was listed as the father. I have a half-brother. Born a month before me. My dad had an affair."

I knew it might be a stretch for her, but I really needed her to be on the same page with me. I stared into her eyes. The wheels were turning; I could see that, but it was happening *veh-reee slow-leee*. Silence unrolled for what felt like forever. First, she wouldn't stop interrupting, now she wouldn't talk.

Finally, she spoke. "Your dad's eyes in a stranger's face. He's your dad's son. The dream and the birth certificate are connected."

"Exactly! But do you understand what this means?"

Liv shook her head.

"He was born a month before me," I prompted.

No response.

I sighed and continued. "I was born about ten months after my parents got married. If he was born a month before me, that means my dad was fooling around with her at the beginning of their marriage." Another thought struck me and I gasped.

"What?" Liv demanded.

"He was born a month before me!"

"You already said that."

"I know, but don't you see? I got Granddad's paintings because there wasn't another heir. Now there is. I've already sold two of the paintings for the down payment on my loan for Black Pearl. I'm looking for buyers for the others in order to pay the rest, but now, since there's another heir, what if I have to share the fortune? He was born first, after all."

"The paintings were all in your house, Lacey. They belong to you."

"But what if they don't? What if he has some crazy claim to them? What if he has a letter or some kind of document that wills some or all of the paintings to him? Something notarized that would make it official—something I didn't know about when I sold those canvases for the down payment?"

"Do you think your mom was aware of this baby?"

I groaned and flung my head back. "Ugh. That's what Ford asked me. I don't know. Maybe not. She probably would've let something slip. You know Alzheimer's sort of stole all her filters. But even though the beach house is mine and I *thought* it included everything in the house, what if that's not the case? If I have to wait to sell any other paintings until I find this mystery brother to make sure he doesn't have a claim to them, I could lose the restaurant. It could bankrupt me. If I can't make the loan payments, Raine might try to get Black Pearl after all— just for spite—and if that happens, I'd have to leave. I couldn't work for her. She'd make my life a living hell after the stunt I pulled."

"She wouldn't do that."

I gave her a look. "Oh, wouldn't she? Perhaps you've forgotten how she's hated me ever since we were kids and how that feeling has done nothing but grow now that we're adults."

"Yeah, but you are the reason she's still alive," Liv argued. "If not for you, she'd be another dead woman on the Lullaby Killer's list."

"Raine doesn't know about that. She knows I can dream things before they happen, but she doesn't know she's alive because of me, that I dreamed of her—of that guy choking her—and it gave me enough details to tell the police where to find her. They got there in time—barely—but she has no idea I'm the one who told them. What she *does* know is that she planned on buying the restaurant from Pearl, and I bought it out from under her. How do you think she feels about me now?"

Liv winced.

"Right," I replied with a grim nod.

She silently opened the bottom drawer again. After handing me another cookie and taking one for herself we lapsed into deep meditative contemplation about half-brothers, lost fortunes, and the many ways Raine might try to destroy me, or at least, that's what *I* was thinking about when someone tapped on the doorjamb on the other side of the curtain.

"Olivia?"

One word, and I knew who it was. Who else did I know who sounded one cigarette away from throat cancer?

"Are you busy, sugar?" The curtain swished open before Liv could respond and Barrett Clatrans stepped through the door. "Oh." He looked surprised to see me there. "I'm sorry. I didn't realize you had company. Great to see you, Lacey." His greeting seemed too exuberant for the situation.

"Good morning," I murmured, eyeing him dispassionately. Barrett wasn't my favorite person in town. He was the new curator at Front & Centre, the art gallery that was appropriately located at the corner of Front Street and Centre Street. He'd only been there about a month and a half, but he'd managed to wow the whole town already. They seemed inordinately impressed by his high-level art connections. I had to agree it was an important quality for a curator to have, especially since I'd placed Granddad's paintings there. He'd managed to find buyers for those first two paintings in record time, and since there were quite a few more to go, I needed that expertise. So, in spite of how I felt, I was stuck with him. I needed collectors; he knew how to find them. Simple as that. It was a business venture. My personal feelings needed to stay out of it. As much as I might like to move the paintings somewhere else so I wouldn't have to deal with Barrett, I knew I wouldn't. I'd keep them local—right here in Granddad's hometown—so folks who knew and loved him could still enjoy his work.

What was it about him that I didn't like? It wasn't that he was rude or arrogant. He was nice. A little gushing and effeminate for my taste, but I guess he couldn't help that. He was slim and average height—five foot five or so. He wore his straight, dark hair pulled back into a sleek ponytail at the base of his neck, and he was attractive, or he would've been if not for the scar that jagged from just under his left eyebrow toward his nose then down to the corner of his mouth. Not a good look for him or *anybody*. Too *Texas Chainsaw Massacre*-ish for my tastes. And then there was his scarf. Maybe it was an attempt to draw attention away from his injury, but he always accessorized with a colorful scarf knotted around his neck. The fashion trick didn't work, though. In fact, it seemed to emphasize his injury, rather than draw attention away. It made me wonder whether the fabric hid something even scarier, and that thought made me shudder. But that wasn't even what bothered me. I couldn't put my finger on it, but there was just something about the guy that rubbed me the wrong way. I guess I needed to tell him to hold off trying to find buyers until I located this previously unknown brother of mine.

As if reading my mind, he said, "Good news, Lacey. I have a buyer for another one of your grandfather's pieces. We'll get—"

"Um, sorry, but we're going to have to put the brakes on sales for a bit, if you don't mind," I interrupted. "A potential problem has come up and until I can get it worked out, we need to let things sit."

His eyes narrowed and a muscle worked in his jaw while he tried to keep his composure from unraveling. Something flashed in his dark eyes then was gone in an instant, leaving me wondering if I'd imagined it. Finally, he swallowed hard, pasted on a forced smile, and purred, "Whatever you say. After all, they're yours."

While his words sounded benign, a wave of uneasiness washed over me. Before I could reply, he turned his attention back to Liv.

"Glad to see you're enjoying my little gift, sugar." He smiled, wrinkled his nose in a way that was probably supposed to look cute, and motioned toward the cookies. "I'll check back with you later when you have time to talk. Ta-ta, girls."

The instant the curtain swished behind him, I swiveled my head and fixed Liv with a questioning stare. "The cookies? *He* gave you the cookies? I thought you said you bought them from the bakery."

Liv's cheeks grew an indignant pink. "They *did* come from the bakery, and I said I *had* them, not that I *bought* them. Don't start, Lacey."

"Start what?"

"You know what. You're in censor mode again. I don't need your permission to choose my friends."

"That's not what I'm doing."

"It's exactly what you're doing. Just like you always do."

"I'm just trying to look out for you, Liv. You don't have the greatest track record when it comes to men."

She rolled her eyes. "Okay, I'll give you that, but just because I haven't made the wisest choices in the past doesn't mean I'm destined to always do that. I'm a grown-up. I don't need you to look out for me. And besides, he's just a friend."

I rolled my eyes. "I've heard that before. He gave you *cookies*, Liv. Does he know how much you love cookies?"

"He might. What if he does? Do you have a problem with a man giving me a gift?"

"No, but—"

"Fine. I don't want to discuss it further. Now, don't you need to be getting to work?"

Liv's reaction seemed way over the top for the situation, but before I knew it, I found myself on the sidewalk outside her shop, wondering what in the world had just happened?

CHAPTER SIX

Ford

On my way back to the police station, I mulled over all that I'd just learned from Lacey. What a mess. I'd never known Dan Campbell, but I'd known his wife. Like so many other Fernandina Beach kids, she'd been my second-grade teacher and in my opinion, she was a saint. He, on the other hand, was the opposite of saint in my book. He was the ultimate lowlife to have cheated on her.

I turned left off of Atlantic onto Citrona and slammed on my brakes. Thoughts of Dan Campbell's unfaithfulness vanished. A battered blue moped sputtered and whined up the street in front of me. The driver was helmetless, and the sunlight glinting off the frizzy blond curls made him look like a giant dandelion puff. I recognized that cloud of hair.

Jobey Greene.

I'd first met him when I was a rookie cop with the FBPD before my five-year stint with the SBI and it appeared that not much had changed. *He* never wore a helmet, but his dog, Bud (short for Budweiser)—a mid-sized mutt of undetermined parentage who rode with him everywhere he went—never rode *without* one. Jobey had retrofitted a child's discarded bike helmet into a doggy-sized version in order for his beloved companion to stay safe. Due to the large amount and frequency of his alcohol consumption, taking this extra safety precaution was a good move on his part.

Under Florida statutes, you can get a DUI while operating a motorized wheelchair, a riding lawnmower, or even a horse. Naturally you could get one on a moped. Unfortunately, some wise guy noticed that you don't need a driver's license to operate an electric helper motor bicycle. Lo and behold, the guy started marketing them as transportation for people whose licenses have been suspended, calling them "DUI scooters." Though it looked like a scooter, and was capped at 20 mph *like* a scooter, it was technically a bicycle powered by pedaling, *along with* an electric motor. Yes, riders could still get pulled over for DUI, hauled in to sleep it off, and fined, but they couldn't lose their license, because they didn't *need* one. Jobey's license had long since been permanently revoked from repeated bouts of driving drunk, but it looked as if he was now the owner of one of those electric bicycles.

He seemed to be attempting some sort of balancing act along the centerline, but the way he was lurching, to and fro—zigzagging, first to the right, then to the left—it was a good thing it wasn't really a tightrope act or else he'd be in the net underneath. Repeated DUIs had taken his driver's license and made a moped his only form of transportation, but from where I was sitting, he might lose that too. While I watched, he groped a hand over his shoulder into an oversized pack strapped to the deeply tanned skin of his shirtless back and withdrew a familiar silver can. Ahh, mystery solved, though it wasn't really a mystery. After all, it *was* Jobey. If I hadn't known why he was weaving before, I did now. Flicking on my blue lights, I hit the siren once. He jumped, swerved wildly, cast a panicked look over his shoulder, and wobbled into the high school parking lot.

I eased in behind him, leaving my lights on to warn other drivers, but instead of parking and waiting for me to approach him like I expected, he dismounted, carefully set the bike on its kickstand, then tore off across the street into the woods. Bud, better behaved than his owner, remained seated on the moped. His helmeted head swiveled around to face me, tongue lolling as he panted. In my opinion it was the doggie equivalent of a shrug. Or was it an eye roll?

"Oh, good grief!" I shoved the car into park, slung my door open, and raced after him.

I gained ground quickly and it was easy to see why. Not only was he barefoot, he was running with his beer in his hand, trying his best not to spill it. If I'd been a spectator, just watching the show instead of having to chase this nut, dodging blackberry briars and poison ivy, it might've been comical. But being a participant in this fiasco, it was starting to tick me off.

A pained *yowl* echoed in the morning air and he stopped abruptly, limping over to lean against a tree. When I reached him, he had the bottom of his left foot turned up and was whimpering as he slowly plucked off sandspurs. He still held the beer, though.

I winced, waiting and not saying a word until he finished the painful ordeal. I had firsthand knowledge of what sandspurs felt like. I was sure the devil sold seeds for those things in hell.

He finally looked up at me, with pain still etching his face, and handed me his open beer. "I'm stupid."

I nodded and motioned for him to turn around while I reached for my handcuffs. "Yeah, Jobey, you are." Before cuffing him, I removed his backpack, which was dripping. A peek inside explained the soggy situation. It was filled with ice and more of those silver cans. "Ingenious beer cooler, though."

He took it as a compliment. "I wanted them to be cold for the party we're having this afternoon. This pack is just big enough for ice and two six-packs."

My eyebrows rose. "You had twelve in here?" I quickly counted the remaining cans in the pack. "I see eight."

He dropped his head and muttered. "I got thirsty."

I rolled my eyes, shaking my head. "You're gonna have to leave your moped here at the school. You have anybody who could come pick it up for you?"

"It'll be okay." He nodded. "My mom is the lunchroom manager here. Ma will look out for it until my friend, Dana, can come pick it up. She's hitchhiking up from Jacksonville this morning. I was actually heading to Dominos to meet her, and to get some pizza to go with that." He nodded his head toward his makeshift cooler.

"My phone is in my back pocket," he continued. "Could you text Dana so she'll know where my bike is? She can drive it home for me. I guess, all in all, this works out better. I was wondering how her, me, and Bud were all gonna fit on the bike. She's one of them 'big-boned' girls, don't ya know."

Any number of replies came to mind. I pressed my lips together to trap them while retrieving his phone from his pocket.

When we arrived at my car, he lifted his chin toward the pack I still carried. "Can we leave that with the bike?"

"In the parking lot of the high school?" My voice shot through an octave. "I don't think so. There's a fridge in the lunchroom." I motioned toward the building. "Why can't we leave them with your mom?"

His face scrunched up and he shook his head. "Could you take them with you? Stick them in the fridge at the station. If I leave them with Ma there won't be anything left to go with the pizza. She's partial to them Silver Bullets, don't ya know."

I bit back a laugh while I helped him into the back seat of my car and slammed the door after him. Once he was inside, I popped the trunk, muttering, "And you think these things will fare better at the station?" After pouring as much of the melted ice as possible out of the backpack, I tucked it into a corner, wedging a set of jumper cables against it, and hoped that would keep it upright.

"Okay," I said after getting behind the wheel and buckling in. "Let me text Dana. Her number is in here?"

"Yeah, under D."

After quickly sending her a message, I was about to place it in my console, when my finger accidentally grazed the camera button. The last picture he'd taken filled the screen. I glanced at it briefly, did a double-take. Was that the cemetery? Yes, those were gravestones, with a crowd gathered around one of them. Wait a minute. Was that Lacey? I zoomed in some. Yes, there was Lacey, with Liv on one side of her and me on the other, all dressed in black. Her mother's funeral. I met Jobey's eyes in the rearview mirror. "Care to tell me why you have a picture of Eve Campbell's funeral on your phone?"

He shrugged, but his expression was somber. "She was my second-grade teacher. I wanted to pay my respects."

I looked at the picture again, remembering that day. As far as I knew, this was the only picture of the event.

Wait! Could Jobey have—? I zoomed in some more. Yes, there in the shadows of a nearby tree was the elusive mystery man.

"Jobey," I said, hitting the send box under the photo and typing in my email address. "I'm forwarding this photo to me. I think you might very well have gotten the only known picture of a person I really need to find." I tossed his phone into the passenger seat when I was done.

"I did?" He looked like he didn't know what to think about that. "Well, that's great. Glad to help."

I gave his bike one more dubious glance and asked, "So you're sure your bike will be okay here until Dana picks it up?"

"Nobody'll bother it. Not with Bud to guard it."

"You're leavin' your dog with your bike?"

"Yeah. He'll sit here and wait for Dana. He knows what she looks like and can ride home with her."

"Okay," I replied, because I really didn't know what else to say.

You wanted "small town USA," I thought as I turned the ignition key and pulled out onto the road. Boy, did you ever get it!

CHAPTER SEVEN

Delilah

*T*wenty-eight years earlier

JD pushed open one of the art museum's glass doors and motioned Delilah through. The same MOCA attendant who'd reminded Delilah of the time earlier was right behind them, herding them toward the exit, nearly treading on their heels in his eagerness to get the door locked behind them. Her eyes briefly met his through the glass as the lock clicked. His expression clearly said, *"Finally."* She shrugged it off and turned.

August's late afternoon air steamed as if freshly ironed, making it hard to breathe. A languid breeze wafted hints of the supper menu from a nearby Mexican restaurant. The smell of onion, peppers, and cilantro mixed with the stench of diesel fuel drifting up from the boats docked on the river. Rainwater rushed along the curbs, carrying bits of debris in its current, before gurgling into drains. The sun had returned and glinted off the wet sidewalks—heat still strong, even after five o'clock. Wisps of steam floated upward, adding even more moisture to the already saturated air. Bruised and angry thunderheads crowded and piled up to the east, pierced intermittently by lightning bolts that flicked like a snake's tongue.

"Wow! Looks like we missed quite a storm," she said, and immediately felt like smacking her head with her palm. *Well, duh.*

He didn't seem to notice. "Uh, do you want me to walk you to your car?" He eyed a rather alarming-looking, very wet individual with long, matted, mostly white hair, standing at the corner holding a sign that read, "Are the other planets flat too?"

She bit her lip, feeling apprehensive. "Maybe?"

"Smart lady. Which way?"

Once she gestured away from the man on the corner, silence descended on them, feeling at least as heavy as the evening air. Try as she might, she couldn't come up with a single intelligent thing to say. Her mind was blank.

JD Campbell was walking her to her car. *The* JD Campbell. Right here beside her, and her brain was filled with fog. She was an idiot. They'd already walked almost a block. They'd be at her car before she knew it and her big moment would be gone. Say something. She gave herself a silent command. Anything. This is your chance and you're blowing it. He's going to think—

"So, what's your story, Delilah?" The question interrupted her mental tirade.

"I-I'm sorry, what?"

"What do you do? What's your line of work?" Then he gave a short mirthless laugh. "That's me trying to make small talk. I do better with paintings. They don't require conversation."

Her laugh sounded nervous. "I thought it was just me. I've been over here wracking my brain for something to say that wouldn't sound stupid."

"Well, I dare say my 'what's your story' comment has already claimed that adjective as its own."

"It wasn't *that* bad," she argued. At his disbelieving look, she added, "Well, *I* didn't think it was."

"Hah!" he scoffed. "You're being kind." He cut his blue gaze toward her. "So?"

"So what? Oh! My job." Her cheeks heated. "I hate to say, since I'm not anywhere near your realm, but I'm a painter, actually. Art has been an integral part of my life—as natural as breathing—since I was a young girl. Part of my heritage, I guess you could say."

His eyebrows rose. "Oh, yeah? What heritage is that?"

"I'm Yup'ik. It's a tribe in Alaska. The eastern part of the state along the Togiak River."

"You-pick?"

She nodded. "It's spelled Y-U-P-I-K, but you pronounced it right."

"Yup'ik," he said, experimenting with the word again. "You said Alaska? How in the world did you get from there to Florida? That's a big jump."

"Long story." She shook her head, unwilling to elaborate. "And even longer journey. Too long to go into now, but it's because I'm Yup´ik that I'm an artist."

He frowned. "What's the connection?"

"When a Yup´ik girl turns four or five, during Elriq—the Great Feast of the Dead—she's given her own story knife."

"They give a knife to a four-year-old?"

She laughed at his incredulous expression. "Don't worry. It's not sharp. Well, sharp enough—more like a spatula carved from whalebone. I was taught to respect it, only using it for one thing: illustrating—in dirt, mud, or flattened snow—all the grandmother-stories that have been passed down through the ages."

"Hmm. Drawing with a knife. Didn't they have pencils in your town?"

"It's hardly a town," she laughed. "Not even a village, really." Then she shrugged.

"Yup´ik are nothing if not traditional. Personally, I think it was their way to ensure all the stories were remembered and passed down to the next generation. Anyway, learning to draw so young filled an empty place in me and when I grew up, I wanted that feeling to continue. So I chose a career that would do that. Most of what I do is freelance work. You know, designing logos, letterheads, some murals, that sort of thing. Occasionally, I get commissioned to do a portrait, and that's always fun. At least it makes me feel like I'm still an artist. It's not much, but I manage to pay the bills." A wry smile tilted one corner of her mouth, then she added, "Most of the time."

JD looked impressed. "A young artist who's able to pay her bills? Not the typical 'starving artist'? You must be pretty good."

She shrugged off his comment. "I'm building a portfolio. My dream is to get into a gallery someday. Probably won't happen, but a girl can dream. Right?"

He nodded. "Dreaming is always good."

The silence was more comfortable this time.

"I'd like to take a look at your work sometime, if you don't mind."

His request dumbfounded her. "Are you serious?"

He nodded. "I am. Like I said before, if you're able to make a living with your art, you must be pretty good. I'd like to see for myself. Depending on what I see, maybe I can put in a good word for you somewhere. What do you think?"

She narrowed her eyes. "What I think is that sounded like a pickup line, and not even a very good one. I may not look street-savvy, but believe me, I am. I've had to be. Mostly hitchhiking across the country made it a necessity."

"It wasn't. Scout's honor."

"You were a Boy Scout?"

"No."

"So you admit lying?" she asked incredulously.

"No. I just told you the truth. I could have lied and said I *was* a Boy Scout, but I didn't. That proves you can trust me." He gave her an innocent grin.

She couldn't help but laugh, and shook her head in defeat. "Very convoluted reasoning, but okay. When did you have in mind?"

"You busy now?"

"Now?"

He shrugged. "*Carpe diem.*"

***

"Well, here we are. Home, sweet home." Was that her voice? Good grief! She sounded like Minnie Mouse. No chance of hiding her nervousness when she sounded like that. Oh well, being nervous was a given.

JD Campbell was in her studio!

"Nice window." He gestured at the five-foot wide by eleven-foot tall bank of glass where a strip of the choppy, gray water of the St. John's River was visible two blocks away. "Amazing lighting." He glanced over his shoulder to where her easel and supplies were set up. "Renovated warehouse?"

She touched the glass. "Yeah, each studio has a window. That's singular. *One* window each. The rest of the room is a cave. But I'm one of the lucky ones. Only nine of the units overlook the river. As far as I'm concerned, this window is the only redeeming factor of this place. Well, that and the price."

"I like it," he said, still studying the window. "The wavy glass makes your view look like an impressionist painting."

She traced one of the undulating lines in the pane. The glass was so old it had run like clear honey. "Did you know that glass isn't actually a solid? It's a liquid. It just moves super, *super* slow. The waves develop over time. Makes it look like it's melting." She glanced up sheepishly, shrugged, and felt her cheeks heat again. "Sorry. You probably already knew that."

She hurried on, trying to bury her embarrassment with words. "But, to answer your previous question, yes, this was a warehouse in its former life. I've been told it was built just after the Great Fire of 1901. 'Distributed dry goods and notions, etc.'" She finger-quoted the statement. "The words are still there, painted on the side of the building. You might've seen them. Not sure exactly what that means they sold, but that's what it says.

"The whole place was renovated several years ago. Somebody with deep pockets turned it into what you see today. This floor is all studio spaces. The third and fourth are condos, and the ground floor is all commercial— several trendy shops, a bar, a restaurant, and the obligatory Starbucks."

He chuckled. "Good ol' Starbucks. What would we do without it?"

"Well, a cup of coffee might still be closer to one dollar than it is to five."

This time he threw back his head and laughed. "Right. And I can remember when a cup of coffee was just a dime!" He turned back to the window. "So, you live here? It's not just your art studio?" At her look, he explained. "I noticed a futon and a small kitchen area when we first came in."

She wrinkled her nose before answering. "Technically, the studios aren't supposed to be *lived* in, but several of us kind of bend that rule." She shrugged. "Management doesn't ask questions as long as I pay them on time."

He smiled, but didn't comment as he stepped over to her worktable, eyeing her painting equipment with curiosity, before motioning toward the empty easel. "No work in progress?"

She joined him beside the table. "Just finished a portrait and delivered it yesterday." Reaching out toward the crock that held all her brushes, she plucked out a ten-inch-long, carved ivory blade. "This is what I was telling you about," she said, handing it to him. "My story knife."

He studied it carefully, turning it over, his fingers running across its surface like he was reading braille. "I'm guessing there's significance to the symbols?"

"Yes. Salmon, seagulls, seals," she said, pointing to each in turn. "Things important in the life of a Yup'ik."

"And this one?" he asked, pointing to the base of the blade.

"My family's totem." One corner of her mouth quirked upward.

He rubbed his thumb over the four-legged image while studying her. She could feel the intensity of his stare. He shrugged when she didn't elaborate, and pointed to another symbol, a circle with a dot inside. "This one is the same one you have tattooed on your wrist. It must be important."

The fact that he'd noticed surprised her. "Yes. The eye and the hole. It's a symbol for the movement between the spiritual world and the physical. Yup´ik boys get the tattoo on their wrist and elbow after the hunting trip when they get their first kill. Girls get it after puberty."

He handed the knife back to her and she dropped it back into the crock. "Would you like something to drink?" she asked as they moved back toward the kitchen area. "I can offer you water, water, or water. Or I could make some coffee."

He laughed. "Some coffee would be nice."

"Coming right up." She hurried to the corner that acted as her kitchen, grabbed the pot, stuck it under the faucet of the utility sink and while it filled, the words tumbled out of her mouth. "Everything I've read about you—the interviews, the articles—they all stressed how you're practically a hermit." She frowned while pouring the water into the coffee maker. "I'm sorry, but the JD Campbell that I've read about and the JD Campbell who is here with me right now, don't seem to be the same person." She looked up, feeling her cheeks burn. "So, which one is the real you?"

She felt pinned in place by the gaze of his blue eyes while the smell of ground coffee filled the air between them.

He finally spoke. "The hermit JD. I'm not good with people, as we've already established. Oh, I do okay one-on-one, once the ice is broken." A frown creased between his eyes, then he added. "That's not entirely true, either. I guess it depends on who that *one* is, but put me in front of a group and I freeze."

"That bad?"

"I could sink the *Titanic*." His expression was deadpan, but there was a twinkle in his eyes that made her smile.

She opened her mouth to reply, but her coffee maker, which heretofore had been emitting soft, rhythmic gurgles as such a device normally made while brewing coffee, seemed to morph from "Dr. Jekyll" to "Mr. Hyde." Spitting, growling, and snarling like a rabid animal, the noise level built until the whole, long, narrow room echoed with it.

"Sorry," she yelled over the deafening growls. "It's almost done. It'll be over in a minute."

He didn't reply, just stared at her, his eyes wide with shock.

While they waited for the fit to end, steam billowed into the air above it, looking like a miniature volcano getting ready to blow. Finally, after a long *pshew*, it was quiet. The air rang with silence.

"Sorry," she repeated with a sheepish look. "I think it's demon possessed."

JD's brows rose almost to his hairline. "*That* was amazing!" he exclaimed while trying not to laugh. "Where did you get that thing?" Wisps of steam still ghosted innocently above the now quiet machine.

Her cheeks felt hot as she gave a noncommittal shrug. "Goodwill. The price was right."

This time he couldn't hold back his laugh. "They should've called in an exorcist before trying to sell it. One thing for sure"—his eyes sparkled with more amusement—"at least you know why the former owners got rid of it. I hope it at least makes a good cup of coffee."

She handed him a mug. "The best. You need cream, sugar?"

"Black's fine." He took a sip. "Mmm. This *is* good, thanks."

After motioning him to one end of the futon, she sat at the other end, slipping off her shoes, tucking her feet up under her. "That's why you don't teach," she said, returning to their conversation. It wasn't a question.

"Believe me, I've been asked." He shook his head. "No, I would have more success walking on water than trying to teach a roomful of students."

"I would've given anything to have you for a teacher," she murmured, more to herself than to him.

They enjoyed their coffee and the silence for a minute or two, until he arched his brow at her. "So?"

"So, what?" she asked, knowing exactly what he meant.

"I can wait as long as you can."

She tensed, then swallowed hard. "Right. You stay here. I'll pull the canvases out and set them up. I'll tell you when I'm ready."

"I'm not going anywhere."

***

"Okay. You can go look, now." Her throat was so tight her voice was nothing but a whisper. "I think I'll stay back here. That way if I shatter into a million pieces, you won't witness it."

"Whatever makes you more comfortable. It won't take me long."

As soon as he was back in the studio area, she collapsed onto the futon, leaned forward, elbows on her knees, and clasped her head, fingers digging into her scalp. JD Campbell was critiquing her work. Right now. This very minute. *JD Campbell was critiquing her work!* Just thinking about it made her queasy. What if he didn't like it? How would she ever get past that? Why in the world had she thought this was a good idea?

Her ears perked. What was that? A groan? A sigh? Oh, no! He hated them. How would he break it to her? Would he be blunt, give it to her straight? Or would he try to soften the blow somehow? What was taking him so long? It shouldn't take that long to look at twelve measly paintings. She'd spoken in jest about falling into little pieces, but now she was afraid it might really happen. How would that look? He'd come back here and she'd be scattered, in little chunks like ice cubes, all across the floor in front of her futon.

Another sound? This time it sounded like "Hmm." A doctor's favorite word. Usually code for bad news. A terminal condition. Stage four, inoperable cancer. Say goodbye to your loved ones. It's over. It's—

"Delilah?"

She jumped to her feet and her mug crashed to the floor, breaking off the handle and sending the remaining coffee spraying in a wide arc. She didn't notice, too intent on trying to read his expression.

"Uh, don't you need to clean that up?" he asked, pointing to the mess.

"Oh!" She snapped out of her trance. "Right. Let me grab a towel." She turned toward the kitchen and was back in a flash. Her thoughts churned while she wiped up the spilled liquid and gathered what was left of the mug. After dropping the chunks of pottery in the trash can, she tossed the towel on the counter and turned to face him, eyes wide, hands fisted, teeth clenched together so hard she was afraid she'd crack a tooth. What was he thinking? What was coming? He'd make a good poker player. His face gave nothing away.

"I had no idea what to expect when I came over here tonight," he began. "And I just want you to know this is not, by any stretch of the imagination, my *modus operandi*. Oh, I've been asked by many art students over the years, but all it took was seeing their work for me to decide." He winced before adding, "You wouldn't believe how many ways there are to paint boring bowls of fruit and vases of flowers. No imagination, at all." He shook his head. "All that aside, I want to assure you that I don't do this, I've *never* done this sort of thing. *Ever*—"

"Just get it over with," she interrupted. "I can take it." She closed her eyes, braced for his next words, every muscle tensed.

After a beat of silence, he asked, "Would you be my student, an apprentice, of sorts? I'd love to teach you what I know."

CHAPTER EIGHT

Lacey

*T*he painting hangs on the wall in a dark room. Its title is Delilah's Lilies, *my favorite of all Granddad's work, and the one canvas Ford and I never found. The water glows with the reflection of a setting sun. Vibrant, jewel tones. The colors are iridescent. They dance and glimmer, as if some sort of glow-in-the-dark substance has been mixed in with the paint. It provides movement and its own light source.*

A paintbrush appears out of the darkness, getting closer and closer to the canvas. But no, not a paintbrush. Some sort of knife. Long and intricately carved. Its blade glows in the light from the painting.

For a moment, all is still, then from the corner of the room comes a low, rumbling growl. A shadow looms across the canvas and I can plainly see the outline of a dog, the pointed snout and ears, the plume of a tail, the sharp teeth when it opens its mouth. I tremble in terror.

A white arc. The blade slashes downward, through the canvas, then across, upward, and back across.

Then it's gone. And so is the painting. All that's left is an empty frame.

The light dims. Then darkness grows into daylight.

My father has a stack of stretched canvases leaning against a table leg on the floor beside him; their dazzling colors warm the shadows. On the table in front of him, there's another stack, but these have been removed from their stretcher bars. They're just heavy cloth panels, dark and thick with paint. I watch him select one from each group, pull the dark painting tightly over the colorful ones, stapling around the edges, covering the luminous jewel tones of Granddad's paintings with the muddied tones of his own.

***

I awoke with a gasp, sat up, and turned on the lamp. Pulling up my knees, I wrapped my arms around them, hugged them to my chest while my mind replayed the dream.

Well, at least *part* of a mystery was solved. Kind of. I knew all Granddad's paintings had disappeared while I was away at culinary school. They were on the walls when I left, gone when I returned. In their place were ugly substitutes—all painted by my father. I knew now that someone had covered all of Granddad's work with my father's. Ford and I had discovered that two months ago. If my dream was to be trusted—and there was no reason for it not to be—I knew Dad had been the one to do it. Which begged the question, *why*? And where was *Delilah's Lilies*? Ford and I had found the rest of them, but not that one.

I snorted. That was the problem with my dreams. Always raising more questions than answers. Did Dad's reason have something to do with the knife slashing the painting out of the frame? Common sense said "yes," but common sense didn't always figure into the dream world.

The knife itself had looked old, the carvings symbolic. Some kind of ceremonial blade? And if so, what kind of ceremony would use something like that? On second thought, maybe I really didn't want to know.

And what about the shadow of the dog? That didn't make any sense. Was that supposed to be part of it, or was it some sort of random addition my weird subconscious decided to throw in?

I shook my head in exasperation, turned off the light, and flopped over onto my side, squeezing my eyes shut. I'd ask Ford about it tomorrow. Right now, I needed sleep. This was Sunday night. I cracked my eyelids open, peeked at the red numbers glowing from my alarm clock. Correction. Monday morning. I had five days to get things done before Saturday. There was more than five days' worth of things on my wedding to-do list, and I was feeling the strain.

***

I tapped on the glass to get Ford's attention when I got to the diner later that morning. When his eyes met mine through the window, I blew him a kiss. Hurrying to the door, I pulled it open and was soon sliding into our favorite booth. "Good morning. Did you order for me yet?"

"Yes. The usual." He motioned for the waitress to pour my coffee. "Another nightmare?" he asked as soon as she stepped away from the table.

"How'd you know?"

"Pale face? Sunken eyes? Definite indicators, but even without them, your face doesn't lie, Lacey."

"Shoot!" I wrinkled my nose at him. "And I thought I covered those dark circles up." I stared at the table top, tracing a pattern on the Formica top before looking up again. "But in answer to your question—yes, I had another nightmare, but this time, instead of raising questions, I think this dream answered one."

"*Answered* a question? Well, that's different. Okay, tell me."

Once the waitress slid our plates in front of us, I gave him an abbreviated version, between bites of scrambled eggs and toast. He snorted when I finished my tale. "So where's the answer? The whole thing is nothin' but questions."

"I saw Dad covering Granddad's paintings."

"Pfftt. We already knew that. Remember? I was there when you dropped that painting. If it hadn't busted the frame all to pieces, we'd have never known your granddad's stuff was underneath."

"Yeah, but we only *suspected* Dad did it. We didn't know for sure."

He gave me a look.

"Well, okay. We *sort* of knew. But we didn't find *all* of Granddad's paintings. My favorite one, *Delilah's Lilies*, is still missing. So, where is it? Did someone steal it? Cut it out of the frame like in my dream? Was that why Dad went to such extreme measures to hide them? And what about the shadow of the dog?"

"Questions, questions, questions. That's what I'm talkin' about. Start dreamin' some answers, baby," he sighed. "I'll do some checkin', see if your dad filed a police report. Then, at least that part of the dream will have an explanation. The part with the knife and the dog?"—he shook his head—"I got nothin'."

"Okay. Well, on that note …" I gathered my purse and slid out of the booth to my feet. "I need to get in touch with my inner Robert Frost. You know, 'miles to go before I sleep' and all that?" I leaned in and gave him a quick kiss. "Thank you."

"Thank you!" He gulped a last swallow of coffee and threw the tip on the table with a grin. "I'll walk you out. I have a surprise for you."

"A surprise? Oooh, I love surprises. What is it?"

He shook his head, still grinning. "Wait 'til we get outside." After paying the bill, he lifted his chin toward the door.

Once we exited, I pounced. "Okay. Tell me."

He snaked his arm around my waist while we walked. "Oh, not much," he stated, his tone over casual. "You remember the mystery man from your mom's funeral?"

I frowned at the question. What did that have to do with my surprise? "How could I forget?" I said, rolling my eyes. "Everybody keeps reminding me of him. What I don't understand is why everybody in town noticed him but me."

"Your mother had just died, Lacey. The fact that you didn't notice a stranger is completely understandable."

"Maybe so, but we should at least have an accurate description of him. With all the eyewitness accounts, we should know exactly what he looks like, maybe even have a police sketch of him. But everyone's story is different. He's anywhere from mid-twenties to mid-forties, handsome or average-looking, lean or heavy for his size, tall or medium height, black- or brown-haired, fair or Latino. It all depends on who you talk to. The only thing they all agreed on was that it was a man, that he slipped in after the service started, interacted with no one, and slipped out before the last amen was spoken. A couple of friends said they think they saw him again at the cemetery, lurking in the shadows of a large oak tree, but they can't be sure. The whole thing seems like something out of a spy novel. Very cloak-and-daggerish. I guess we'll never find him."

"Never say never." His drawl was soft as velvet.

His tone made me glance up at him. He was wearing a smug expression, laughter danced in his eyes. Mine narrowed. "Wait a minute. Is there a particular reason why you brought up the mystery man?"

"We-ll," he drawled the word out, his tone as casual as a fistful of daisies. "I just might've tracked down a lead."

"What?" I stopped in the middle of the sidewalk, eliciting some audible bits of exasperation from a group of tourists who, in my opinion, were following too closely behind us anyway. They moved en masse, like a school of fish, sped up to pass us single file on the left, then spread back out again, taking up the entire width of the sidewalk. They looked choreographed. I pushed Ford over toward the wall so we wouldn't be in the way.

"How? Where?"

"You know Jobey Greene?"

"The guy on the moped whose dog wears a helmet??"

He nodded, while reaching into his pocket for his phone. "He was there—at your mom's funeral—and took a picture with his phone of the graveside service." Pressing a couple of buttons, and using his fingers to enlarge the photo, he held it out for me. "See? In the shadows under a tree?"

I took his phone for a closer look. Sure enough, here was concrete proof that the mystery man existed. I couldn't make out any details, but there was definitely a man standing in the shadows. Was this the brother I never knew existed until I saw that birth certificate? My heart beat faster at the thought. And what if it was?

"I'm going to see if I can get Myron to enhance it." Ford continued talking, unaware of where my thoughts had headed. "Maybe he can make it a little clearer so we'll at least have a face to work with."

I gave his phone back and mustered a smile, cupping my hand to the side of his jaw before kissing him. "My hero," I whispered.

"Careful, now. PDA on Centre Street with the chief of police? What will people think?"

"PDA?" I questioned. "What's that?"

"Police-speak for public display of affection." A devilish gleam lit his eyes and he grinned, leaned in, and kissed the top of my head. "I'm not a hero, but you make me feel like I am. I don't want to be anybody's hero but yours, Miss Campbell. Now,"—he kissed the top of my head again—"go give Robert Frost a run for his money."

***

Since Monday was my day off, I didn't have to go by Jeb's to place my seafood order for that night's menu. Good. It allowed me a valuable chunk of time. I could use it to run by both the bakery and the florist to pay final installments on my cake and flowers. After that, I'd head to Liv's. She'd practically shown me the door after getting into such a huff over the cookie thing with Barrett the day before, so we never got to talk about wedding stuff, and it needed talking about. I'd apologize. That's what friends did when they hurt each other, even unintentionally. Liv was my best friend and I didn't want something as stupid as Barrett giving her cookies to stand in the way of our friendship. I'd had no idea she was so touchy about it.

I stepped out of the florist's, turned toward Liv's shop on Second Street, and nearly crashed into Raine Fairbanks walking arm in arm with none other than the cookie gifter himself. Though Raine was taller than Barrett by a good three or four inches, it didn't seem to bother her in the least. Hmm. Things looked mighty cozy between them. I wondered if Liv knew they were friends.

"Oh, Lacey." Raine's smile was that of a crocodile and her eyes shot daggers at me. "Fancy bumping into you."

I forced a smile of my own. "Just on my way to see Liv."

"Ah." Something flickered across her face—here, then gone. It happened so quickly, it made me question whether I'd really seen anything after all. "Well, give her my best, will you? By the way, your ears must've been burning just now. Barrett and I were talking about you, or at least about your grandfather's paintings."

"What about them?"

"Oh," she trilled. "Not really about the paintings themselves, mostly about the commission he'll get when they sell. He just told me how they've stirred up so much interest among Campbell collectors already, that he's considering an auction."

I turned my attention to him, eyebrows raised. "Oh, really? That's the first I've heard about it."

Barrett had the grace to blush. "Yes, I've been meaning to schedule a meeting with you to talk about what our next step will be, Lacey."

"I'd appreciate that," I replied. "There's something I need to discuss with you as well." I flicked my gaze to Raine and back to him. "Privately. I'll be in touch." Then I brushed by them and continued to Liv's.

***

"Where is she?" I demanded before the wind chimes atop the shop's front door stopped ringing, startling Monica, who almost dropped her phone.

She motioned her head toward the back and I flung myself through the curtain.

Liv stood on a ladder and nearly lost her balance when I entered. "Good heavens, Lacey! Don't you knock? Where's the fire?"

"Knock?" I asked, nonplussed. "Since when do I need to knock?"

"Since you almost made me fall off this ladder!"

"I'm sorry. Here, I'll hold it steady. Come down. I have something to tell you."

As soon as both her feet were on the floor, I swept her into a crushing hug. "I'm so sorry for yesterday. Please forgive me. I wouldn't hurt your feelings for the world."

"Okay! Let go! I can't breathe, and I think you broke a bone or two." She rolled her eyes when I released her, rubbing her ribs. "It's all right. Don't worry about it. I was in a mood because of that note, and your comment set me off."

"What note?"

"I never got to show it to you, but I got another one today." She hurried to her desk, opened the center drawer, and withdrew two envelopes. "This one came yesterday."

I slid the single sheet of paper from the envelope and unfolded it. Individual letters of all colors, sizes, and typestyles had been cut from magazines and glued to the paper to spell out *Lacey knows.*

I squinted in confusion, flipped the envelope over. No address, and no postmark. "How did you get this?"

"Someone slid it under the shop's front door."

"Under it?"

Liv shrugged. "They're the original wooden doors. They're not airtight. There was enough space. Go figure."

"Lacey knows?" I read the words aloud. "What am I supposed to know?"

"That's what I wondered," she replied. "Then I got this one today."

I repeated the process. This time the cartoonish letters spelled out *Ask her about your dad.*

My look shot up to meet her quizzical expression. "Liv, don't look at me like that. You know I don't know anything about your dad. I would've told you. I haven't seen or heard anything from him since he disappeared. I swear." I remembered Liv's dad as a handsome man with blond curls and a ready smile, both of which she inherited from him. He was good-natured, always kidded around, and tended to have a Peter Pan, 'I-don't-wanna-growup' personality. When we were sophomores in high school, he'd left for work one day—same as usual—but this time he never came home. No letters. No phone calls. Nothing. Just *poof*, and he was gone.

Liv's shoulders sagged. A sheen of unshed tears glazed her eyes, but she nodded. "I know. You'd never keep something like that from me. You know how much—" Her voice cracked and she swallowed hard, then shook her head, unable to finish her sentence.

I handed the envelopes back to her, then rubbed her arm in sympathy.

"But who could've done this?" Though her voice was back under control, the hand holding the fanned-out letters trembled with suppressed emotion.

"I have no idea." I was mystified. "Why would someone try to mess with you—no, mess with *us* like that?"

She shook her head, just as puzzled.

"So, we're still friends?" I finally asked.

"Yes," she said, nodding. "We're still friends. Now, what in the world has you in such a tizzy?"

"I have news. Sit." I pointed to her chair while I took mine. "First, Ford has a picture of the mystery man from Mama's funeral."

Her mouth dropped open. "How?"

"Long story, but he's getting his computer geek down at the station to work on it—enhance it, like Abby on NCIS. We can't see enough details to tell who it is yet."

"Oh, good. Hopefully, it'll be what we need to solve that mystery."

I nodded. "Exactly. Next thing—I had another dream."

"Another one?" she groaned.

"That's exactly what Ford said and exactly how he said it."

"Well, let's face it, your dreams are generally not harbingers of good news."

"This one is. Sort of."

"Sort of? Okay. Let's have it."

Liv listened intently, eyes wide, without interruptions, which was a first.

"So," she said when I'd finished. "Do you think the knife slashing the painting out of the frame had anything to do with your dad hiding your granddad's work?"

"That's my take on it. And since we didn't find that painting, but found all the rest of them, I think it was stolen. Ford is going to check today to see if Dad filed a police report."

"What about the dog?"

I shook my head. "That part makes no sense."

"The knife and the dog imply a threat, which is kind of scary," she mused. "The last thing in the world we need to be dealing with is another serial killer situation. Especially not with your wedding this Saturday. And speaking of wedding, we need to discuss things. We didn't get to do that yesterday, because, well, you know."

"Right." I made a face, then continued. "I went by and paid the florist and bakery this morning on my way here, so that's taken care of. How are you doing with plans for the bachelorette par—"

I was interrupted by a discreet tap on the doorframe behind the curtain.

"Olivia? Are you busy, sugar?"

"Not again," I moaned when I heard the rough, low voice. He knew I was there. I'd just told him I was on my way to see Liv. I gave a huge sigh, flung my head back, and glared at the ceiling with my lips pressed tightly together.

"Shush." Liv gave me an exasperated look. "Come in, Barrett."

The curtain parted and Barrett ducked in. His big smile faded a little as soon as he saw me, then returned, but it seemed a little fake. "Oh, you *are* busy," he said with mock surprise. "I'll drop by later." He turned to leave.

"No, it's all right." Liv gave him a bright smile. "What do you need?"

"Oh, I saw something this morning, and I immediately thought of you." He pulled a cute gift bag from behind his back and handed it to her. "I hope you like it." He lowered his eyes, and long, dark lashes fanned across his pinkened cheeks. This only seemed to emphasize the jagged scar.

"Another gift?" she fluttered.

My eyebrows shot up. Did she like this guy?

He wrinkled his nose and gave a slight shake of his head. "Just a little something."

Liv removed the pink tissue paper and her face lit when she pulled out a small book. "*A Thousand Shades of Pink*? Oh, this is perfect. Thank you." She beamed.

I squirmed in my chair. When was the last time I'd given Liv anything? Yes, I bought our weekly lunches most of the time, but what else? I knew giving thoughtful gifts was important to her. That was obvious to anyone simply by looking at the things she stocked in her store. But I never realized how important *receiving* gifts was to her. Or maybe it was the fact that this gift was given by a man. A certain man, perhaps?

"I'm glad you like it, sugar," Barrett replied. "I'll go now and let you get back to"—he sent a look my direction—"your meeting. See you later?"

Liv nodded, a warm smile still lighting her face. "Yes, later." Feeling my eyes on her, she turned and held up a hand. "Not a word. Not a single word."

I gave her my most innocent look. "About what?"

She narrowed her eyes and stared at me a minute before turning her attention to her iPad. "Drag your chair over here, will you? I'm pulling up The Knot, so we can keep tabs on where we are." Her fingers tappity-tapped across the keyboard a bit. "Okay, here's our checklist for today . . ."

CHAPTER NINE

Nick

Enough was enough. Nick was done trying not to think of the beautiful blonde in Fernandina. That disastrous date with Marilee—if one wanted to call it a date with her dad lurking behind them the entire evening—had been the catalyst. Of course, she'd explained the reason behind her father's overprotectiveness—a former, slightly psychotic boyfriend had stalked her until she'd had to get a restraining order. He understood how such a fiasco had made her dad cautious, but in the end, her explanation just didn't matter. He was taking a hiatus from the dating scene for a while. The idea that a mere date could take his mind off of the blonde bombshell from Fernandina was ludicrous anyway. That battle had been lost before it'd started.

She played a starring role in his dreams, both night and day. His sleep had suffered, which in turn caused his work to suffer. He couldn't continue like this, not if he expected to keep his job. She was sure to be taken—married, engaged, or at least with a boyfriend. There was no way a girl who looked as drop-dead gorgeous as she did wasn't snatched up. But he knew himself well enough to know that the only way he'd get over this infatuation was by actually meeting her. The state of limbo he'd been living in for the last eight weeks wasn't a place he wanted to stay. It was time to do something about it.

There was a problem with that, though. He knew nothing about her. Not even her name, though she must have said it when she spoke at the funeral. It was certainly no surprise that he missed it, what with his heart pounding like a big bass drum. That kind of noise would drown out anything. Did she even live in Fernandina Beach? Knowing his luck, she was probably a third or fourth cousin of the family who lived several thousand miles away on the other side of the country. Or worse, on the other side of the world. But whatever the case, he knew he had to find her.

Then, first thing at work that morning, he had gotten an email that seemed to give his decision affirmation. It had to do with the library's new computer program. Due to a generous endowment, the entire public library system of Florida had a new interlibrary computer program. Since he was a bit of a computer geek and considered the go-to guy for all things technological at Jacksonville's main library, he'd gotten his library staff proficient with the new system in record time. Word had spread. Soon he was having training sessions for all of Jacksonville's branch libraries, then all of Duval County. This morning's email was from his boss's boss thanking Nick for his efforts in bringing the county libraries into compliance with the rest of the state. Because of his outstanding efforts, it went on, they were expanding the area he was responsible for to include Nassau County, which included Fernandina Beach. The offer was sweetened with a bonus and per diem.

Serendipity.

He'd already decided he would drive back up so he could nose around a little. But this would legitimize the trip. The last thing he wanted was to come across looking like a stalker. The town wasn't big. Surely someone could help him. Once he finished the training sessions, he'd play curious tourist. Who knew? Maybe he'd luck out and find someone who knew her.

It was worth the try. The training session was scheduled for the next day and he could hardly wait.

CHAPTER TEN

Delilah

*T*wenty-six years earlier

Delilah stepped back from her easel and gave her painting a long, critical stare before turning her attention to the painting on the easel to her right, the one JD had painted and given her as a gift for her twenty-fourth birthday. Her eyes flicked back and forth between the two, comparing stroke for stroke, top to bottom, left to right, searching for some small difference between them. Then she smiled.

There was none. Even the signature was the same. JD wouldn't be able to tell them apart.

Some might call it fanaticism. She preferred to call it devotion. It hadn't been his goal to create a clone. No, he'd encouraged her to be herself, to use his technique, but to paint in her own style. But this *was* her style. Ever since she was nine years old and had read that first magazine article about him, seen his work. All she'd ever wanted was to paint like JD Campbell.

She glanced at the stacks of canvases leaning against the wall. They were like marks on a doorframe marking growth. They chronicled her growth as a painter. They were the ones JD knew about. She'd kept this project to herself.

Having him for a teacher for the last two years had been better than she could've ever dreamed. He'd started with the importance of *planning* a painting before starting with a brush, not just diving right in like she normally did. The first step was to work out the composition and color combinations that would most effectively capture the drama of the landscape. Only then was it time to start painting and only with a limited palette—

no more than five colors—mixing those into a wide variety of hues and values that complemented each other.

He had taught her everything he knew about open impressionist painting. How to use expressive color and loose brush stokes—wet-on-wet. *Premiere coup*. French for "right the first time." With that technique, she was able to use as few brush strokes as possible to capture the emotional movement of a landscape. It allowed the texture of each mosaic-like, side-by-side brush stroke to be seen. No layering and no thinning colors with turpentine. The results were stunning: a vivid palette—more symbolic than realistic—done in a highly abstract style that practically pulsed off the canvas with vibrant movement, emotions, and light.

He'd even taught her how to mix paint like the old masters. Why bother? she'd asked him. Art stores would be more than happy to sell you oils in nice, convenient tubes. She'd never forget his answer: "Commercial oil paint to that which you mix yourself is what fruit juice drinks are to fruit juice. Every pigment has its own personality, Delilah. You have to learn their quirks."

So she'd learned which pigments were toxic, filled with things like cadmium, cobalt, lead, mercury, cyanide. She'd learned which ones to avoid at all cost, and which to use with caution. She'd learned the proper way to handle them; which powders required the use of a mask and gloves and which ones didn't. She learned how to grind the pigments with a mortar and pestle, how much linseed oil to use, and the trick of using a little beeswax with ultramarine blue to keep it from getting stringy or runny during storage. That vibrant blue was the most difficult color for her. The pile of powdered lapis lazuli always formed a crumbly mass when linseed oil was added, then suddenly, and without any warning at all, it became soft and fluid. Too fluid. Every time. Even now, it caught her off guard.

She learned the eccentricities of every pigment because JD said to, and she did it because she loved him. Not as a student loves her teacher, not as a child loves her father. No, she loved him, wanted no one else but him, for the rest of her life. She'd kept her feelings to herself for two years. It was time to let him know. She would tell him tonight.

***

Delilah swept the door open wearing a brilliant smile and a brand-new dress. The color was a deep, rich red. JD had told her he liked her in this color once; that it went well with her skin tone, her dark-brown hair and eyes. Tonight would be special. It deserved a new outfit.

JD's eyes widened and he grinned. "Wow! You look great. What's the occasion?"

She dimpled up at him. "Do we have to have an occasion for me to dress up a bit?"

"No, I guess not, but I feel kind of underdressed compared to you."

"Don't be silly." She closed the door. "Would you like a glass of wine?"

"Wine?" He gave her a curious look. "What happened to water, water, or water?"

"Well, I added wine as a choice tonight because I have a surprise for you, and I want to make a toast first."

"A surprise? What kind of surprise?"

"The good kind." She smiled as she poured pinot noir into two unmatched coffee mugs. "Sorry about this." She wrinkled her nose, handing one to him. "They're all I have to drink from."

"Not a problem." He grinned. "What are we toasting?"

She held up her cup. "Two years ago, today, you asked me to be your student, and I wanted to celebrate it as the beginning of the best two years of my life."

Surprise lit his blue eyes. "Has it really been that long already? Wow!" He clinked his mug to hers. "To an amazing student."

"To the best teacher in the world," she countered and took a sip.

After swallowing, he said, "I should take you out somewhere, show off that dress."

She shook her head. "No, I have Chinese takeout in my little fridge. All I have to do is nuke it a little. I have it all planned."

"'All planned,'" he grunted and turned toward the futon. "I remember my wife saying almost those exact same words on occasion before she died. It always made me nervous."

"No need to be nervous," she said, following him and taking a seat. "You've never mentioned your wife before. Why?"

He stared down into his mug, and suddenly seemed far away. "She's been gone a long time, died when my son was fifteen years old, ten years ago."

"You never thought about remarrying?"

"No, painting like crazy to pay the bills, and keeping up with a teenage boy while trying to keep food on the table took up all my time. Now that he's grown and gone, I'm too set in my ways."

She didn't like his saying things like that, so she tried to steer the conversation in a different direction. "You never talk about your son either. Are the two of you close?"

"Close to Dan?" he scoffed before taking another gulp of wine. "Hardly. He's a painter, too, though not a very good one. I tried to give him some pointers, teach him techniques. You know, like I've done with you."

From the look on his face his memories weren't pleasant ones.

"Let's just say he had his own ideas and wasn't interested in any of mine. At. All. I'd tell him one way, and he'd do the opposite." He took another sip. "He just got married. Sweet girl named Eve. Teaches second grade. I didn't think he was ready to settle down, but he always did like to prove me wrong. I just hope he married her for the right reason."

"What's the right reason?"

He looked up, surprised. "Because he loves her, not just to prove something to me."

She gnawed at her thumbnail while he stared moodily at nothing in front of him, absently rubbing his left arm, a frown creasing his brows. This definitely wasn't going the way she'd planned. Maybe he was hungry. She could go ahead and get the food ready, but the light would be fading soon and she wanted him to see her surprise before it got too dark.

She jumped to her feet and took his mug from him. Setting both of them on top of the microwave, she turned and held out her hand. "Time for the surprise," she said with a mysterious smile.

He allowed her to pull him up, following as she dragged him toward the front of the room where the backs of two easels stood side by side.

"What's going on?" he asked. "Why do you have two easels?"

"It's my surprise. Close your eyes. No peeking. Here." She reached up and covered his eyes, walking him awkwardly around until they were standing directly in front of the two paintings. "Okay, ready?"

"Mm-hm."

"Ta-dah!" She removed her hands and stood over to the side so she could see his face, read his expression.

His eyes flicked back and forth between the two paintings. Back and forth, over and over. He stepped closer, bent so he could see the details of first one, then the other. Was he comparing brush strokes? Could he see how identical they were?

The comparison continued. Right, then left, then right, then left. It was like he was following a tennis match on television. Back and forth, massaging his upper arm like he'd pulled a muscle or something. Then he stepped back to where he'd started, not taking his eyes off the paintings, not saying a word.

Her excited smile faded and, as the silence stretched, her stomach slowly tied itself into knots. What was he thinking? His expression gave nothing away. He still had a good poker face. That hadn't changed in the two years she'd known him. Trying to read him made her feel blind without the knowledge of braille.

Finally, when she was ready to scream, he turned his head and looked at her, his blue eyes boring into hers, confused and bewildered.

"Why?" he whispered.

"It was an experiment." She tried to smile, but didn't succeed. "I wanted to see if you could tell which one was yours and which one was mine. Can you?" she asked. "Can you tell which one I painted?"

"But why?" he persisted. "I wanted to give you the skill, to learn the technique, but to have *your* style, to allow *your* paintings to sing. I could see your potential that first night I was here, when I first saw your work. You had a voice then—*your* voice. I just wanted to teach you the technique, not take your voice away."

"And all I wanted was to paint like you."

"But you're *not* me."

"I know, but I love you." The words escaped before she could stop them. She clapped a hand over her mouth and stared at him with wide eyes. If only there was a way to snatch those words back. But there wasn't.

His head jerked back as if she'd slapped him. "Like a dad," he said, as if trying to convince her. Or was he trying to convince himself? "You've been without a dad for so long, you're using me as a substitute."

"Don't try to tell me how I should love you," she replied, and her eyes welled with tears.

"Delilah, I—"

She shook her head. "No! You need to hear this. I never talk about my childhood because I'd just as soon forget it. I never knew my parents. My grandmother raised me until I was eight, but she died. After that, I bounced around foster homes until age sixteen. That's when I ran as far away from Alaska as I could get."

"I didn't know. I—"

She swiped angrily at the tears streaming down her cheeks. "Let me finish. I worked hard. Finished school. Didn't end up on drugs, or alcohol, or prostitution. I could have, you know. No one would've been surprised either. That's exactly what happened to so many of my friends. But I didn't want that. I worked two jobs, sometimes three, just to make enough money to take art classes at a community college. And do you know why?"

He shook his head.

"It was while I was living in one of those foster homes that I found a magazine that had an article about you in it. That's when I got my first glimpse of one of your paintings. I still have that article. I cut it out and saved it, put it in a scrapbook along with all the other articles I found written about you over the last fifteen years. And ever since then, all I wanted was to paint like you."

She flung her arm out toward the easels while tears streamed down her face. "Now I can. Don't you see? I can finally do it. And it's because of you. I love you, not as a dad, not as a teacher, but as a woman loves a man. I love you, JD Campbell." She took a step toward him, touched the corner of his eye where a single tear was trapped in his lashes.

His mouth tipped up in a tender smile. He opened his lips to speak, then gasped. His right hand clutched his left arm, his knees buckled, and he crashed to the floor.

Her scream echoed against the high ceiling, the brick walls. She stared at him, filled with horror and panic, while shock rendered her immobile for several terrible seconds. Then she ran to her kitchen, grabbed the cordless phone, and sprinted back to where he lay gasping on her floor. She blinked away tears so she could see and her trembling finger punched 911. Tears dripped from her chin while she waited for someone to answer. When they did, she gave the details they asked, a robot answering their questions, all the while stroking his face, smoothing his hair back on his forehead.

When she realized he was trying to speak, she dropped the phone.

"Delilah—"

His voice was weak. Barely above a whisper.

"Yes, I'm here."

"So sorry—"

"I am too, but the ambulance is coming. They'll be here soon. They'll get you to the hospital and you'll get better." Her voice cracked. No, no, no! her frantic thoughts screamed over and over. This can't be happening. This wasn't how this night was supposed to go.

"'lilah—"

She could hear the emergency responder questioning, "Hello? Hello? Please stay on the line until the ambulance gets there. Please—" Her finger pressed the red *x* to stop the annoying voice. She needed to hear what he was trying to say.

". . . love you."

She gasped. He loved her. "I love you, too, JD. You stay with me. Don't you leave me, you hear? You can't leave."

"Something . . . missing . . ."

"What? I didn't understand what you said. Can you say it again?"

"Paint . . . recipe . . . missing . . . 'gredient."

"Missing ingredient? To your paint recipe?"

He nodded, then his face contorted, jaw clamped, lips pressed into a straight line for a long, gruesome minute. His breath hissed in a long, slow exhale, like air escaping a balloon. He didn't move again.

Her eyes widened in horror. No! No, no, no! She pressed her fingers against the side of his neck, desperate to feel a pulse.

Nothing.

"No," she wailed, trying the other side, getting the same results. "Please, God . . . no!"

She became aware of banging on the door, hollow, echoing. Muted voices yelled. The pound of shoes on wooden floor. The clatter of an easel, then another one. Someone pushed her out of the way.

Garbled voices.

Someone starting CPR. Counting. *One, two, three, four, five, six . . .*

Static from a radio.

More counting. . . . *seven, eight, nine, ten . . .* would it ever stop?

The metallic rattle of a gurney.

Shoes pounding again.

Voices ebbing.

Silence.

CHAPTER ELEVEN

Lacey

*G*randdad's painting, Delilah's Lilies, *glows against a dark wall, again. One spot of brightness in a sea of black. But how can that be? Hadn't someone cut it out of its frame last night? How could it still be here?*

Right. This was a dream, just like before. Would this be a repeat of last night? A rerun? It must be. Everything looked the same.

No, not exactly the same. Something was different . . . a change of viewpoint. This time I'm the painter. Well, not me, but I'm looking through the eyes of the painter. Am I supposed to be Granddad? Even for a dream, that's crazy.

A hand reaches out from the blackness. Is it mine? No. It's not a man's, but it's not mine, either. Bright-red nail polish on smooth oval nails. It's holding the carved ivory knife again, but while I stare, the blade turns into a paintbrush and starts daubing oil paint on the canvas. Then the paint turns into gemstones—sapphires, emeralds, rubies, topaz, amethyst, garnet, jasper, opal—dazzling facets of light.

I hear a shuffle and scrape behind me in the dark. The dog shadow is back. I know it without turning. I hear it growling, panting, getting closer and closer, feel its hot breath against my neck.

***

My eyes popped open and I jerked away from the hot breath of my dream, but there was nothing there, just my empty room. The only sound was the crash and pound of the waves outside;

no panting. Besides that, all was quiet. I willed my heartbeat back to normal.

For two nights in a row, I'd had basically the same dream. The painting, the knife, and the dog. I was sure it meant something, but for the life of me, I couldn't figure out what it might be. But with a track record like mine, where a dead body was always the main character—it made me understandably nervous, like I was waiting for the other shoe to drop. I thought briefly about calling Ford and telling him about it. He still rented the apartment upstairs, which I'm sure some people thought was silly. I could practically hear them saying, "You're engaged. Going to be married in a few days. Go ahead. Live together." It was a common mantra anymore, but we wanted to wait until we were married. Some might call it "old-fashioned," but we were both Christians, and we decided that was the right thing to do.

We'd talked about whether he should find somewhere else to live after we'd gotten engaged, but decided against it. It was only for a couple of months, we reasoned; it would be silly for him to move for that short of a time.

For the most part, it worked, but sometimes—like now—I wasn't so sure. He'd be down here in a second if I called. I knew that. It was the reason I nixed the idea of calling him. I remembered how sexy his voice sounded in the middle of the night. I'd heard it before, while he was working the Lullaby Murders case and I'd called him to let him know I'd dreamed of another young woman being strangled. His gruff, sleepy voice sounded good then, *too* good. In my current emotional state, calling him wouldn't be wise. It was better to wait. I'd see him in the morning for breakfast and tell him then. No sense in both of us being awake in the middle of the night anyway. My life wasn't in immediate danger.

Then the images of the ivory knife and the terrifying dog shadow flashed through my mind and I swallowed hard. At least I hoped I wasn't in danger.

CHAPTER TWELVE

Nick

"This is stupid," Nick Bradford muttered aloud, while waiting for the left turn signal to allow him to turn onto Centre Street. "Stupid, stupid, stupid! What am I doing back here?"

He was in Fernandina Beach for the second day of training at the library, though two days hadn't really been necessary. The library staff there was brighter than some he'd worked with. They'd grasped the new computer system almost immediately. The only reason he'd come back was to give himself another chance to find the woman he hadn't been able to get out of his mind.

What had he expected? That she'd just magically appear in front of his eyes? He scoffed. That was the *only* way he'd find her. He had no name, no address, no clue whatsoever other than the fact that she'd been sitting up on the family row at Mrs. Campbell's funeral. It would take a miracle, and the last time he'd checked, those didn't happen much these days. He was a fool. He knew it, and if he started asking about her all over town like he wanted to, everybody else would know it too. Or worse, they'd think he was a stalker and call the cops. No, he'd finish up the training this morning, spend the rest of the day being a tourist—ask a question or two, see what he could find out—then he'd go back to Jacksonville and go on with his life. Or at least, he'd *try* to.

Finally, the green arrow. His foot shifted from the brake to the gas. Just as he began his left turn, a flash of bubblegum pink blurred past him.

"What the—?" He blinked, blinked again to make sure he wasn't seeing things. A woman—wearing pink from head to foot, including a halo, tutu, and big pink wings—whizzed down the street on a bicycle the exact color of her outfit. Sunlight glinted off the woman's blonde curls and he gasped, feeling as if he'd been hit with a Taser. It was her! The woman from the funeral.

A horn honked behind him, jolting him out of his stupefied state. He completed his turn, speeding up as much as he dared, desperate to keep her in sight.

All along Centre Street tourists filmed and snapped pictures of the pink vision as she rode by. They'd need proof to back up the story of their alleged sighting once they got back home, otherwise no one would believe them. He hardly believed it himself, and he was seeing it in real-time, not a photograph.

Everything was fine until an ancient, gas-guzzling Cadillac—probably from the '70s judging by the fact that it was the size of a small European country—backed out from a parking spot right in front of him, then proceeded to creep down the street at a snail's pace. Great! Because his truck sat higher than the land-yacht, he had a perfect view of the vision in pink moving farther and farther away. Oh, how he longed to lay on his horn but he was afraid it might send the ancient driver and his equally ancient wife into cardiac arrest and that would *really* back traffic up.

After an agonizing block, the Cadillac turned, but by then it was too late. She was gone.

But wait! There was a group of folks crowding on the next corner laughing, aiming their phones and pointing down the side street. He zoomed forward, fingers crossed that no one else would back out in front of him and that all local law enforcement was busy elsewhere. A flash of pink let him know he was back on her trail. She was looping a chain around a telephone pole in front of a little shop. He drove past her but kept her in his sights in his mirror. He breathed a sigh of relief when he saw her enter the store.

A little voice in his head was screaming for him to whip into the nearest parking spot. She wouldn't be hard to find. It wasn't like she could blend in, not in that get-up. But a glance at his watch gave answer to that little voice. The library staff was waiting. He couldn't be late to a class *he'd* set the time for. He glanced up at the sign. Par-a-dux. He should be able to remember that.

After one last longing look at the store, he reluctantly turned left on Ash Street so he could loop back around to the library. At least, he consoled himself, picturing that vision in pink, he knew what to ask now.

***

At noon, he exited the library and hurried toward his truck, armed with valuable information and a destination in mind. Before beginning the training session that morning, he'd mentioned seeing the unusual lady in pink to the library staff. With that as a starting point, all it had taken was a few casual but strategic questions and voilá! He not only knew that her name was Olivia Hale, he knew that the shop he'd seen her chain her bike in front of was a toy store and that she owned it. Now he knew where to go. Perfect.

"Hey!"

The shout came from behind him and he turned instinctively, though he was certain whoever it was wasn't calling for him. How could they? Nobody here knew him. Well, except for library staff, but they were all in the building.

A block away, a uniformed man strode in his direction. Sunshine glinted off the badge on his chest. The police? Nick peeked back over both shoulders. No one else nearby. Turning back, he pointed to his chest, raised his eyebrows in mute question. *Me?*

The policeman's answer was a brisk nod, while his long, ground-eating strides quickly closed the gap between them.

Nick groaned. Now? Really? What had he done? Had he parked where he wasn't supposed to? He hadn't seen any No Parking signs. He glanced around again to make sure. No, nothing. So, what? He ground his teeth in frustration. All he wanted to do was find Olivia—see her up close, introduce himself.

While he waited, he studied the figure approaching him. He was tall and lean—obviously worked out—with a shank of blond hair pushed back from his forehead, giving him a sort of surfer-dude look. The knife-edged crease of his khakis would slice bread. Spooky-green eyes, he noted when the man got close enough to see them. He wore a stern, determined expression.

When the man stopped in front of him, Nick could see the name engraved on a silver bar attached to his pocket. Ford Jamison. He nearly snorted out loud. Sounded like the name of one of those cheesy, soap opera heartthrobs. Then he paused. It sounded vaguely familiar. Had he gone to elementary school with this guy? "May I help you, officer?"

Jamison's eyes narrowed. "I need to see some ID, please."

Nick frowned. "Have I done something wrong? I didn't see any meters. Is this a pay lot?"

"ID, please," the officer repeated a little more firmly.

Nick reached into his back pocket to retrieve his wallet, flipped it open, and slid his license out, handing it to the waiting officer, who studied it like a KGB agent, glancing up several times to compare the photo to the real thing standing in front of him.

Nick shifted uneasily. What was his problem? He could practically feel waves of suspicion radiating off this guy. And they were attracting attention. Already, several curious passersby had stopped to listen in.

The officer finally handed him back his license. "So . . . Nick Bradford." Jamison's voice was neutral, but had a definite edge to it. "You mind tellin' me what you're doing here?"

Nick's brows shot up. "What?"

"Just answer the question, please."

Nick's ears heated at the guy's attitude. Was this normal? He glanced around at the steadily growing crowd. No help there. One of the onlookers was holding up his phone, obviously recording the interaction, while a couple senior ladies, fresh from their weekly salon visit—judging by their hair-dryer pink scalp visible between neat rows of curls—exchanged loud whispers back and forth behind their hands. He scowled when he caught the words "shiftless" and "riffraff." What he *wanted* to do was tell this guy—and those blue-haired biddies—where to get off, but decided that probably wasn't a good idea. He forced a smile, instead. "Look, can we do this somewhere else?" He gestured at the circle of spectators. "Somewhere a bit less public?"

After a brief look at the group, Jamison nodded and motioned him down the street to where Nick could see a police car. There was an audible murmur of disappointment as the group dispersed.

As soon as they reached the cruiser, Jamison chirped the doors unlocked. Nick took a seat inside the stifling interior and immediately started sweating. The engine roared to life and Jamison cranked the AC on full blast before pinning Nick with a penetrating stare. "Well?"

"I hope this isn't how you treat all your visitors," he quipped, trying to lighten the thick tension in the air. If anything, Jamison's expression grew harder. Okay, enough with the comedy routine. Better just tell him. "I-I just finished training your library staff," he stammered in explanation. "You may not know, but Florida public libraries, statewide, have a brand-new computer system that connects them all together thanks to a grant that bought new software. My job is to train library staff how to use it."

The green eyes narrowed suspiciously. "So, you're a computer guy."

"Well, not exactly," Nick replied, then hurried to continue when the other man's look sharpened. "I'm actually head librarian in downtown Jacksonville, but I understand this new system so well that the powers that be asked me to head up training all of Duval and Nassau counties' library staffs."

"First time here?"

Nick shook his head. "No, I used to live here." Uh-oh. The suspicious look was back. This guy had some serious issues. "Back when I was a kid. Your name sounds familiar, so I think we might've even been in elementary school together. My family moved to Ocala right before I went into sixth grade and I haven't been back here since then. That is, until two months ago."

"Two months ago?" The words were razor sharp.

"Yeah. I returned for a funeral." Geez. He'd better not mention his date with Marilee.

"Why?"

"What do you mean, why?" Nick demanded. "I wanted to pay my respects to my second- grade teacher. Not that it's any of your business." He'd about had it with Jamison's interrogation tactics. "The last time I checked, attending a funeral wasn't against the law."

"You were one of Eve Campbell's students?"

He answered with a terse nod.

Without warning, a lazy grin spread across Jamison's face. "Mystery solved."

"You lost me," Nick replied sourly. "What's that supposed to mean?"

"I guess livin' in the big city for so long has made you forget how things are in a small town. Here, everybody knows everybody. So, when a stranger shows up at the funeral of someone as beloved as Eve Campbell, well, let's say people notice. You, Mr. Bradford, have been the subject of untold speculations for two solid months."

"I have?"

"You have. Someone even got a picture of you on his cell phone at the cemetery. That's how I recognized you. And since Eve Campbell's daughter is the woman I'll be marryin' this

Saturday, you could say I had a vested interest in findin' out who you were."

Nick snorted. "Finally! Something that makes sense. So, are we done here? Am I free to go?"

"Yes, Mr. Bradford. You're free to go. Enjoy your day."

***

Wind chimes tinkled when Nick pushed open the door of the toy store, and his mouth dropped open in awe. He felt like he'd entered a fairytale.

Frothy material in purples, pinks, white, and silver draped from the ceiling like clouds, sheathing tiny blinking, white lights that mimicked thousands of fireflies. Hundreds of fairies and butterflies—in every color imaginable—dangled from the ceiling by invisible threads. It was easy to see why the place was packed with children. His eyes scanned the interior, searching for a telltale flash of pink.

There she was! A mere fifteen feet away.

His heart began thudding against his ribs, making it impossible to draw more than half lungsful of air.

He was finally going to meet this incredible woman. It was going to happen. Today. Now. He took a step forward.

And stopped.

Hold on! A skinny little man wearing his dark hair pulled back in a ponytail at the base of his neck stood close to her talking in a very animated manner. He couldn't tell what the guy was saying, but whatever it was made her blush. Nick's eyes narrowed and shot daggers at this unknown rival. When the guy handed her a gift bag and she smiled a pretty "thank you," Nick barely kept from growling. He suddenly knew exactly what it meant when someone described jealousy as a "green-eyed monster." At that moment, his vision seemed suffused with that color and he felt like the Hulk, capable of tearing the man limb from limb. Who *was* he and what did he think he was doing with Nick's girl?

Without a word, he spun on his heel and yanked the door to the shop so hard the wind chimes jangled in protest. Stalking back to his truck, he flung himself inside. His hands gripped the steering wheel so hard his knuckles bleached white. His breath rasped in and out, too loud in the confines of the truck's cab.

What an idiot he'd been. Of course someone besides him was interested in her. She was the most beautiful creature he'd ever seen. How could men *not* be flocking around her? What had he expected?

It took several minutes before he could breathe normally, and when he was finally able to draw a deep breath, it was tinged with regret.

That was that. Time to head back to Jacksonville where he belonged.

Backing out of his parking spot, he turned his truck toward home.

CHAPTER THIRTEEN

Delilah

Twenty-six years earlier

At the funeral, Delilah sat with the rest of the friends and acquaintances, not in the front row where the family sat, where she should sit . . . where she belonged.

Instead of black—the usual funeral color *and* the way she felt—she wore her red dress. JD was the reason she'd bought it. He'd liked it, so she'd wear it to say her goodbyes. When she got home, she'd burn it.

The church was packed. The town of Fernandina Beach wasn't that big. Of course, being world-famous like he was, people knew him beyond the confines of this place. Many who were here might very well have traveled great distances to pay their respects, but she was willing to bet every Fernandina Beach citizen had showed up. JD Campbell was one of them. They would see him off the best they knew how.

She noticed a young dark-haired man sitting beside a woman with short auburn hair in the front row, closest to the center aisle. That had to be JD's son, Dan, and his new wife, Eve. She'd seen photos of him at JD's beach house, each one chronicling Dan at various ages, from baby to teenager, but nothing after that. After he'd graduated from high school and went off to college, the tenuous relationship between them finally broke. Dan moved away to somewhere mid-state, according to JD. She'd never met him in person, but she could see he was built like his father. She was sure JD's hair had once been dark like that, but straight and fine. Those curls must've come from the mother. Her thumb ran across her fingertips. She could still feel how silky JD's hair felt when she'd run her fingers through it the night he died, smoothing it back from his beautiful forehead. Spun silver.

Her fists clenched the feeling away. She'd never feel that softness again.

Hot tears ran in paths down her cheeks, dripped from her chin to puddle on her white-knuckled fists before seeping through them, marking damp circles on the rich, red cloth of her dress. She didn't bother to blot the tears. Just let them go where they would. It didn't matter anyway.

Then the pastor's droning stopped, followed by the mournful whine of organ music. The sound echoed her own inner wails. The man with the dark curly hair, the redheaded woman, and a few other people stood and filed out into the aisle, gliding slowly back toward the doors of the sanctuary.

She lifted her eyes and studied the young man. His head was bowed, dark lashes fanned against bronze cheeks. Handsome. His face had the same planes, chin, jaw, and same nose. JD's son.

He raised his head and looked up. She gasped. The same cerulean-blue eyes. JD's eyes! Her own welled with tears and spilled a fresh wash down her cheeks. She choked back a sob.

Then those eyes met hers and she stilled. There were questions in their depths. A crease appeared between them, identical to the one she'd seen on JD's face. Her heart stuttered for a beat or two before thundering against her ribs. The sensation confused her. How could her heart beat like that when it was shattered?

Finally, he and the redhead swept past and were gone. Gloom settled like fog, trapping her.

***

She watched the small group of about ten gathered under a tent-like canopy that bore the letters she couldn't read from where she stood, a white blur against forest green. She stayed hidden behind a massive oak tree whose lower branches drooped so low they nearly swept the ground in places as if tired from all the years of holding themselves up.

Ah. Finally. It must be over. The group began breaking up, drifting away from the tent one or two at a time after giving goodbye hugs and air-kisses to JD's son and his wife. Then it was down to three. She watched the pastor shake their hands, offer his pantomimed condolences, then he too, strode toward the parking lot. The couple stood there a moment longer before following the path the pastor had taken. She waited until she saw their car exit the lot and turn left, toward town.

Her attention swung back to the tent. There was already a truck pulled up nearby and two uniformed men were busy stacking the folding chairs into the open tailgate. She took a deep fortifying breath before mentally commanding her feet to move her forward.

The workers looked up in surprise when she neared them. "I'm sorry to interrupt your work, but could I have a minute alone?" she asked in a voice barely above a whisper.

The men looked at each other questioningly, then shrugged. "Sure, lady," one of them replied. "Don't matter none to us. We're on the clock. We'll wait in the truck. Take all the time you need."

"Thank you." She forced one corner of her stiff lips to tilt up. It was all the smile she could muster.

She closed her eyes, waiting. She heard the truck's doors open, then one slammed shut followed by the other. A hard swallow, another deep breath, and she turned woodenly toward the casket, stepped forward until she could lay a trembling hand against the cool metal surface.

"Hi, JD," she said in a voice that wavered. "It's me." She blinked away the sudden well of tears. "I wore the dress you liked. I didn't think you'd mind it being red instead of black." The hand pressed against the casket suddenly clenched into a white-knuckled fist. "It wasn't supposed to be like this," she choked out. "Not the way I planned it at all." Hot tears streamed unchecked down both cheeks. Her shoulders shook with her sobs.

After a long moment, she lifted her head, used both hands to wipe her tears away, and sniffed. "Thank you for being the greatest teacher in the world," she murmured. "For giving me the tools to fulfill a dream—to paint like you. And even more than that, for loving me. Two things that no one can ever take away."

She leaned down and pressed her lips to the cool metal. "Goodbye, JD. I love you. You'll live on through me."

***

Delilah's rubber-soled sandals thudded quietly against the sun-bleached boards of the pathway toward the ocean. Once she descended the stairs, she removed her shoes, hooking a finger through the back straps, and stepped out into the fine, silky sand. Its velvety softness, warmed by the late September sun, cradled her feet.

The habit of coming here had settled to once or twice a week, down from the daily trips right after JD's funeral. It brought her comfort to walk in the same sand he had trod, to view scenes that his eyes had seen—perhaps even painted— to be within sight of his beach house. It made him feel closer somehow.

When the blocky white structure came into view, she was surprised to see activity around the place. From where she stood, she could see figures moving back and forth from the open back end of a large truck to the house. Someone was moving in. Had it been sold? She'd never seen a realty sign posted out front. She'd been careful to keep a check on that, though what she would've done if there'd been one, she had no idea. She could no more purchase a place like this than fly.

She was so intent on watching the activity in front of the house, she didn't hear the approach of the man until he spoke right behind her.

"Can I help you?"

She whirled, hand to her throat, then her knees nearly buckled when her eyes met a pair of blue ones so exactly like JD's it was like seeing a ghost. Curly brown hair, tousled by the sea breeze, whipped around his head, a white smile in a tanned face.

He reached out a hand to steady her. "Whoa. Careful there."

Then a look of concern clouded his expression, and she wondered what she must look like. "S-sorry. I didn't hear you come up. You surprised me."

"I'm the one who's sorry. I forget. Walking in soft sand gives one ninja-like stealth."

She laughed, brushed her hair out of her face, and then pointed toward the house. "Someone must be moving in there."

"You're right. I am."

"You?"

He nodded. "Me and my wife. My father recently died, and he left it to me."

It felt like a giant hand squeezed her heart. She blinked away a sting of tears.

His eyes narrowed. "I remember you. You were at my father's funeral. The girl in red."

She gasped at the word "funeral." It was like a punch in her stomach. She almost doubled over with the pain. Any progress she might've thought she'd made getting over JD's death was gone, obliterated with a single word. The steady blue gaze missed nothing. While she tried desperately to hold herself together, his expression went from curious to suspicious. Finally she nodded.

"And afterward at the gravesite. I saw you there too."

Her startled eyes met his but she didn't speak. She couldn't.

"My wife accidentally left her purse by her chair. I came back to get it and saw you just as you were leaving. I couldn't mistake that dress."

His smile was tinged with a leer and she felt the hair on the back of her neck rise.

"Just how *well* did you know my father?" he asked.

The question held a hint of suggestion and it sent angry heat burning in her cheeks. "He was my teacher and a very dear friend."

"I see."

The suggestiveness he infused into those two words jerked her chin up, and her breath caught again when she met his eyes. "From your tone, I don't think you do," she snapped. "Your father was a fine man and one of the most amazing artists this world has ever known. Losing him . . ."—she swallowed hard before continuing—"There's now a great, dark hole in the art world where JD Campbell once stood."

He didn't answer. She turned and faced the ocean, staring blindly at the waves, her mind consumed with thoughts of JD.

He touched her arm and she glanced up sharply, once again caught in that blue gaze.

"Hey, sorry. That was out of line. Let's start over." He held out his hand. "I'm Dan Campbell and you are . . . ?"

She studied him a long moment, tried to gauge his genuineness before finally reaching out to shake his hand. "Delilah Edmunton."

"Nice to meet you," he grinned. "I saw you standing out here staring at my house and thought I'd better check things out. You know you can't be too careful these days," he said with a laugh. "All kinds of crazies roaming around. You from around here?"

"Not too far."

"Well, I'm kind of busy today." He gestured toward the house. "With moving in and all, but maybe we could get a cup of coffee sometime. What do you say?"

A tiny voice in her head began shrieking a warning so loudly it was hard to think. She didn't trust Dan Campbell, not one bit. The only thing he had in common with his father was the color of his eyes. If she were smart, she'd turn and walk away and never look back. Yes. That's what she'd do. She'd refuse him and do just that, but when she opened her mouth, she heard herself say, "Okay," in a voice that trembled slightly. "Call me when you get settled."

What? Why on earth had she said that? It was the opposite of what she'd meant to say, what she *should've* said. He was bad news, and she knew she'd regret having anything to do with him, but she couldn't help herself. He was JD's son, had JD's blood flowing in his veins. He was the nearest thing to JD that she had and for now, that was enough.

He smiled at her answer, pulling a pen and a scrap of paper from his pocket. "What's your number?"

***

He called right before she fell asleep three days later and scheduled to meet her the following day at Busy Beans, a coffee shop in the little town of O'Neil, just west of Amelia Island. For the next ten hours she argued with herself about whether or not to keep the appointment.

It's just coffee, one side argued.

He's married, the other side countered shrilly. A newlywed, for heaven's sake. Remember? JD told you they hadn't been married long the night he died. You can't date a married man!

It's not a date, she insisted. It's a meeting. For coffee. That's all.

For now. You know how he is. You saw how he tried to make your relationship with his dad into something sordid. His nasty, suggestive insinuation. Do yourself a favor and stay away from him.

One cup of coffee, a little bit of conversation. That's all.

Think about his wife. What if the shoe were on the other foot? Would you like it if you were the wife and she was the "coffee date"?

She was ready to shoot back a retort to her own question, but it made her pause. How *would* she feel? She didn't have to think about it. She already knew her answer. She shook the argument away and pulled her phone from her pocket. She had a call to make.

Then she remembered the way his eyes had sparkled, just like JD's, and she put her phone away.

Her internal debate continued until she pulled into the coffee shop parking lot the next morning. Well, she thought while staring at the building, no more time for controversy. Besides, it's just coffee. She took a fortifying breath, then opened her door and got out.

***

Delilah stared in shock at the blue line showing on the plastic handle of the pregnancy test she held in her numb fingers. She scanned the instructions again, making sure she'd done everything exactly right. Seemed pretty idiot-proof. Remove cap. Pee on a stick for eight to ten seconds. Replace the cap. Set it on a flat surface with the result window facing up. Wait five minutes. If you see a line, the test is positive.

She had hoped her period was just late, but that hope shriveled up and disappeared when she looked at the display window again. There was no mistaking that bold blue line.

The plastic clattered to the floor. She clutched her head, grabbing handfuls of hair. No! This couldn't be happening. It was never supposed to happen. Not this. How had the relationship progressed from "just coffee" to a blue line on a pregnancy test?

She knew how. It was his eyes. Somewhere along the way in her mind he'd stopped being Dan and become JD. That was the only explanation.

Affairs don't start in bedrooms. They start with conversations. She'd read those words somewhere, remembered scoffing at them at the time, countering it with the familiar excuse, "It's just coffee."

But each time they met, he became less Dan and more JD until eventually . . .

She sat up quickly; one hand going protectively to her stomach. She knew what she needed to do.

Hurrying to her phone, she quickly dialed his number, something he'd told her never to do. He was always the one to call. But this was an emergency. He'd want to know he was going to be a father.

"I thought I told you never to call me," he whisper-shouted.

Not exactly the response she'd hoped for. "I'm sorry. I didn't have a choice. Can you talk?"

"Hold on."

Sound muffled on his end. She heard a low, muted rumble once, twice. Then he was back. "Okay." He sounded breathless. "I told Eve I had to run out to the store. Now, what is so important?"

"I'm pregnant," she blurted. She hadn't meant to tell him over the phone. She'd wanted to meet him, tell him in person, see his eyes when she said the words, but she panicked, and it just came out.

"What?"

"I'm going to have your baby."

There was a long moment of silence in which her heart hammered furiously. Then, of all the reactions she might've imagined, he did the one thing she wasn't expecting. He laughed. Not just a chuckle, but a rolling belly laugh that ended on a slightly hysterical note. When he finally stopped, he sounded out of breath. "You're sure?"

"The way that blue line on the pregnancy test was screaming, I'd say it's pretty sure."

"Wow." In the silence that followed, she could imagine him running a frustrated hand through his curly hair. "Maybe they should make this into some kind of national holiday or something."

"Why do you say that?"

"It's not every day that a man hears the words 'I'm pregnant' from two different women he's involved with."

The words sank in slowly, one word at a time. "Are you telling me Eve is pregnant, too? I thought you said you were getting a divorce."

"We were."

"Then how did something like this—" His words registered, and her stomach plummeted to her feet. "Wait. 'Were'?"

The heavy silence told her everything she needed to know. "You're not leaving her." It wasn't a question.

"You know I can't. She's carrying my baby."

The universe tilted. It felt as if the floor dropped from under her feet. Then rage, more ferocious and violent than she'd ever experienced, exploded in her head.

"So. Am. I!" she screamed, then threw the cordless phone across the room. It hit the wall and shattered. Pieces of plastic flew in every direction. She sank to her knees, sobbing.

***

The next day found her sitting cross-legged on neatly manicured grass. Less than two feet in front of her was a granite grave marker. The autumn sunshine reflected off the quartz in the stone, making it appear as if someone had sprinkled a layer of glitter over it. She reached forward to trace the deeply engraved letters.

Jackson Daniel (JD) Campbell
Born: July 16, 1946 – Died: August 10, 1993
Without art, earth is just eh.

"JD," she whispered brokenly, pressing her forehead against the cool stone, pretending it was his shoulder. "That's how my life feels right now—'Eh.' I don't want to live in a world without you in it. I don't know how to do that." She pressed her lips against the hard surface before continuing. "I've done something stupid—so incredibly stupid, and I'm ashamed. I can't even tell you what it is because I don't want you to think badly of me. I have no idea what to do about it right now, but I'll figure it out. I have to. I don't have a choice."

She rubbed her forehead back and forth against the stone's coolness as if trying to smooth out her wrinkled thoughts, mentally picking at the knotted tangle in her head. "I'm confused. I've been pretending for too long. I'm at the point where I don't know what's real and what's not anymore. No matter where I look, I see your blue eyes and I can't tell if they're real or remembered. I can't tell whose are whose."

Miserable tears welled up, spilled over, and ran down her cheeks. "Tell me what to do," she wailed. "I don't know what to do." Her shoulders shook as sobs wracked her body.

***

The next seven months passed more quickly than she could have imagined. She was fortunate to have a job she could do from home. With only a month more to go before her baby arrived, she was as huge and unwieldy as a barge, and very thankful she didn't have to get up and dress for work each day.

She cocked her head, listening to the pound of the storm. The mid-Atlantic states were being buried in record-breaking snows. Thankfully, Jacksonville was only getting rain, but a lot of it. The cold, nasty kind that seemed to seep into your bones, making you never able to get warm. What she *wanted* to do was stay holed up inside all day, wearing sweats, and preparing her nest for the baby boy they assured her she was carrying. But what she *had* to do was go to her doctor's appointment. As much as she hated to venture out into this storm, she wanted to make sure everything was going well. Baby boy hadn't been moving around as much as normal, and it made her nervous. A checkup by the doctor would calm her fears. So she finished getting ready, applied a coat of lip gloss, and fluffed her hair.

As much as she loved JD, she hated Dan for what he'd done, but she'd finally found a way to deal with those feelings by altering reality. In her mind, this baby wasn't Dan's son at all. It was the son she and JD should've had together. She'd discovered a beautiful truth: if you think something long enough and hard enough, and often enough, eventually it becomes your reality. Though his birth certificate wouldn't back up her claim, in her heart of hearts, this baby belonged to her and JD.

***

It was raining so hard she could hardly see the front of her car. The windshield wipers flapped furiously, slinging water everywhere but were unable to handle the blinding deluge fast enough. The only way she could see a thing was by keeping the red taillights of the car in front of her in her sight. It was a balancing act; staying close enough to see, but far enough apart to be able to stop in time if there was a need.

A watery blur of green caught her eye. The traffic light. The color told her it was safe to go, so she proceeded through the intersection at a crawl. A large dark shape trundled along beside her on her left. Its size told her it was a truck, but the rain hid any specifics.

Without warning, brilliant blue-white light sizzled between her and the truck at the exact instant a crash of thunder shook the air, the road, her car—everything. The smell of ozone burned in her nostrils.

In the same instant, another vehicle's tires sent a wall of water pluming like a tidal wave, across her windshield, completely obliterating what little sight she had. Blind! Her wipers flailed in desperation trying to catch up. She clutched the steering wheel like a life ring, and prayed for the wipers to hurry. When she could finally see again, it felt as if the large, dark blur to her left was leaning her way at an odd angle, crowding into her lane. But before she could move to avoid it, her world exploded.

Metal screeched and crunched. Glass filled the air inside of her car. Shards of it flew everywhere. She was instantly drenched. Pain . . . so much pain. And blood. Someone was screaming over and over and over. She realized the shrieks were coming from her just before everything went black.

CHAPTER FOURTEEN

Ford

I couldn't remember the last time I wasted time on Facebook and I had no idea why I clicked the little white *f* inside the blue square this morning, but I had a few minutes before I was supposed to meet Lacey for breakfast and—who knew?—maybe I'd see something interesting.

Scrolling mindlessly through my feed, a name caught my eye. I scrolled back.

Well, I'll be darned. Greg Donovan. I hadn't seen him since SBI training school. Back then, he'd been tall and gangly and extremely uncoordinated, with feet that seemed much too large for his body. Though only in his twenties, he was already going bald, and his pink scalp glistened through his thin, blond hair. We'd dubbed him Big Bird. The name just seemed to fit.

Greg was third-generation law enforcement. With a grandfather and dad who were FBI men and an older brother who was a state trooper on the fast track to follow in their footsteps, there was never a question of whether Greg would join that field. He was expected to excel in his SBI training on his way up the law enforcement ladder. In their eyes, nothing less would do. Before the driving test, I remembered Greg blowing his own horn, bragging about his driving skills, boasting that he was going to blow all of our socks off, that the SBI program had never seen driving like his before.

This was true. Never in the history of the SBI training program had a cadet totaled his car.

One might think such a thing would tone down his braggadocio, but it only seemed to increase it.

Firearms testing was next. He vowed he'd make up for his "one bad day" of driving with his firearms skills. He claimed his abilities would make John Wayne, Clint Eastwood, and Walker, Texas Ranger look like amateurs. Never mind that all of these were fictional characters. According to Greg, he was a crack shot; said he'd set records with his marksmanship. And boy, was he ever right.

He was the only one in the history of SBI training whose targets could be reused because he didn't hit them. Not once.

He blew it off, claiming "faulty sights." No worries. He was certain he'd make up for it in defensive tactics.

Not to sound sexist or anything, but he was knocked out cold by the only female in the program.

Even with something as simple as running, he lagged a quarter mile behind the slowest participant. My theory? It was those Big Bird feet of his. Imagine trying to run while wearing snow shovels. He took a lot of ribbing but never more than on the day we dubbed "Operation Bird Drop."

The rest of us had long since finished our run and were waiting for Greg to bring up the rear, as usual. The trainer's scowl grew worse each time he checked his stopwatch. Finally, we caught sight of Greg in the distance and breathed a collective sigh of relief. It was just as he crossed the finish line that a bird with digestive issues and a sadistic sense of humor decided to use Greg's shoulder as his toilet. The mess splattered against his dark blue T-shirt, then oozed like melted ice cream down both his chest and back. The trainer lost it. He got right up in Greg's face and screamed, "Look at you, Donovan. You're so slow, the birds are stopping to crap on you!"

Yet, Greg somehow managed to pass the program, which in my opinion didn't speak very well for the SBI. I wondered what he was up to. I clicked on his picture and then the Messenger icon.

Hey man, remember me? Your name popped up in the "People you might know" list and I thought I'd touch base.

I'm getting married Saturday. If you're ever in the Jacksonville area, give me a call. I'm up in Fernandina Beach. Later, dude.

I hit the send arrow and got a response almost immediately. Looked like someone else was wasting time that morning.

Course I remember you. Good to hear from you. Married, huh? Who is she? Anybody I know?

I replied, *Lacey Campbell, local girl. You don't know her.*

He responded right back, *Campbell? From Fernandina? She any kin to the artist, JD Campbell?*

Well, that was weird. How did Donovan know about Lacey's granddad?

He was her grandfather. Why?

I barely got my finger off the send button when he wrote back, *Send me your phone number.*

I typed it in, too curious to do anything else.

My phone rang immediately.

"Ford, hey man. Sorry to be calling you like this, but I can talk sooo much easier than I can type."

"Believe me, I understand," I chuckled. "So why'd you ask about Lacey's granddad?"

"Well, it's really kind of ironic that you sent me that message this morning with all that's going on."

"What do you mean, 'all that's goin' on'?"

"Where do I start?" he muttered. "Okay, let me give you some background. You know I'm not with SBI anymore, right? I'm federal level, now."

"Wow! FBI. You made it to the big time. Congrats."

"Thanks, but it's really just the same thing on a bigger scale. You wouldn't believe the bureaucratic red tape."

"I hear that," I laughed. "So, you were saying . . . ?"

"Right. I doubt you know this, but since Campbell's death twenty-four years ago, we've had occasional forgeries of his work pop up."

"*What?*"

"Yeah, I didn't figure you knew."

"How many are we talking about?"

"I don't have the exact number in front of me, but there've been several."

"But how?"

"They have ways. You wouldn't believe the lengths these guys go to. They even had legitimate looking COAs."

"What's that?"

"Certificates of Authenticity. They include all the details about a piece of art. You know, the medium used, name of the artist, title, dimensions—that sort thing, and then verifiable contact information of the person who signs the certificate. Can't be just some Joe Blow off the street. They have to be legit."

"Makes sense. Go on."

"Anyway, the paintings were all excellent. To the naked eye, they looked exactly like Campbell's work, but when they tested them, they all lacked a key ingredient in the paint. Seems the old guy mixed his own oils and added some secret substance to make it sort of his signature so that no one could ever copy him."

"Smart guy."

"Well, it's not an original idea. He sort of borrowed it. Some of the old master painters did stuff like that."

"So, you haven't caught whoever's doing the forgeries?"

"No, and since nothing's come across the radar for a while, we're sort of at a standstill with the investigation. No one knows how to proceed. I'm telling you, catching forgers is a lot tougher than you realize, man. The average person has no idea how many of the famous paintings out there are fake. The estimate is twenty percent of all the stuff hanging in museums the likes of MOMA—oh, sorry, that's the Museum of Modern Art—the J. Paul Getty, the Gardner, you know, all the famous joints—are *fake*. The Fine Arts Experts Institute in Geneva says that seventy to ninety percent of the pieces brought to them for examination are inauthentic and, based on their research, they say that as much as half of the artwork out in circulation today may be forgeries."

"Half? How is that even possible?"

"I wish I knew. There's all sorts of testing that's supposed to sniff out forgeries of the old master paintings; digital wavelet decomposition, atomic absorption, mass spectrometry, but the crooks find ways around them faster than we can keep up. A perfect example of that is the hot needle test."

"Sounds like a DEA matter, not art forgery."

Greg chuckled. "Yeah, well, not the same kind of needle. In this case, if we have a suspect oil painting, we apply rubbing alcohol on it, then poke the paint with a hot needle. New paint can be punctured. Old paint can't. That used to be enough, but they've figured out a way to get past that now."

"How?"

"They mix a type of plastic into the paint, something called Bakelite. It dries hard enough that the needle can't poke through. So now there's an extra step. We have to test to see if there's plastic in the paint."

"Good grief!"

"Yeah, they've even figured out how to fool carbon dating. All they have to do is use canvases of not-so-important artists from the same time period and strip the paint off the canvas down to its sizing."

"What the heck is sizin'?"

"It's where those little crackles come from. You've seen them in old paintings."

"Oh, okay. Yeah, I've seen what you're talkin' about. Looks like leaf veins."

"Yeah. It's called *craquelure*," he replied, mangling the pronunciation, following it with a wry laugh. "Foreign words. They 'bout kill me. I barely passed Spanish in high school. Anyway, after they do that and an excellent forger paints over it with the right kind of paint, they bake it in these big ovens, and you can't tell the difference between old and new. *Voilà.* Instant masterpiece painting."

"Sheesh. I'm glad I never had to deal with the forgery angle."

"Yeah," Donovan agreed. "And it's even worse trying to catch the more modern stuff. Some of the forgeries are so good they can even fool the artist themselves."

"What?"

"There was this case in South Korea where an artist claimed thirteen suspected forgeries were his own work. They even had the confession of the indicted art dealer admitting they were all counterfeits, but the guy refused to be convinced. I'll never forget his quote. 'An artist can recognize his own piece at a glance.' Those ten words are the epitome of why this job is so hard. They say a painter's brushstrokes are as unique as a person's handwriting, but I'm here to tell you, it's hard to catch a good forger."

"Do I need to be worried? We have Lacey's granddad's collection on display at a local art gallery, here in town."

"We know."

I laughed nervously, a little taken aback. "Um, of course you do. Do you think you could keep me informed on this?"

"You bet. And do me a favor, will you? Keep your eyes and ears open. The big dogs are getting antsy because we haven't cracked this case yet. They're saying we're not doing our job. I might've overstated a few things. You know me."

"Yeah," I laughed. "I remember."

"Anyway," he continued. "Let me know if anything comes up on your radar."

"You got it, man. I hope you catch a break on the case."

"Thanks. And best of luck Saturday."

I hung up the phone, my mind trying to piece together this information with what I learned yesterday. *Delilah's Lilies,* the painting from Lacey's dream, *had* been stolen. I had looked up the police report earlier that morning. It had been cut right out of the frame, just like Lacey dreamt it. Could it somehow be connected with what Greg just told me? I wondered if he'd email photos of the forgeries that had popped up over the years. It would be very interesting to see if that painting was one of them.

***

Lacey was waiting for me on the landing when I locked up my apartment and headed down the stairs. Her face was pale and she looked a bit hollow-eyed, a sure sign that she'd had another dream.

"Hey, sweetheart." I wrapped my arms around her, pulling her close, smiling when I felt her arms go around me. She laid her head against my chest and we stood like that for a long minute. Finally, I tipped her chin up and gave her a kiss before studying her with concern. "You should've called me. I would've come down."

"I thought about it." Her brown eyes sparkled like someone had sprinkled glitter in them. "Then I thought better of it."

"Smart girl," I said with a grin. "I might not have left. I guess, in hindsight, I should've found someplace else to live for two months. Havin' an apartment just upstairs from your fiancée isn't the greatest idea. I know we agreed to wait, but this close-but-yet-so-far living arrangement is wearin' awfully thin."

"Yeah. It's a good thing we're so tough," she laughed.

I groaned, "If only that were true."

After a quick kiss, we continued down the stairs. I opened her car door and as she got in I said, "Meet you at the diner?"

"See you there."

***

The waitress poured our coffee and moved to another table. I took a large, fortifying swallow, then looked at Lacey expectantly. "Okay, it's safe for you to talk now."

She shook her head and smiled. "I wonder if there's an AA meeting for coffee addicts. CAA? Caffeine Addicts Anonymous? If so, you and I both need to attend. Okay," she said after taking her own sip. "Last night's dream was basically the same as Monday night. The dark room, Granddad's painting glowing on the wall, the shadow of the dog."

"Has that ever happened before? Havin' the same dream like that?"

"No, but it wasn't *exactly* the same. There were a couple of differences. This one felt like I was seeing it through *my* point of view, like I was acting in it, rather than watching it happen in front of me. And when the hand showed up holding the knife? It was a woman's hand. At first I thought it was mine, but the nails were painted red, and were longer." She glanced down at her own hands. She wore her nails cut short, filed into neat curves, the nails of a chef.

"Then the knife was suddenly a paint brush, and I was daubing paint onto the canvas, but each time, the paint turned into gemstones. The canvas was covered with them, all different colors. It was beautiful."

She stopped talking and took another sip of coffee and I noticed her hand was shaking. "What happened then?" I asked.

"The dog's shadow. This time I could hear it panting. It got closer and closer to me. I could feel its warm breath against my neck. Even after I woke up." She shuddered and looked up at me.

"Can you do me a favor? Please try not to dwell on it."

She gave an uncertain nod.

"Okay, time for a subject change." I rubbed my hands together briskly. "Good news. I know the name of the mystery man from your mom's funeral."

"What? How?"

"You know I got Myron to enhance the photo I showed you. Wasn't real clear, but clear enough. And yesterday, right here in town, I saw a man who I thought looked very much like that picture, so I stopped him and asked him a few questions."

"So, who is he?" Her brown eyes were clouded and uneasy. I knew part of her wanted it to be her half-brother and part of her didn't.

"Nick Bradford."

She frowned. "I don't know any Nick Bradford."

"He was one of your mom's second graders. Said he wanted to pay his respects to the woman who'd made such an impact on his life. He's head librarian at the main library in downtown Jacksonville. Said she instilled such a love of books in him that he never even considered another vocation. For him, there was no other choice."

Tears welled up in Lacey's eyes, but she blinked them away. "Mama would be so proud to know that."

"I think she knows. I'm sure God told her. Anyway, at least that mystery is solved. Oh, and I almost forgot to tell you. I found out that *Delilah's Lilies was* stolen, just like you saw in your dream."

Her eyes widened. "Cut out of the frame?"

I nodded, watching her. I didn't want to tell her what I'd learned from Donovan until I had more to go on. No sense giving her more to fret over. She had enough on her plate trying to get things set up for Saturday.

"So?" she asked.

"So what?"

"Are you going to tell me how you found out, or am I going to have to start guessing?"

"Oh. Right." I stalled, thinking fast. I couldn't let myself slip up. "I did some checkin' on old police reports. Dan Campbell reported a break-in—you would've been away at culinary school—and the only thing missin' was a paintin' titled *Delilah's Lilies*. It fits."

I waited for her to say something. When she didn't, I reached for her hand. It felt cold. Wrapping both of mine around it, I hoped some of my warmth would act as a defroster. "Try not to worry, okay? I know that's easy for me to say since I'm not the one havin' the dreams, but we'll get this worked out. I promise. Now, is there anything on that weddin' list that I can help with?"

CHAPTER FIFTEEN

Lacey

I could hear the screaming a half a block away and assumed it was a carful of teenagers blasting some weird new kind of music, but the closer I got to Par-a-dux, the louder it got. Uh-oh. I had a bad feeling about this.

I could see the blur of bodies whizzing past the window inside the shop, and the noise was crazy loud, even with the door closed. Curious onlookers stayed safely on the other side of the street, but craned their necks to see the show. Smart move, I thought, wishing I had the same option. I didn't, though. Liv was my friend. I had to see what in the world was happening and help her if possible.

I couldn't believe my eyes—or ears—when I opened the door. It was what I imagined the seventh circle of hell might be. Kids were running and screaming everywhere, harried adults—parents, grandparents, and others—were shouting, trying to round up their offspring, but it was like herding cats. Liv, in a flash of pink with wings fluttering at Mach 1, trailed around, nearly in tears, waving her wand as if hoping it really was magic and could somehow bring order to the bedlam.

"Don't just stand there!" Liv shouted as she darted past me. "Do something!"

My hands flew up in the air. "What do you want me to do?" I bellowed over the piercing screams, sounds that only small children's vocal cords were capable of making.

"Catch it!"

It? What the heck was "it"? I was standing there, mouth hanging open in amazement, watching an entire three-ringed circus crammed inside her small store, and wondering if it was safe to join the melee, when something furry darted right between my feet. I screamed and lunged in the opposite direction, crashing headlong into Liv as she was making yet another lap. "What *is* that thing?" I yelled.

"A guinea pig!" she panted, pushing a drooping curl out of her face and raising her voice to be heard. "There are actually two of them. Some little girl wanted to take her pets on a 'field trip' and, somehow, they escaped their cage. I have to get them out of here before those kids destroy my shop."

"Okay," I hollered back, assessing the situation. "I'll open the door, you herd them toward it."

"The guinea pigs?" she wailed. "I don't know where they are!"

"No, the children!"

"Oh, okay." She eyed the pandemonium doubtfully. "What about the guinea pigs?"

"That's the least of your worries. If you don't get these kids out of here, they'll be guinea pig pancakes . . . if they aren't already."

She looked stricken at the thought, but nodded. "Right. Let's do it. Open the door."

It took several more minutes, and a lot more screaming, but eventually we got everyone outside, panting and sweaty, some more the worse for wear than others. A frazzled older woman, whose hair had been teased and sprayed to within an inch of its life and was in dire need of some repair work, was patting a sobbing little girl on her back. The child wept and carried on like she was dying, wailing over Muffin and Cupcake, which I assumed weren't bakery items, but rather were the names of the still-missing rodents. I hoped guinea pigs had nine lives like cats, and that these two had enough brains to find a good hiding place out of trampling reach. I also hoped the grandma of the little fiend who had caused all this hullabaloo had a platinum credit card, because she had quite a bit of destruction to pay for.

Liv put her small sales crew of Monica, Judy, and Lindsey to work setting the place to right, then retreated to the back room. I followed right at her heels.

She scrambled through her desk drawer, found a bottle of Ibuprofen, shook out a couple, and then handed it to me. We shared a bottle of water to wash them down and then collapsed in our chairs.

I groaned, then asked, "How long had that been going on before I got here?"

She'd scrunched down and tilted her head back, leaning it against the back of her chair and holding the bottle of water against her forehead. "Not that long. A few minutes. You got in on most of the fun."

"Fun," I snorted. "Right. Is that girl's grandma going to pay for the mess?"

"She apologized profusely then wrote me a generous check. Even gave me her phone number. Said to let her know whatever additional costs there might be." Removing the bottle from her forehead, she looked up at me. "How much you want to bet that little girl never takes her guinea pigs on a 'field trip' again?"

"There's no way I'm betting against that. She'll be lucky if she gets to keep the things."

"Well, I'm glad we found them and that they weren't too traumatized."

"Yeah," I nodded, remembering how they'd looked when I found them hunched together, trembling violently in the shop's stuffed animal display. It reminded me of that scene in the movie, *ET.* "They're probably going to need some kind of therapy. Maybe a guinea pig whisperer."

Liv looked worried. "Is there such a thing?"

"Mmmm . . . no, I was kidding." Poor Liv was so "blond" sometimes. "Anyway, who knew guinea pigs were smart?" I added, wishing I'd kept my mouth shut about getting psychological help for a rodent. "I mean, their brains can't be much bigger than a quarter, right? If they hadn't been quivering like they were I would've never noticed them. I guess they thought there was safety in numbers or something, but whatever the reason, it was a great hiding place." Maybe it was the relief that the fiasco was over, maybe it was something else, but I was suddenly struck with the hilarity of it all and I pressed my lips tightly together to keep a bubble of laughter from escaping. "I didn't realize their eyes could get that big. And those twitchy little noses . . ."

Liv must've seen the humor in it at the same time because she put her hand to her mouth to trap her giggle and failed.

That's when I lost it. "I wish you could've seen yourself. Running around and around in circles like you were doing laps in a NASCAR race — your wings flapping—I thought you were going to fly away," I howled.

"It was a freak show!" She squealed with laughter. "A mad and crazy, upside down and backwards version of the Pied Piper, with guinea pigs instead of mice." She wheezed in a breath, then shrieked, "Mass chaos!" Unable to continue, she leaned forward, and dropped her head to her crossed arms atop her desk. Her shoulders shook up and down with hysterical giggling.

Tears were streaming down my face and my stomach muscles hurt from all the unaccustomed usage. "Ah," I gasped. "Have to stop. Need to breathe."

Liv drew a deep quivering breath and let it out. "I think everybody needs to laugh like that every once in a while. It releases toxins." Her statement was punctuated with a couple of leftover giggles.

"You're right." I nodded, wiping my eyes. "I feel totally toxin-free. Now's the perfect time to tell you the good news."

"What is it?"

"Ford found out who the mystery man is. The one from the funeral."

Liv's eyes grew wide. "Is that a good thing or a bad one? Is it—?"

"My half-brother?" I interrupted. "No. It was one of my mother's second-grade students from years ago. Nick Bradford. He's all grown up and is head librarian in Jacksonville."

"Wow. One mystery down."

"About time, right? He said he saw Mama's obituary in the paper and wanted to pay his respects to the woman who had such an impact on his life."

"Aww. That was sweet of him."

"Yeah, but I guess I don't understand why he didn't say something at the funeral, introduce himself. Not just flit in and flit out without speaking to anyone."

"Maybe he thought it was just for family and close friends and didn't think that would include him."

"Maybe. At any rate, Mama would be proud that she caused someone to choose a career associated with reading. She was the 'Reading Lady,' after all."

Liv smiled and reached over her desk to squeeze my hand. "Her legacy lives on."

I squeezed back, swallowed the lump in my throat, and whispered. "I miss her so much. It's like waves, you know. I'll be fine, then all of a sudden it hits me like a tsunami. She's gone, and I find myself floundering, struggling, crying."

"Oh!" Liv released my hand, and immediately began scrambling through a pile of papers on her desk. "That reminds me. I saw a meme someone posted on Facebook and I copied it down. It made me think of you. Here it is." She pulled out a scrap of paper. "Someone named Jamie Anderson wrote this. 'Grief is really just love. It is all the love you want to give, but can't. All of that unspent love gathers up in the corners of your eyes, the lump in your throat and in that hollow part of your chest. Grief is just love with no place to go.'" She looked up at me, eyes full of unshed tears, and smiled.

I couldn't speak for several minutes. I finally whispered, "Thank you, Liv."

She nodded, took a deep breath and said, "Now, let's talk wedding stuff."

"Right," I answered. "But before we start, how are you coming with the bachelorette par—"

I was interrupted by a familiar *tap-tap-tap* on the doorframe. The sound set my teeth on edge.

Liv sat up quickly, smoothing her hair and swiping at the tears from her cheeks with a sleeve. I hurried over to the curtain and slung it aside, startling Barrett.

"Surprise, surprise. Look who's here. Again," I said.

To my eyes, his thousand-kilowatt smile seemed to dim a bit when he saw me, but he recovered quickly, beaming brighter than ever. "We keep running into each other," he gushed.

"Yes, we do." I cocked an eyebrow at him. "But I have a reason to be here. I'm getting married Saturday. Liv is my maid of honor, as well as my wedding planner. We have a lot to do, so it makes sense that I'm here. The question is —why are you?" It wasn't very subtle, but I was past that. He was getting on my nerves.

He nodded once, radiating invisible 'drop dead' vibes that only I seemed to be able to feel. "Right. I won't be a minute. I just heard about what happened this morning and I wanted to check on Liv." He pushed past me. "Are you all right, sugar? Do you need me to do anything for you?"

Liv gave him a sweet smile. "No, thank you, though. We'll get things set to rights soon. My ladies are working on it up front."

"Good." His gaze flicked to me again as I returned to my chair, then back at Liv. "Well, I guess I'll let you get to it then. See you later."

Liv finger-waved and the curtain flipped behind him.

I waited until I heard the wind chimes announce that he'd left, then turned to her. "Is there something going on between you two?"

Liv's eyes shot to mine. "Don't start that again."

"I'm concerned, Liv."

"Well, you don't have to be. I'm an adult. You're not my mother. I already have one of those and one is enough." Her jaw hardened while spots of angry pink bloomed across her cheeks. She took a deep breath, visibly trying to calm down. "Besides, it's not like that. He's a *friend*," she added, stressing the last word. "He happened to be walking by when I got here this morning. Someone had slid another one of those notes under the door. I was upset and he helped me."

"Another one?" I ignored the 'friend' comment, concentrating on the note. "Good grief. What did this one say?"

"It said, 'She's lying.'" Her blue eyes—now as hard as her jaw—seemed to drill into my brain.

A flash of anger shot through me. "Is that what you think? That I'm lying? And, what?—you and Barrett are BFFs and he just came over to talk to you about it?"

"Barrett has more time for me than you seem to anymore. He listens to me, which is something you don't seem to be able to do."

I was too busy floundering with her accusation that I was lying to follow her. "What do you mean by that?"

"You don't listen. You *say* you do, but your actions say otherwise. You think I'm a dumb blonde, don't you? No, don't deny it. I see it in the way you treat me. But what does that say about you?"

"What's that supposed to mean?"

"You chose me to help you plan your wedding, and I'm doing a good job at it too. I'm the one who checks The Knot account daily to keep you on track, but apparently, I'm still dumb because I don't choose friends you approve of."

"Hold on," I answered, raising both hands in surrender, trying to keep my cool. I wasn't going to bring up how I'd seen Raine—our mutual enemy—all arm-in-arm friendly with Barrett yesterday. I *wasn't.* "I just don't want you to get hurt."

"Why do you automatically think I'll get hurt? I told you, I'm not a child you need to take care of. I'm a big girl. I can take care of myself. You just don't like him."

"It's not that I don't *like* him. It's that I don't *trust* him."

"What's not to trust?" she demanded. "What's he done that makes you not trust him?"

"It's just a feeling I have." Don't bring it up, I told myself. Don't.

"A feeling? I'm supposed to let your feelings determine whether I can have the friends I want?"

"No, that's not what I'm say—"

"I think you're jealous."

"What?" I sat up straighter in my chair, my temper flaring. "Now, you're just being ridiculous." Do. Not. Bring. It. Up.

"Am I? I don't think so. You don't want me to be friends with him because you don't want me to have any friend besides you."

"Where in the world did *that* come from?"

"You have Ford, but I can't have Barrett for a friend?" she continued as if I hadn't spoken. "I'm not saying I'm romantically interested in him. I'm not. He's too old for me. You know that. But if I want to have him for a friend, I will, and there's nothing you can do about it!" she declared, her eyes shooting blue sparks.

I jumped to my feet, ears burning, my own eyes flashing fire as well. Okay. She asked for it. "You want to know why I don't trust Barrett? Well, I'll tell you. Guess who I happened to see strolling along Centre Street yesterday? Give up? Well, I'll tell you. Barrett and"—I drummed my hands against the edge of her desk—"*Raine.* Yes, there they were, waltzing down Centre Street, like arm-in-arm best buddies. Think about that for a minute. Hmm? He's best buds with Raine? You and I both know she can't be trusted, especially not after I snagged Black Pearl out of her clutches. And if he's in cahoots with her, then he can't be trusted either. And if you can't see that, we have nothing further to discuss."

Then I turned on my heel and stormed through the curtain.

***

Being in the kitchen of Black Pearl wasn't helping my mood any. I felt my sous-chef, Mia's, gaze as I furiously chopped a small mountain of onions, following it with one of carrots. I needed them for that evening's prawn pasta with bisque sauce. I looked up when I reached for the celery. "Don't you have some shrimp to peel, devein, and chop into chunks?" I snapped.

Her brows disappeared under angled bangs. "My, my, aren't we in a tizzy tonight."

My only answer was a glare.

Without a word, she strode to the refrigerator, snatched one of the large stainless bowls piled with the shrimp Jeb had delivered just before I'd arrived, dropped it on the counter with a *thud*, and set to work.

Silence hung in the air between us, thick with unsaid words. I let it drag on for as long as I could stand it, then sighed. "I'm sorry I'm such a grouch."

The tenseness left her shoulders. She glanced sideways at me. "So? You want to talk about it?"

I poured some olive oil in the pan to start it heating. "Not really. It's nothing you can do anything about."

Mia's eyes sparkled and she grinned. "C'mon. If you don't tell me, I'll just start guessing." When she got no response, she laughed. "Don't say I didn't warn you. Did Ford change his mind? Decide to have a big blowout stag party because Liv is throwing you one?"

I shook my head. "No. He wasn't sure of the protocol in regards to inviting the guys who work for him at the police department. Jonas can't come down until Friday night for the rehearsal and since the only other guy in the wedding party is Chief Craig, he decided against it."

"Okay, then—"

I cut her off before she could voice her second guess. "Can we just not do this?"

"Tsk. Honey, it's a good thing your bachelorette party is tomorrow. It's time to blow the soot out."

"Ugh, don't remind me."

"What?"

"The bachelorette party," I answered, rolling my eyes.

Mia looked surprised. "What about it? I'm looking forward to it even if you're not."

"It's not that I'm not looking forward to it," I said as I scraped the chopped vegetables into the heated oil, stirring as they sautéed. "It's that Liv's in charge and . . . well, you know Liv."

Mia snorted. "I see your point. If she dyed her hair brunette, she'd have artificial intelligence."

"Mia!"

"What?"

"Be nice."

"That *is* being nice!"

"Liv is not dumb," I insisted. "She happens to be a very savvy businesswoman, running a successful retail enterprise. You can't deny that."

I could tell by the way she pursed her lips that she was biting back a retort, but she managed to keep it to herself. I knew I shouldn't have, but couldn't help adding, "I'll admit, she can be a little scattered—"

"Scattered?" Mia exclaimed, unable to contain it any longer. "That's what you do with grass seed. She's beyond that. She called an avocado a 'guacamole ball,' for crying out loud." She flung another shrimp head into a growing pile, and added under her breath, "If pink and glitter were vitamins, that girl would be the healthiest pers—"

"Anyway," I spoke over her muttering. "Liv is my best friend, but she's mad at me—won't talk about it, or anything else for that matter. Discussing the party is out of the question, so I guess we'll have to wait and see how it all pans out."

Mia's only answer was a grunt.

Silence allowed us both to settle down. Once the onions were translucent, I added some water and I looked up. "Hand me those prawn heads and peels, will you?" After adding them to the mixture and stirring well, I explained, "This needs to simmer for about an hour, then I'll strain all that out and add the cream."

Mia sniffed appreciatively. "Smells good already."

It was her version of an olive branch, and I readily accepted.

"It's going to taste even better than it smells," I said, smiling. "Straight from the farm veggies melding all those delectable flavors into a creamy sauce poured over sautéed shrimp and pasta? Yummy. Okay, next, I need you to chop up the crabmeat for the she-crab soup and get those green beans trimmed up and ready for the red snapper. I'll start the béchamel for the soup."

We worked in comfortable silence until Mia finished the beans. "I have one more thing to say about Liv and the party." She held up her hand when I opened my mouth. "It's not bad. I promise."

At my uncertain nod, she continued. "I understand your nervousness, and believe me, I'd feel the same way if I were in your shoes." She grinned and the sparkle was back in her eyes. "But even with Liv in charge, I have to say I'm looking forward to tomorrow night."

CHAPTER SIXTEEN

Delilah

Twenty-four years earlier

Delilah awoke in a dimly lit room. Curtains were pulled closed over the single window. She had no idea whether it was day or night. The only lights were from the bank of machines that beeped and clicked at regular intervals, displaying rows of digital numbers that meant nothing to her.

Plastic tubing snaked upward from the back of her left hand. Her eyes followed the tube to the IV stand that towered beside the bed. That tube junctioned with a jumble of others, each one leading to its own bag of clear fluid. Some were plump, some not as much. They dangled from stainless steel hooks like ripe fruit. A similar tube led to her nose. Oxygen. She could feel cool flow.

White gauze covered most of her arms and hands. Her head too, she discovered when she slowly lifted her right hand to touch her face.

She fought a wave of nausea, dizzy with the effort of even that slight movement.

Her mind felt blurry, thoughts whirled together. What happened? Why was she here? She could tell it was a hospital, but why? She closed her eyes and drifted.

Driving. She'd been driving in a storm. Why? She should've been home, where it was safe. There must be a reason—an important one—but it hurt to think what it was. Like bumping a painful bruise. She shied away from it, trying to retreat into a shadowy corner of her mind without success.

The rain had been a white curtain so thick she couldn't see through it. A flash of lightning, the world tilted, then chaos.

Thoughts and images spun together in a blur, overloading all her senses. Glass was everywhere. And blood. She could taste it. Someone screamed over and over and over.

She jerked, and her right hand clutched the blanket over her flat stomach. The machines went wild. Footsteps hurried into the room. A moment of panic. Then nothing.

CHAPTER SEVENTEEN

Delilah

F *our years earlier*
Delilah stuck her lunch in the fridge at the office before heading back to her cubicle. After hanging up her jacket and putting her purse away, she turned on her computer and typed in her password. Her eyes went to the large calendar on her desk where she jotted notes about appointments and deadlines and such so she'd have it right in front of her at all times. Since the accident, her short-term memory needed such prods. The brain was complicated, the doctors had explained, and there was much more that they didn't understand about it than they did. Sometimes, in spite of their best efforts, connections didn't return to normal. Such was the case with her brain.

She stared at the date. Twenty years ago today. She only knew what they told her. The driver of the truck carrying a load of windows for a new high-rise that was under construction had lost control when the lightning had struck. The frightened driver had swerved crazily, the load shifted, and the truck started overturning right into her lane. She would've been able to veer out of the way, but fate stepped in. A dump truck, approaching perpendicularly to the intersection, ran the red light, claiming he never saw it due to the torrential rain and blinding flash of lightning. He plowed into the side of her car without hitting his brakes at all, trapping her in the path of the toppling glass truck. She was in critical condition when they brought her in, having lost almost half of the blood in her body.

Broken and battered, somehow she had lived, but her baby hadn't been so lucky. Though born alive, he'd died two days later. One of the large shards of glass that had pierced her abdomen had badly injured him. And though they'd tried valiantly to save him—starting an immediate transfusion and whisking him away to surgery—it was too late, he'd lost too much blood. Maybe if he'd been full term he'd have been strong enough to make it, but being a month premature, his tiny body couldn't fight hard enough.

Losing her spleen and part of her liver was nothing compared to the loss of her son. She wished she had gone along with him. He would've been a young man now, in college, like Dan's daughter. Tall and handsome like his father and grandfather. Blue eyes—she always imagined him with blue eyes.

She'd spent time in the psychiatric ward of the hospital when she realized she'd lost him. The trauma had been too much for her to handle in her injured state. Her mind refused to accept reality. With time, though, she'd made it back.

Her fingertip traced the outline of the number on the calendar, then she sighed.

She blamed it all on Dan. It would never have happened if he'd made the right choice. The fact that his wife still had her child when Delilah had lost hers was like a cancer eating her soul.

Trips to Fernandina Beach happened regularly. She'd go, find a secluded spot just down from the beach house, and watch . . . unobserved. It was how she'd learned his daughter's name was Lacey. Thank God she looked like her mother. She couldn't have borne it if she'd looked like Dan, like JD.

It was a dichotomous life, living part of her life vicariously through Dan and Eve Campbell, who were able to watch Lacey grow from a young child to a beautiful young woman. It made her hate them because they had what she didn't, but fate would win someday. She believed that with all her heart, comforting herself with the assurance that they would eventually get what they deserved.

In the meantime the thing that got her through it all was the decision she'd made while locked away in that room. She would continue JD's legacy. If a writer could continue a book series for a famous author by writing under that author's name, then why couldn't she do the same with JD's art? She knew she had the skill. Even *he* hadn't been able to tell their paintings apart. All she needed was the missing ingredient for the paint.

She felt her luck had finally turned when she landed a job as an administrative assistant with Wasserman Fleischer, an insurance company whose specialty was insuring famous artwork for museums and wealthy collectors. The knowledge she gleaned was filed away for future use.

In her free time, she continued trying to figure out the secret ingredient to JD's paint. Her experimentation had become almost an obsession. First she tried using other oils besides linseed: walnut, poppy seed, safflower. None of them worked.

She tried adding rabbit glue to her sizing, underpainting with yellow ochre, and mixing egg tempera into her medium. She'd even tried adding powdered pearls, hoping to achieve the "glow" always visible in his paintings.

Each attempt was a failure.

She tried encaustics, tempera, marble dust, and calcium carbonate. None of these worked either.

She managed to get her hands on some plumbonacrite, something she discovered while researching. It came from lead oxide, the substance car manufacturers used as a color preserver for red and orange car paint. It was also the secret ingredient found in Rembrandt's paintings. But even that wasn't right.

She tried natural resins and plant gum. They didn't work. Then after reading that some old masters used animal protein, she got some goat's blood from a local butcher and experimented with that. Not only did it not work, it stunk to high heaven even though she didn't use that much.

Most of her attempts ended up bagged up in a heavy lawn and leaf bag and stuffed down the trash chute of her warehouse loft, but she didn't give up. Instead, she took Thomas Edison's attitude. She didn't call it failure, but ten thousand ways that didn't work. Each of her attempts just renewed her determination to discover his secret.

As she experimented, she painted. On rare occasions, she came up with something she deemed "Campbell-worthy." That's when she used some of the tricks and tips she'd gleaned from her job.

Her first hurdle was faking a certificate of authenticity or COA. At first, she'd gone to the trouble of finding an expert who could guarantee the authenticity of the painting. She'd found someone with legitimacy to his name, but was also known to be an avid Campbell fan. He was so enamored with the idea of a new Campbell being discovered, he tended to cut corners on the technicalities. She'd almost been caught that time.

That's when she learned that there were no laws governing who is or is not qualified to write COAs. Nor was there a standard with respect to what types of statements, information, or documentation it must include. Finding an official COA template online, she simply filled in the blanks, and voilà— instant provenance. And she could change the names and info as needed. All it required was keeping her identity a secret online with an anonymous proxy server she found on ProxySite. com, using a savvy broker and, suddenly, one of Campbell's "personal collection" was birthed into the art world. She had no trouble finding buyers. Truly fanatical collectors were so gullible. They believed that having that seemingly official paper legitimized a piece of art. Either that, or they didn't care. To them, if it looked like a Campbell, then it was. All they wanted were bragging rights.

In each case, the deception was eventually discovered, but she herself never was, and she never gave up. One day, she would discover that elusive ingredient. Until then, she'd keep trying. And painting.

***

Delilah lowered her makeup's applicator sponge and studied her reflection in the mirror, tilting her head from side to side. She didn't like using heavy makeup, but there was no way around it. Damage control, she called it. But she'd been through a lot. And she was forty-four! She couldn't expect to still look like a twenty-four-year old.

She brushed on some blush and added another coat of mascara. There, that would have to do. She needed to get dressed. She mustn't be late.

She had a date. Not a romantic one. She'd given up on that long ago. But this had been weeks in the making and she had to admit she was looking forward to it.

She'd met Chuck Newton at work. He was a forensic art investigator for a firm that specialized in testing art for forgeries all over the world. He'd been called in to Wasserman Fleischer to test some of the pieces they insured. She'd spoken to him several times on the phone, even seen him through the glass in the conference room at work, but since she held a more secretarial position and he was in the field, they'd never met in person. That is until the day she had "accidentally" spilled a cup of coffee on him.

It seemed a hokey thing to do, perhaps merging into the desperation realm, but since she hadn't been able to come up with a better idea, it was the route she'd chosen. She had to meet him. Period. She had to find out if the rumor she'd heard was true—that he'd been in on the Campbell forgery investigation. If he had, it was possible he might inadvertently share some vital information she'd have no other way of getting. He could even have access to the missing ingredient of JD's paint recipe. It was a risk she had to take.

Picking up her curling iron, she tested it to see if it was hot enough, and allowed the scene of the staged coffee spill to replay in her mind while she styled her hair.

***

She paused outside the door of the conference room and took a deep breath, trying to calm her racing heart. Chuck was in there. She'd seen him walk by her office earlier. This was her chance. She had to make it work. She gulped another deep breath, before tapping on the door. Her boss, Peter Wasserman, opened it. "Coffee, sir?" She gestured to the loaded cart.

He almost waved her away, but then he spied the plate piled with a variety of Krispy Kreme's finest. "Donuts, too, Delilah?"

"I knew you had a big meeting this morning, so I picked some up on my way to work. I thought it might be nice to have them with your coffee."

She knew blueberry cake donuts were his weakness, so she'd purposely stacked a couple of them right on top. She bit back a smile when his eyes lit up. He'd spotted them.

He eyed the plate with obvious anticipation. "Just don't tell my wife. She's got me on this no sugar, no fat, and no flavor diet and it's about to kill me." He swung the door wider so she could push the cart inside, and announced to the group, "Gentlemen, before we get started, my secretary has graciously provided us with refreshments."

There was a chorus of appreciative sounds and she smiled. So far, so good. Now, how was she going to manage the coffee spill?

"Dibs on the blueberry ones," Chuck said, wearing a huge grin, and plopped both of them onto his plate. "I hope no one minds, but these are my all-time favorite and I haven't had one in ages."

He may not have had a blueberry donut in ages, but from the looks of him, he didn't abstain from much else. A physique that had looked merely chubby through the distant conference room glass told a different story up close. He was probably a hundred pounds overweight—seventy-five, at least. If he'd had his legs crossed, Indian style, he could be a stand-in for a Buddha statue.

She glanced quickly at her boss who appeared to be fighting the urge to snatch the coveted donuts from Chuck's plate. She hurried over and murmured near Mr. Wasserman's ear, "I have two more of them in my office. They wouldn't all fit on the plate. I'll be right back."

Relief washed over his face and he gave a brief nod.

She was back in an instant with the remainder of the donuts on another plate. Pausing just inside the door, she scoped out the situation. Chuck's seat was to Mr. Wasserman's right, and his cup of coffee was in the perfect spot. Good.

She stepped forward, offering the plate to her boss, who all but snatched his favorites from it in case Chuck tried to get them too. Then, with her heart in her throat, she leaned in to set the platter on the table. She only had one shot at this and it had to look natural. If anyone suspected otherwise, not only would her plan blow up in her face, she'd lose her job for sure.

Just as one side of the plate touched the table, she fumbled it the slightest bit so that the edge of it bumped against Chuck's full cup of coffee. It teetered, but he failed to notice. All of his attention was focused on the first delectable bite of that donut, which delayed his reaction time. His eyes had time to widen in horror, but it was too late. A wave of blistering liquid washed over the edge of the glossy conference table right into Chuck's lap.

Chaos ensued. Chuck shrieked and leapt to his feet, expletives and donut crumbs hissed through his clenched teeth. His face contorted in a grimace of pain while he plucked his steaming pants away from scalded legs. The room was filled with the hum of voices all talking at once. Someone ran for a towel, while she gushed apologies and shoved napkins at him so he could mop up. Mr. Wasserman didn't say a word, but the gleam in his eye seemed to say that Chuck got what he deserved for claiming those blueberry donuts.

The meeting was postponed. Chuck made a beeline to the men's room, his mind probably focused on damage assessment. She followed him down the hallway. "Mr. Newton, I'm so, so sorry. I feel terrible. Please forgive my clumsiness. Is there anything I can do to help? Anything?"

He waved her away like he would a fly. "It was an accident." His voice sounded strained. "You didn't do it on purpose," he muttered just before pushing through the men's room door.

As the door swished shut, she whispered triumphantly, "If you only knew . . ." Phase One of her plan had gone better than expected. She hoped Phase Two would do the same.

***

She'd waited until the next day to call him. "Chuck Newton?"

"Speaking."

"This is Delilah Edmunton, from Wasserman Fleischer."

There was a brooding pause before he answered, "Yes?"

"I won't keep you, but I haven't been able to stop thinking about yesterday's terrible incident, and I wanted to apologize again."

"No need. I put aloe on the burn when I got home and that fixed everything right up. I'm good as new. No blisters."

"Oh," she breathed the word. "I'm so glad to hear that. I was worried."

"Well, now you can rest easy."

"Good." She gave a nervous laugh and added, "I was going to get you a gift card for a meal at a nice restaurant, but gift cards seem so impersonal to me. So I was thinking, what if I treated you to a nice meal."

"Um, that's . . . nice of you, but it's not necess—"

"Please?" she interrupted him. "It really would make me feel better."

"Well . . ." He sounded uncertain.

"You can choose the place," she added, sweetening the deal.

"Well, okay, if you're sure."

"I am."

"How about Jack's Chop House? Down on Bay Street. They have the best steaks in Jacksonville."

"Great. How about tomorrow night? Does seven sound good? I can meet you there."

"It's a date."

She hung up wearing a smile. Mission accomplished. Now, all she had to do was see if he was privy to something useful, but even if he wasn't, at least she'd enjoy a good steak dinner.

***

He was sitting on the bench outside the restaurant when she arrived. Bent over his cellphone, he was focused intently on the small screen. Sweat glistened on his bright pink scalp through thin, sandy hair.

"Chuck?" she asked and he lifted his head, seeming reluctant to tear his attention from the screen. Her eyes flicked down. Candy Crush? *O-kaaay.* His hazel eyes peered up at her through round Harry Potter-type frames. He struggled to his feet, seeming flustered. She held out her hand. "Good to see you again." She glanced down towards his lap, and back up. "No ill effects?"

He shook his head. "Good as new."

His clammy hand felt a little spongy when it wrapped around hers. His eyes traveled over her face as if only now seeing her and she saw his Adam's apple bob up and down once as he swallowed. She kept her smile in place and gestured to the door. "Shall we go in?"

He held the door open for her and the hostess soon had them seated in a quiet corner.

Once the waiter left with their drink orders, she gazed around with curious eyes. "Sorry for gawking, but I've never been here before. Always wanted to, but never made it. I can't get over the coffered ceilings and all this gorgeous heart-pine wood, and the arched windows. It's beautiful."

"It is," he agreed. "And it's even better from the roof."

"The roof?"

"Yeah, there's a rooftop lounge up there with a spectacular view of the Southbank skyline. I would've reserved us a table there, but I was afraid the heat would be a little too intense."

"No, this is better. I'm more of an AC kind of girl."

"Me too," he agreed. "Well, not a girl, but . . ." His face turned pinker, and he used his napkin to mop his forehead. "You know what I mean. Uh . . ." He seemed to be desperately casting around in his head for something else to talk about. "Did you know this building used to be a bank?"

He visibly relaxed when she shook her head. "It's one of the lucky few in downtown Jacksonville that survived the Great Fire that turned so many to rubble. I think they did an outstanding job restoring it."

"They certainly did," she replied, her eyes dropping to her menu. "So, any recommendations?"

"Well, they're known for their steaks, so anything off that section will be good, but everything on the menu is top-notch."

***

As soon as the waiter poured their wine and left, she asked, "I know you're affiliated with Wasserman Fleischer in some way, but what do you do for a living, Chuck?" She already knew what he did. That was why she was here.

"I'm a forensic art expert."

She faked a look of awe. "Forensic art expert? Whoa. That sounds pretty official. What does that mean?"

Her words had him sitting a little taller, his chest puffing up. If he'd been a peacock, his tail would be unfurled, fanned out and proud. Oh brother! She mentally rolled her eyes. Men were so easy. Puff up their ego and you could get them to do anything. Faking rapt attention, she clenched her fists so tightly under the table, her fingernails dug into her palms.

"We do a series of tests to see if a piece of artwork is authentic or a forgery—UV fluorescence, optical microscope, x-rays, infrared reflectography."

He rattled off the big words in an obvious attempt at sounding important while Delilah kept her reactions under tight control. "Oh, my. What does all of that mean?" she asked. He was dying to expound on them. Why not let him?

"You sure it won't bore you?" At the shake of her head, he continued, settling into it like a hog into mud. "As they age, paints and varnishes develop fluorophores, a fluorescent chemical compound that when irradiated with long wavelength UVA lamps, will show areas of luminescence. In layman's terms, the original work will shine brighter than retouched or restored areas. With the optical microscope, we can see the fine details on the surface of a work, from brushstrokes and tiny cracks called craquelure in the varnish, to the ink patterns of a lithograph. The super-high magnification allows us to detect the attempt at mimicry."

"Fascinating," she murmured when he paused and took a sip of wine.

He nodded in agreement and continued, "X-rays and infrared reflectography allow us to unearth underdrawings and materials underneath the surface of a work. Did you know that prior to 1910, white paint contained lead carbonate?"

"No, I didn't know that." She shook her head, eyes wide in wonder. *Yes, she knew.*

"Not many people do," he preened.

Heaven help her. She was having a hard time keeping her face under control.

"So," he continued, "a pre-1910 painting without any lead white pigment is likely to be a forgery."

"Why, you're a regular Sherlock Holmes of the art world." It was easy to see that he liked that comparison. If his chest puffed any more, he'd explode. "Have you found any forgeries lately?"

Chuck smirked a little. "We find them all the time. A recent one was supposed to be by this local guy, JD Campbell. You familiar with his work?"

She took a sip of wine before answering to give herself time to get her breathing under control. If she wasn't careful, she'd give herself away. "Yeah, I've seen his name in some of the paperwork that's come across my desk."

"Well, I've got a file on the guy this thick." There was about a two-inch space between his index finger and thumb. Chuck continued expansively, obviously enjoying the spotlight. "To the naked eye, it looked like the real thing, passed all the obvious tests, brushstrokes, the medium used, style, where and how it was signed, stretcher bars, etcetera, but when we tested the paint, it was like the others."

"Others? You mean this isn't the first one?"

"Oh no. Every once in a while, over the past twenty years or so—ever since this guy died—we'll get one. They're all supposedly from his 'personal collection.'" He made the finger-quote motion with his hands. "We see that as a red flag anymore. They're excellent forgeries, really. Whoever does them paints exactly like the man, but it's the paint that always gives them away."

Exactly like him. She basked a moment in the compliment, then faked a puzzled look. "What do you mean, the paint gives them away? Paint is paint, right?"

"The average person would think so, but the experts . . . *we* know better." He sniffed self-importantly. "Campbell was a sly one, all right. He mixed his own paints like all the old masters during the Renaissance used to, but he added a secret ingredient to his mixes. Guess he didn't want anyone to get away with copying his work."

"That's sneaky," she replied with wide eyes. "Sneaky, but ingenious."

Chuck nodded as if he'd thought of the trick himself.

She savored her next question before allowing herself to verbalize it. She was looking forward to sticking a pin in this man's self-inflated ego. "So? Did you catch the forger?"

She had to pinch the inside of her thigh to keep from laughing. He deflated like someone had let go of the end of an overfull balloon.

"No. Not yet."

Not wanting him to dwell on that failure, she sighed and said, "The whole idea of secret recipes appeals to me. You know, like the secret recipe for Kentucky Fried Chicken or Frosted Flakes. I like the story about the Neiman Marcus cookie. Have you heard it?"

He shook his head.

"The story goes that a mother and her daughter were lunching at the Neiman Marcus café and had these wonderful cookies for dessert. The mother was so impressed with them, she asked if she could get the recipe. 'Sure,' the waitress said. 'For only two-fifty.' Agreeing that it was worth it, she left with the recipe. When her credit card bill arrived later in the month, the woman was astonished to see that she had an almost $300 charge from Neiman Marcus. It seems the recipe cost her two hundred and fifty dollars and not the two dollars and fifty cents she had thought. Though she tried to get her money back, the company wouldn't budge. She got her revenge by posting it on the internet and it ended up going viral."

"Serves them right," he laughed. "That kind of reminds me of that *Friends* episode about Phoebe's grandmother's perfect chocolate chip cookie recipe. It was supposed to be this big family secret. Ended up being the one printed on the back of the bag of Nestle's Chocolate Chips."

"I remember that episode." Her laughter joined his. "I think it would be so exciting to really have some kind of secret like that. It would make you feel like you were in a spy movie or something. But you probably feel like that all the time, right?"

A frown creased his brow. "What do you mean?"

"The secret ingredient for JD Campbell's paint. You know what it is, right?"

"Well," he faltered. "I do, but it's classified."

Classified? Give me a break, she thought. "Classified? Oooo. You mean like top secret? How exciting."

The waiter chose that exact time to bring them their food. Delilah gritted her teeth, fuming. Of all the times to be interrupted.

The next couple of minutes she spent focused on her food felt like an eternity. She wanted desperately to get back to where they'd left off, but didn't dare rush it for fear of making him suspicious. She waited until after she had swallowed her first mouthful to pick up the conversation. "So, do you? Feel like a secret agent or spy?" At his nonplussed expression, she added, "Knowing the secret?"

"Oh, right. Mm . . . maybe a little," he said, grinning.

Her eyes sparkled with excitement and she leaned forward. "I've always wanted to be a female James Bond." She glanced quickly over each shoulder. "Think you could tell me?" she asked.

His attention dropped to his plate, and he squirmed a little, looking very uncomfortable. "Uh, I don't think that's a good idea."

"Oh, c'mon. It's like a game. Play along with me. Besides, who's going to know? And who would I tell? I'm just a lowly secretary at an insurance company, for heaven's sake."

"Well . . ."

Her heart beat faster. She sensed him breaking. "It'll stay between you and me. I promise."

He studied her a long moment, frowning a bit as he did so. She strove to keep a smiling, cajoling look on her face while she fought the urge to wrap her hands around his neck and squeeze until his eyes popped out.

He finally shook his head. "Sorry. I can't. I hope you understand."

Nooo! She barely managed to keep the wail inside her, to keep her nod from seeming curt. Instead of screaming, she concentrated on her food, chewing automatically, but all she tasted was disappointment. He'd been ready to tell her. The words had been on the tip of his tongue. If he'd have opened his mouth for something besides putting food in, she probably could've seen them. What happened?

She picked up her glass and took a slug of wine, staring at him dispassionately while he shoveled in his steak and baked potato. Well, so much for her plan. She should've realized how much his job meant to him. It was the single most important thing in his life, the only thing that gave him a measure of self-respect and worth. He'd never risk losing that for a woman he'd just met.

So, she needed another plan, but was fresh out of ideas.

He'd mentioned having a file on JD and the forgeries, one that was two inches thick. Probably exaggerating, but even if he was, he was talking about a *paper* file. A computer file couldn't be two inches thick. That gave her hope. She might be able to get her hands on a paper file, but where might it be? He carried a briefcase. He always had it with him for his appointments at Wasserman Fleischer. Had JD's file been in that briefcase? Had she been in the same building as the file that contained JD's secret without even realizing it? That thought made her a little sick, but she shook it away. She had to get her hands on that file. Where else might it be?

If not his briefcase, there were two other obvious options: he kept it at work, or in his home office. The first one might be a problem, but she'd cross that bridge later. So, what about door number two? Finagling her way into his home would allow her to check two of the three places: his briefcase and his home office. Yes. She needed to make that happen.

"Did you save room for dessert?" The waiter's question made her jump.

Chuck opened his mouth to reply, but she spoke first. "Heavens, no!" she exclaimed. "I couldn't possibly eat another bite."

Her date looked disappointed. Apparently, he'd saved room. He acquiesced, though. "If you're sure—"

"I am," she interrupted. "Here." She shoved her credit card at the waiter, who took it and hurried away. She curved her lips into what she hoped was a seductive smile and whispered, "I thought we could get dessert at your place."

"My place?" His eyes went wide and he gulped. "Really?" His voice squeaked on the second syllable like an adolescent boy's and his face turned hot pink.

"Mm-hmm."

Sweat glistened across his forehead.

The waiter returned, laid a leatherette folder on the table, and wished them a pleasant evening. Delilah scrawled her name on the merchant copy and tucked the other one into her purse. "Ready?"

Chuck scrambled to his feet and tossed a ten on the table before gesturing to her to go ahead of him. "After you."

***

Since they had met at the restaurant, they were in separate cars. Good. She needed time to think. After punching his address into her GPS, she stared through the windshield through narrowed eyes. What was she supposed to do when she got to Chuck's place, pray tell? Even if the information was out in plain sight, how would she get her hands on it? Chuck was good at his job. Maybe not as good as he thought he was, but good enough that she needed a plan. Her problem was that she didn't have one.

Hold on. Maybe she did. She yanked her purse from the seat beside her and began rooting through the contents. She still had occasional anxiety attacks from the accident, and so kept a bottle of Klonopin with her at all times, just in case. One tablet always did the trick for her, putting her out like a light. They were small, and if she could somehow smash them into a powder, they should dissolve quickly in a glass of wine.

Ahh . . . she breathed a sigh of relief when her hand closed around the answer to her dilemma. A quick shake gave a reassuring rattle. There were still plenty. Just what she needed.

***

Chuck swung the door open, wearing a nervous smile. "Come in. Come in," he urged and closed the door behind her. "Welcome to my humble abode."

She surveyed the room and then side to side and top to bottom fighting to keep her mouth from dropping open. The largest wall was lined from floor to ceiling with shelving that contained row after row of rubber ducks in all sizes and colors, as well as in all different costumes.

"Not what you were expecting, I know." Chuck's face was hot pink again. From embarrassment, maybe? "I've been collecting them since I was a kid, and I'm up to forty-two hundred. My dream is to make it into the *Guinness Book of World Records*, but I have a ways to go. There's a woman who has five thousand six hundred and thirty-one of them."

She dared not reply. She could tell he was serious about his collection and anything she wanted to say would be sure to offend him. Attempting to appear interested, she walked forward to get a better look. "Some of these don't look like they're made of rubber."

"They're not," he said proudly. "I have a porcelain one, a silver one, and even a gold one."

"Impressive," was all she could manage. Her gaze took in the rest of the room. Magazines fanned out in a perfect arc on the coffee table. Several remotes were lined up large-to-small, under the arc in the dead center of the table. A storage tower of CDs stood beside an elaborate stereo system. DVDs, visible through the glass doors of his entertainment console, were in alphabetical order. But it was with the books he had on shelves along another wall that made her smile for two reasons. One, his having CDs, DVDs, and physical books rather than Alexa, Netflix, and a Kindle reinforced the notion of his being old school. He was definitely a paper file kind of guy. And two, the alphabetizing meant he kept things in meticulous order. Any files would, no doubt, be alphabetized too.

Wait. She glanced around again. No desk or file cabinet in sight, so hopefully there was a separate office or the files were in his bedroom.

"Could I get you something to drink?" His voice sounded anxious.

She glanced up and smiled. "I'll take a glass of white wine if you have it."

"White wine coming up."

He removed two glasses from a cupboard and set them on the granite countertop. Once he'd pulled the cork from the bottle, she held out her hand for it. "Here, I'll pour. You go choose some music for us."

"Okay." He turned toward his CD collection. "What are you in the mood for?"

"Oh, anything," she replied, shoving her hand into her pocket to retrieve the tissue that held the four Klonopin tablets she'd managed to grind up before heading to his place. "Surprise me."

Keeping one eye on him and one eye on the task at hand, she hurriedly emptied the powder into one of the glasses. She had considered giving him five, but decided four was enough. She only wanted to knock him out, not kill him. The powder dissolved so completely when she poured in the wine, stirring wasn't an issue. She had been worried about that, and now, smiled in relief.

Chuck inserted several discs into the CD player, picked up one of the remotes from the coffee table and pressed a button. Soft jazz spilled from every corner of the room. "Ah, my man, Miles Davis. Gotta love that trumpet."

She approached him with a glass in each hand, giving him the one in her left. "Here you go. Cheers." She clinked her glass to his and pretended to take a sip.

Eyes wide, she watched him take a big swallow, followed by another, which nearly drained his glass. When it was empty, he bent over and set it on a table at one end of an L-shaped sofa, careful to use a coaster from a little wire rack beside the lamp. He held out his hand. "Do you dance?"

The question surprised her. She wouldn't have pegged him for a dancer. She winced. "Not very well, I'm afraid."

"That's okay," he chuckled. "I do."

She set her glass beside his—purposefully not using one of the coasters as a sort of experiment—gave him her hand, and waited. It wasn't a question of whether or not he'd be able to leave the glass there coasterless. It was how long?

The muted trumpet music wrapped around them like quilt batting, soft and warm.

He pulled her into his arms and began moving her around the open floor in rhythm to the music, but she could tell his attention was divided. She knew without looking that he was staring at her glass, fighting an inner battle. She began mentally counting. One one thousand, two one thousand, three one thousand . . .

Suddenly, he whirled them close to the end table where he snatched a coaster from the rack, set it beside his glass, smoothly set hers on top of it, and then whirled them away, as if he'd choreographed the whole thing.

Six seconds! To keep from laughing, she murmured, "You *do* dance well. Did you take lessons or are you just a natural?"

"My mother was a dance instructor. She insisted my brother and I learn, whether we wanted to or not. Which we didn't. I was interested in playing football. My brother's sport of choice was basketball." He grimaced and added, "Let's just say dance lessons weren't always amicable."

"Your poor mother."

"Poor mother, nothing! She was a tyrant when it came to *dance*." His voice turned breathy and exotic on the word, pronouncing it, "dahnce," flinging his head back, fluttering his eyelashes.

She had to laugh at his imitation. "But you're glad now, right?"

"Very," he growled and pulled her close enough that she could feel waves of heat radiating from his body.

Uh-oh. Those pills needed to kick in, like yesterday. This dancing interlude would only last so long. Then what? She'd thought that grinding up the tablets would have sped things up. If they were already dissolved and didn't have to dissolve in his stomach, they should get into his bloodstream faster, right? It made sense. Had she used enough? The directions on the bottle said one tablet twice a day. She'd used four. Maybe that wasn't enough. He was a big guy, and he'd eaten quite a bit. It was all guesswork aimed at him, hopefully, becoming unconscious. Four tablets wouldn't hurt him. Would it? No, of course it wouldn't. Stop worrying.

Hold on. Were they moving slower? She waited a few beats and her pulse sped up. They *were* moving slower. It was starting to work.

A minute later he cleared his throat. "Delilah, I'm sorry, but I'm not feeling so great. I think I need to lie down."

She leaned back to look at him with fake concern. "Are you okay?"

"Yeah. Just feeling really weird. I hope it's not food poisoning. I've had that before and it's no fun. Now that I think about it, that steak might've tasted a little off. I think if I just lie down for a few minutes . . ."

"Here, let me help you."

She turned and draped his arm across her shoulders, trying to reach her arm around his waist, but couldn't quite make it. They stumbled across the room toward an open door that she assumed was his bedroom. Somehow she managed to get him to his bed, where he collapsed with a huge sigh, like a giant grizzly settling into a long, winter's hibernation.

"Chuck?" she called softly.

Nothing.

"Chuck?" louder this time.

Still nothing.

She reached out and shook his shoulder, yelled his name. "*Chuck!*"

A whiffling snore rose from the bed.

She straightened up with a smile. Perfect.

***

Thirty minutes later she was back in her car. It had taken her next to no time to find what she was looking for. To the right of the front door was a second bedroom that he obviously used for his office. Behind his large desk was a credenza that included a double-drawer lateral file. Just as she'd expected, everything was meticulously in order, alphabetized and color coded, though she didn't know what the colors meant. JD's file was the first one behind the letter *c*. She didn't dare take the whole file—or even part of it. Chuck would miss it and there'd be no question as to who had taken it. No, she couldn't take that chance. She'd find what she needed, take photos as necessary, and leave the file where she found it.

While she scanned the pages, her ears stayed tuned to the slightest noise that might be the announcement of the end of Chuck's nap.

Her heart skipped a beat when she finally spotted it. She'd stared at the words with jaw-dropped amazement, then a smile curved her lips. "Gold," she breathed. "Of course. He ground it into a powder and added it to the paint. Why didn't I think of that? It all fits." Then with hands that shook so badly she was afraid the results would be unreadable, she used her phone's camera to take several photos, replaced the file exactly where she'd gotten it, and hurried out of Chuck's apartment.

She drew a deep breath, hardly able to believe she finally had it—the elusive secret ingredient from JD's paint recipe—the one she'd been trying to find for years. She finally had it.

Nothing could stop her now.

CHAPTER EIGHTEEN

Ford

My plans for the evening included plopping down in front of the TV, watching a game, and enjoying a plate of whatever Lacey had left for me in the fridge. Having a fiancée—and soon to be wife—who worked as a chef, meant we rarely enjoyed dinners together, but the fridge was always stocked with amazing leftovers that tasted nearly as good zapped in the microwave as they did fresh from her kitchen.

Of course, there was a drawback to Lacey feeding me so well. It wasn't my imagination that was making the waistband of my pants feel snugger. No, it was all that good food combined with my running schedule, or should I say the *lack* of it. Since becoming the chief of police, my running had been sporadic at best. It didn't help that there were always Krispy Kreme "energy rings," as the guys at the station called them, on the counter in the break room. I could usually resist them, but not always. I knew time spent in running gear equaled a fit body and mind, and I owed it to the good townsfolk to be at my best. My hit-or-miss exercise regimen needed a lot more hit and a lot less miss. Dinner could wait.

Seven minutes later, I was on the beach. Ahh. I savored a deep breath of the salty air, feeling better already. I could practically *see* streams of toxins releasing and blowing away in the sea breeze behind me. Right now, it didn't even bother me that there was more about this case that I *didn't* know than I *did*. It felt too good to be out, hearing the crash of the surf, the laughter of the seagulls wheeling overhead, the *thud* of my shoes squeaking against the hard-packed sand. Who cared that there were so many blanks in this case that even a tidal wave of endorphins couldn't fill them?

Okay, yeah, I cared, but I was trying not to let it get me down.

I forced myself to think of something else.

Lacey's bachelorette party was that night. I couldn't help a wry smile at the thought. She wasn't looking forward to it. Definitely not her style. But most of her dread was because of the rift between her and Liv. What was that about anyway? She hadn't given me the details, only something about mysterious notes slipped under Liv's door and Barrett Clatrans causing problems.

Hmm. Thinking of the two things together like that made me wonder if they might be connected. The notes showing up at the same time Lacey and Liv were arguing seemed a tad too coincidental to me. I didn't believe in coincidences. I knew Barrett was the cause of the arguments. Was he sending the notes? Wanting to add fuel to a fire?

Maybe. But why would he do that? It would be stupid on his part, like shooting himself in the foot. Lacey had chosen Barrett's gallery to display her granddad's paintings. JD Campbell's private collection! It was his claim to fame, a major coup for his gallery. And he was handling sales too. He'd have to be as dumb as dirt or crazy as a bedbug to take a chance on making Lacey mad. Barrett must realize that doing that might cause her to yank the paintings out of his gallery and place them somewhere else. He couldn't take that kind of loss. It would kill his credibility. Word would spread and no one in the art world would have anything to do with him. Front and Centre would be washed up.

No, it couldn't be him sending the notes. But who?

I pounded a few strides, waiting for another possibility to flash through my brain.

The anonymity of the notes themselves seemed to indicate some sort of a threat. The purpose seemed to be causing division between Lacey and Liv, but a threat was in there too.

I groaned at the thought. It had only been two months since I'd almost lost her to the Lullaby killer. The last thing I wanted to think about was her being in danger again. Better just file that idea for now.

All righty then. How about the forgery thing Greg had mentioned? The missing painting from Lacey's dreams? Her mystery brother? Delilah Edmunton?

Nothing.

I mentally sighed, then made a wide U-turn and started back the way I'd come. Might as well go get some dinner. The endorphins must've already packed it in for the night. There were still too many missing pieces for me to see the whole picture—*yet.*

CHAPTER NINETEEN

Lacey

I arrived for the party a couple of minutes before the scheduled seven o'clock. If anything, my nervousness about the evening had grown. It wasn't the location that was making me anxious. No, St. Elmo's was a popular spot right on the beach, and it had a decent menu. Not as good as Black Pearl's, but then I was a tad prejudiced.

It was because I hadn't talked to Liv since our blowup yesterday and I wasn't sure what to expect. As my maid of honor, this party was her baby. She was in charge of planning the whole thing. I knew Liv was normally a little ditzy. I didn't mind that. It was part of her charm, what made Liv—Liv. But things had been a little shaky between us lately, with the wedding stuff and then this difference of opinion about Barrett. Maybe the planning and executing of something this big was too much for her, a lot of responsibility on top of everything else. It was anybody's guess how this evening would go. I was nervous, an understatement if ever there was one.

My wedding party was small. Liv was my maid of honor, and my friend Noelle Christmas—yes, her real name—was my only other attendant. I met her at culinary school and we became close friends. Ford's college roommate and best friend, Jonas Holmes, was to be his best man, and surprisingly, he'd asked Sergeant Craig to be an usher, and I couldn't believe it, but he'd actually agreed.

That was it. The ceremony was to be on the beach behind my house, weather permitting. I'd been praying for perfect weather ever since we chose the date, but if Mother Nature frowned on us, the covered outdoor dining area at Black Pearl was our backup plan. I was afraid to talk about—even *think* about—a backup for fear of jinxing it, but it was there, all the same.

All day long I'd had women from all over town barraging me with comments about how much they were looking forward to helping me celebrate that night. As the number of them grew, so did my apprehension. So much for having a small, intimate gathering like I'd hoped. My reasoning? With only a few people, it wouldn't be so bad if the party tanked. But with a crowd? Well, let's just say my experience with the gossip that my dreaming murders provoked had shown me how much the good folks of Fernandina liked to talk. And from the sounds of it, Liv had invited every woman in town, including those we didn't even know. Knowing her, she probably hadn't wanted to hurt anyone's feelings by making them feel left out. So, now if things went badly, it would be one for the record books and would probably be hashed out for years to come.

Noelle was waiting just inside the door. With her dark-brown hair lustrous as mink fur, cut in short layers, and eyes the color of the ocean in a Caribbean travel brochure, she looked as elegant and chic as one would expect of a French chef. We squealed and flung our arms around each other. "You made it!" I exclaimed.

"What? Did you think I'd miss this?" She laughed. "Not a chance."

"When did you arrive?" I asked.

"I drove up today," she answered, a little too chipper.

I frowned. "Drove? Am I missing something? They haven't built a bridge over from Paris while I wasn't paying attention, have they?"

"I'm in Miami now."

"What? I couldn't have missed seeing such a life-changing event on Facebook. When did you—" I took in her forced smile, and knew something was wrong. "We'll talk later, okay?"

She nodded, but I could see the glint of tears in those opulent blue-green eyes. Uh-oh. Noelle had been engaged to the owner of the restaurant where she worked in Paris. Looked like there was trouble in paradise.

Mia and my favorite waitress, Sarah, entered next and, after hugs and introductions, Mia asked, "What are we standing out here for? Let's go get this party started."

"I was sort of waiting for Liv. I thought she'd be here by now."

"Oh, she's coming," Mia answered. "I saw her pulling into the parking lot when we arrived. The rest of the girls from the restaurant were right behind her. Thanks for closing Black Pearl tonight so we could all come. Now, it's time to par-taaay!" She laughed, grabbing my hand and dragging me back to the private room that Liv had rented for the occasion.

I glanced helplessly back over my shoulder, searching for my friend's bright blonde curls, but couldn't see her.

A cheer erupted when we entered the room, and my mouth dropped open. The place was packed. I panicked for a minute, scanning the mass of faces—some familiar, some not so familiar. Oh, Liv!

Pink and black and white balloons were everywhere. Each one said something, but I only caught a glimpse of one that exclaimed, "Sip-sip-hooray." Some hands were dragging me, some pushing ever closer to my spot at the end of the room. Behind my chair, a huge banner covered nearly the entire wall. The phrase "The last fling before the ring" was written in enormous script across it.

Someone pressed a cheesy veil on my head, while someone else draped a sash that said, "Bride to be" over my shoulder and still another shoved a glass of something bubbly into my hand.

Liv . . . I saw her blonde curls glinting in the lights as she entered the room carrying a large tote bag full of who-knew-what. I tried to catch her eye, but she wouldn't look at me.

She picked up a glass, and tapped a knife against it. I could see her mouth moving, but couldn't hear her voice. The noise level didn't change at first, but eventually, the ringing got everyone's attention.

"Whew," she said with a smile, her face flushed. "I can see we have an excited group here tonight. I'm glad you all came to help celebrate Lacey getting married."

There was a chorus of squeals, whistles, and clapping, but Liv still wouldn't look at me. She tapped the knife against the glass again until the noise let up. "I'd planned some games, but I don't think we can manage them with this big of a crowd."

This was greeted with a chorus of boos. She held up her hand. "I know, I know. But I do have a special surprise lined up a little later that might make you forget about the games."

My jaw dropped at her suggestive wink and arched eyebrow. Who was this woman and what had she done with Liv?

That wink was met with a lot of wolf whistles and she laughed. "Until then, there are all kinds of goodies to snack on and plenty to wet your whistle, so eat, drink, and be merry, y'all."

Then instead of joining me at the head of the table in the spot that was clearly labeled "Maid of honor," where she was supposed to sit, Liv hurried out of the room.

I chewed my lip, eyeing the double doors she'd slipped through. Worry niggled at the back of my mind. Did I need to start thinking about a backup plan for my maid of honor too?

I got up from my chair and started weaving through the crowd, trying to make my way to the exit, intent on finding her. We needed to talk. But it was slow going. Every person along my path either congratulated me, patted me on the back, gave me a hug, exchanged air kisses, squeezed my hand, or some combination of that list.

I was worn out when I finally made it. I turned the corner and was nearly plowed down by someone hurrying the opposite direction.

"Oomph!" My hand flailed out and grabbed for the wall to keep from falling. I struggled to recover the breath that had been knocked out of me. "You!" My eyes bugged out when I recognized who'd just run into me. "What are *you* doing here?"

"I was invited," Raine snapped. "Every female in town was. Clever," she sneered. "Good way to get more presents."

Her words stunned me. Then my ears nearly burst into flame. "For your information, people don't generally bring gifts to bachelorette parties, Raine. And it wasn't my idea. Liv put this thing together. I thought it was going to be a small gathering with a few close friends. But you know Liv. I guess she didn't want anybody to feel left out and invited everybody. But just because you were invited didn't mean you had to come."

"Hmph." She gave me a nasty smile. "Don't flatter yourself. I'm meeting someone here for dinner. I just came to get my drink. Excuse me."

Before I could take another step, someone grabbed my arm and hustled me back to my chair. My shoulders slumped. All that effort to get to the door down the drain. I was never going to be able to talk to Liv.

The noise level had lowered, and glassy-eyed ladies scurried to their seats, trying not to spill whatever was in their glasses. Clearly something was up. The lights dimmed and loud music—mostly bass beat—began vibrating the air. My eyes went to my drink and I could actually see the bubbly liquid trembling in the glass. Was this Liv's surprise? I suddenly had a bad feeling about this.

Glancing around, I noticed every set of eyes in the room was trained on the doorway through which Liv had just exited. Now was my chance. No one would notice if I slipped out the back, so to speak. While I couldn't use that door, there was an exit to the outside deck. I was fairly certain I didn't want to be part of whatever was coming next.

As I turned to leave, a deafening police siren joined the bass beat. I looked back over my shoulder and saw a spotlight zoom over to the big double door where a balding man with more than a slight paunch posed suggestively in a skin-tight police uniform. He was obviously wearing one of those head microphones, because when he opened his mouth to speak, his low voice boomed Danny DeVito's line right out of the *Friends* episode depicting one of Phoebe's most embarrassing moments. "Did someone call the long arm of the law?"

My mouth gaped in horror, then I turned and fled to the deck. I was going to kill Liv.

Mortified and cowering in the darkest corner I could find, I prayed no one would come looking for me. The crash of nearby waves was loud, but not loud enough to drown out the music, the cheering and whistles. I groaned when someone squealed.

"No, no, no," I muttered. "Oh, Liv, how could you do this to me? And why? You know this isn't what I wanted and it's not something you'd think up either. I thought you had a bunch of silly games with cheesy prizes lined up. That's who you are. Not this."

The music stopped with a shocking suddenness that would've made me think I'd gone deaf, if not for the sound of the ocean a hundred or so feet away.

My breathing stopped with it, ears straining for a clue. I wanted to know what was happening, but was too ashamed to look. I could hear the low murmur of a voice but not what was being said. After a moment of silence, the rumble of voices grew to a crescendo of many excited women talking at the same time. What just happened? Did I dare take a look? Curiosity finally won out.

I peeked through the door as unobtrusively as possible. It wasn't nearly as crowded as it had been and those who remained were leaving *en masse*. It looked like the party was over.

"There you are!" Mia exclaimed when she spotted me. "Where were you?"

I tilted my head toward the deck. "Out there. Hiding. Praying for a power outage or a stray tidal wave—something— anything to stop him." I took in the shell-shocked expressions that Noelle and Sarah wore. "Was it really bad?"

Mia barked a laugh. "I almost lost it when he sailed that stupid police hat into the crowd and it hit old Mrs. Byrd right in the face. Gave her a nosebleed."

"Oh, no!" I moaned, hands pressed to my suddenly blazing cheeks. "Is she okay?"

Mia waved away my concern. "Oh, yeah. She's fine. I'm sure her nose has stopped bleeding already. She had a tissue pressed to it and plenty more to choose from if she needed another one. All those little old lady friends of hers were digging around in their purses, pulling out their tissue packs, waving them in the air at her." She giggled. "It was kind of funny, like it was some sort of competition and they'd win a prize if she chose theirs."

"Why in the world didn't the guy stop when that happened?" I asked.

Mia shrugged. "You know what they say, 'The show must go on.'"

Noelle gave Mia a look. "I think we should drop it."

"No way!" Mia argued. "Tell her about him taking off his shirt!"

"Mia!" Noelle said with a glare.

"No!" I gasped. "Ugh! He took off his shirt?"

Mia nodded, wearing a huge grin. "Yeah. Picture a nine-month-pregnant belly jiggling like Jell-O while he whirls the shirt around and around over his head."

"A lot of women left then," Sarah piped in.

"Is that supposed to make me feel better?" I moaned, horrified.

"It should," Mia replied. "At least they didn't see his back when he turned around."

"Mia," Noelle's voice held a warning.

"The guy must be kin to Sasquatch," Mia continued, ignoring the threat. "Positively furry!" She made a face. "Disgust—"

"That's enough, Mia!" Noelle ordered.

Mia gave her a sullen look. "Fine. Liv stopped it then, anyway."

I looked up in surprise. "Liv stopped him?"

"Yeah." Sarah's voice wasn't much louder than a whisper. "But most of the women had already left by th—"

"Yes, Liv stopped it," Mia broke in. "Shoved him right out the door and then apologized to the group."

"She apologized?" I asked. "What did she say?"

"That it wasn't supposed to be like that, and to please forgive her. Then she ran out of the room," Noelle answered gently.

My ears rang in the silence that followed. We were the only ones still there. Then I laughed without humor. "Well, at least Raine wasn't here to witness it."

When I heard the clapping, I knew I'd spoken too soon. It was slow and deliberate, with a pause between each one. Clap . . . clap . . . clap . . . .

She stepped out of the shadows wearing a malicious smile. "Think again, sweetheart. I wouldn't have missed it for the world." Then she turned and strolled out, her taunting laughter echoing behind her.

I removed the veil and sash I still wore, folding them carefully. "On that note," I said, tucking them in my purse while blinking back tears, "I think I'll say goodnight."

***

The room is pitch black. This time it's a different one of Granddad's paintings, one I've never seen before. It glows bright against the darkness. Swaths of golds, oranges, reds, and purples paint a sky over water shimmering the same hues.

I hear a sound behind me. A whimper? I whirl, and it's Liv! I can see her wide blue eyes staring in terror at something just out of my sight. What is it? What does she see that I don't? Whatever it is plainly has her scared to death. Her face is white with fear.

A low growl makes the air tremble around me and Liv screams. Her face is etched with horror. Now I can see what was hidden before. First, I see the shadow, then the dog himself slinks into view. Real this time, and dangerous. I long for it to just be the shadow again. He has shaggy, grayish-tan fur and pointed ears. A long plume of tail follows him. His snarl is filled with sharp, deadly teeth and something else. What is in his mouth?

The knife. He carries it like a bone. I can see its carved ivory handle glinting between those razor-sharp teeth.

He stalks closer and closer. The growl grows in volume, filling the air, vibrating louder and louder, filling the room. I put my hands to my ears and scream.

I jerked awake, but was too scared to move. I lay there, muscles tense, listening for the rumbling growl that still seemed to fill the room. It took several minutes for me to work up enough nerve to actually sit up. When I did, I hugged my knees to my chest, mind racing.

Liv was in danger. The certainty of it rang in my mind. I had to talk to her, make her listen, warn her. She must hear what I had to say!

CHAPTER TWENTY

Delilah

our years earlier
FJD had given Delilah a key to his house years before, back when she was his student. She could still remember when he had pressed it into her hand.

"This way," he'd said, grinning that special grin, "if you get here for your lesson, and I'm set up out on the beach, you can take a shortcut through the house instead of walking all the way around, lugging your painting gear over the dunes and down to the beach."

She was gambling that Dan hadn't changed the locks. If he had, she would need to come up with Plan B, but if he hadn't . . .

She inserted the key in the door and turned it.

Click.

She smiled and quickly ducked inside, closing the door silently behind her, listening in the dark. The only thing she could hear was the muffled crashing of ocean waves. She knew Dan used to have a dog—a big black Lab that he'd gotten when his daughter was born. She remembered seeing him play Frisbee with it out on the beach, but that one wouldn't still be around. He'd be too old. Of course, he might've gotten another one. She waited a moment longer.

No telltale clicking of dog toenails against the wooden floor. Good.

She pulled her cell phone out of her pocket, switching on the light. She needed to get her bearings. She swept the walls of the foyer with the resulting beam and stopped.

There! Hanging over a hall table just left of the door. She hadn't been sure it would still be there, but it was right where she remembered.

She kept the light on a moment longer so she could take it in. The shimmering colors she remembered so well sang to her. A love song from JD.

She switched off the light and pulled the knife from the sheath at her side. Gone was the almost spatula-like edge it had always had. The blade was now honed razor-sharp in preparation for that night's purpose. Her thumb rubbed against the intricately carved designs along the handle, touching first the circle and dot on the blade then the one on her wrist. It seemed fitting to use her story knife for this job. She was so glad she'd kept it all these years. According to Yup´ik tradition she was supposed to have gotten rid of it with her first cycle, but she'd clung to it stubbornly. It'd been the only thing she'd had left of her own when her grandmother died, and she'd been thrust into the nightmare of bouncing from one foster family to another, each worse than the previous one. The reason for keeping the knife was even clearer, now. JD had held it in his hands the first night she'd met him. Because of that, she believed his spirit was here with her. Tonight, the spiritual and physical world would work as one. They would do this together.

Quickly, but oh, so quietly, she used the sharp blade to cut the canvas free, careful to stay as close to the frame as possible. She didn't want to harm his beautiful work.

Sheathing the knife, she rolled the canvas up, slid it into a long, narrow, plastic sleeve, then turned and exited as silently as she'd entered.

Seven minutes later, she was in her car zooming back to Jacksonville.

***

She was ready. Her heart pounded as she squirted linseed oil into the pigment powder atop the large glass tile JD had taught her to use for mixing. Scrape and mix, scrape and mix, add a bit more oil, some beeswax to prevent darkening, and mix some more. When it reached the right consistency, she lifted the mortar bowl that held the gold dust, sprinkled some in, and then repeated the scrape-mix routine until the glimmering stuff was completely incorporated. The paint was right this time. She could tell.

After placing the prepared mixture into an airtight container and cleaning the glass tile with turpentine, she repeated the process for each color she would need. When they were all done, she prepared her palette. She lifted her brush like a sword in front of an opponent, poised in front of the empty canvas.

"Begin," she murmured, and dipped her brush.

She had two weeks of vacation from work. That was all. So, for almost two weeks, time ceased to mean anything. She barely slept and ate only when her stomach growled so loudly she couldn't hear JD's voice in her head. Three easels sat in front of her studio window. JD's painting in the center and one on either side. She worked maniacally on one for an hour, then switched and worked on the other. Back and forth. Back and forth. Thirteen days later, there were three identical paintings. She added a tiny black dot to the back bottom left corner of the original. It was the only way to tell them apart.

She cleaned her palette, washed her hands, and collapsed onto her futon. She slept for twenty hours straight.

***

Using the things she'd learned from her job, the paintings were soon authenticated and hit the market. Both copies sold to collectors as JD Campbell private collection pieces, one in Asia, the other on the West coast. The whole operation went off without a snag. Testing of the paint helped ensure their authentication.

Not long after that, she stood in front of the original and smiled. She knew what she would do. The money from the sales had given her freedom to begin Phase Two of her plan—to steal the rest of JD's paintings from Dan. Once she had them, she would do the same thing, keeping the real ones—the ones that JD had held his own brush to—for herself.

***

Her previous success made her bold. She would break in during the day. She could work faster that way. Dan was at work and so was his wife. His daughter was away at college. That's where her son would be if he had lived. But she couldn't stop to think of that. She had to concentrate, keep her mind focused, her eye on the goal.

She pulled into the parking area under the house. No sign of anyone, just like she planned. This was going to be even easier than before.

The door swung open on silent hinges. It didn't surprise her that he hadn't changed the locks. Dan was cocky and sure of himself. She knew he'd believe no one would have the audacity to break in a second time. Oh, how she longed to see his face when he realized he'd gambled and lost.

She eased the door closed behind her and listened. Again, there was nothing. She laughed softly. Still no dog. He was *daring* her to do it. And she would.

The wall was empty where *Delilah's Lilies* had been before. They'd removed the empty frame. He hadn't replaced the picture. She smiled to herself. There would be many empty walls when she was done there that day.

The dining room was past the foyer to the left. One of JD's masterpieces was there. She remembered it well. She smiled in anticipation, stepped into the room, and froze.

A massive seascape hung over the server on the long wall. Paint was spread on thick with a palette knife—a good technique when done well—but this one *wasn't*. The paint was over-mixed and muddied—beyond ugly. The resulting color palette reminded her of decomposing vegetables. A glance at the signature told her what she'd known the second she saw it. *Dan Campbell*. She felt sick.

She hurried to the living room where the walls had once been full of JD's artwork. Her heart pounded in her throat with sudden foreboding.

Her legs nearly collapsed at what she saw. Painting after painting—hideous canvases—crowded every wall. She checked the corner of each one. *Dan Campbell*.

Where were JD's paintings?

She dashed from room to room, fighting the urge to scream and break things as she went. She looked in closets, under beds, anywhere the original canvases might be hidden, but found nothing. All of JD's beautiful work was gone, replaced with the ugliest things she'd ever laid eyes on, too ugly to even be called paintings, and much too ugly to bother slashing them with her knife. She didn't want to desecrate the blade.

Fury raged inside, her blood boiled. How could he do this to her? He'd already taken so much. Had he sold his father's paintings, or had he destroyed them in a petty temper tantrum? She prayed they'd only been sold. She couldn't bear the thought of JD's talent being damaged in any way.

With the imagined ring of Dan's laughter filling her head, she raced out of the house, slammed the door. No thought of silence now. Pounding down the stairs, she flung herself in her car and quickly spun out of the parking spot. The crushed oyster shells along the driveway popped and pinged against the underside of her car. When she hit the pavement, her tires chirped, then she roared away and never looked back.

CHAPTER TWENTY-ONE

Lacey

After a few hours of fitful dozing, I finally gave up and got out of bed. Between the terrifying dream, the fiasco bachelorette party, and all the stuff going on with Liv, my brain just wouldn't shut off.

I stumbled to the bathroom and gave a little shriek when I saw my reflection in the mirror. Dark circles drooped under my eyes, giving me that oh, so familiar raccoon look. Thank goodness Ford had a meeting this morning, and wouldn't be seeing me, but if I didn't start getting a little more sleep, I was going to look haggard Saturday. I didn't want him to turn tail and run when I started down the aisle toward him. I had tonight and tomorrow night for emergency catch-up sleep, and that wasn't a lot of time.

After fixing myself a cup of coffee and a slice of toast slathered with crunchy peanut butter, I took my breakfast out to the deck to eat. I sank back into the depths of the low-slung Adirondack chair with a sigh.

Fingers of gold poked through openings in the purple-and-peach-tinted clouds, sending bands of sunshine dancing across the ocean surface. The beams of light gave the illusion that the clouds were tethered down with golden rope—like a herd of hot-air balloons—so they wouldn't float away.

The previous night's dream seemed just as tethered to my brain, something I couldn't shake. Four dreams in four nights. And even though the wallet dream hadn't included the dog and knife, I was sure it was connected.

That last dream, though . . . I shivered, remembering the look of terror on Liv's face as the dog approached her. I needed to talk to Liv—the sooner the better—whether she wanted me to or not. I'd head over there as soon as I finished breakfast.

I took another bite of my toast, chewed it slowly, my mind busy picking at the threads of my dream. *Delilah's Lilies* had featured in the previous two. This time it was a completely new painting, one I'd never even seen before, and it begged the question—why now? Not—why a different or unfamiliar painting? I knew Granddad had been a prolific painter and there were bound to be many pieces I knew nothing about. A couple of those mystery paintings had been among the ones Ford and I had discovered a couple of months ago. But I couldn't help wondering, why this new painting now? Was there some significance?

Maybe it was just the combination of it all—the painting, the terror of finally seeing the dog, instead of just hearing its growl and seeing its shadow, and the fear on Liv's face. Not to mention the knife.

I glanced at my watch before popping the last bite of toast into my mouth. Time to talk to Liv. I hoisted myself out of the deck chair. It was Thursday—her day off. This early, I'd be sure to catch her at home, even if she had a whole list of errands to do, and I'd still have time to get by Jeb's to order seafood for that night's menu and meet Noelle for coffee before heading to work. I only hoped I could get Liv to listen to me.

***

Liv's house was on the corner of Ash Street and South Seventh, a couple of blocks off Centre Street in the historical district, an easy bike-riding distance from her home to her toy store. The house belonged to her parents—well, her *mother* owned it now, since her father's disappearance. I hated to even think it, and I'd never dream of saying it in front of Liv, but I never blamed her dad for cutting out. Edith Hale was a difficult woman to be around—had been for as long as I'd known her. I couldn't imagine being married to her. To say Liv's parents were polar opposites wasn't drastic enough. How the two of them had ended up together was a mystery to me.

While Liv's dad was happy-go-lucky and fun to be around, her mother was strict and analytical, a no-nonsense type of person with dull, stick-straight, mud-brown hair. She was a pediatrician, of all things. She didn't even *like* kids. I'd had the misfortune of having her as my doctor when I was little, and to this day, I still dread getting sick, tending to put off getting medical help until I'm nearly at death's door. I blame that attitude on Dr. Hale's horrible bedside manner.

Liv moved out right after high school graduation, or at least as soon as she found a job making enough money that she could pay rent. It was the sketchiest studio apartment imaginable, in a questionable part of town. And it was so small she could stand in the middle of it and reach almost everything in it. The size didn't matter to her, though. Nothing could be as bad as the thought of remaining in that house with her mother.

She had upgraded to somewhat bigger places a couple of times since then, and everything was going great. Then several years earlier, Great-Aunt Jill, Liv's grandmother's only remaining sibling, fell and broke her hip. Dr. Hale had dropped everything in order to head to South Carolina to care for her. She'd been there ever since. I knew a broken hip wasn't considered the "death sentence" it used to be in older people, so I wondered about the length of her stay, and I'd come to my own conclusion. Maybe I was wrong, but knowing Dr. Hale, I believed it gave her the perfect excuse to not have to deal with child patients anymore, and two—it allowed her free rein to be a tyrant. Keeping Aunt Jill an invalid gave her the control she craved. Poor Aunt Jill.

Liv moved back to her mother's place in order to keep an eye on things, but even then, she couldn't bear to move into the actual house. Instead, she chose to live in the small apartment over the garage. It was sunny and cute, and matched her personality perfectly. In her mother's absence, Liv's self-confidence had blossomed and she'd come into her own. I hated to say it, but I really hoped that Dr. Hale never returned, and I'm sure her daughter echoed that sentiment.

A small sign hung on the wall to the left of the door, right above the doorbell. "This is my happy place," I read and smiled. Appropriate. Liv was one of the most upbeat people I knew. I reached a finger out toward the doorbell.

But before I touched it, the door swung open. Liv jumped in surprise, then her brows drew down and I faced an unfamiliar scowl on a face that was usually cheerful.

"What are you doing here?" she asked without a hint of welcome.

"Um . . ." The question rattled me a little. "It's your day off. I needed to talk to you." I shook my head. "What do you mean, what am I doing here? Do I have to have a reason to come see my best friend?"

"I don't want to talk about it," she snapped.

"You don't even know what I'm here to talk about."

"Yes, I do. I'm not stupid."

I felt flummoxed. "Well, apparently I am, because I don't know what you're talking about."

She rolled her eyes and shook her head in a disbelieving manner. "The bachelorette party? The 'entertainment'?" She finger-quoted the word.

"Oh, right. I guess I was sort of trying to forget about that," I replied with a weak chuckle. "But now that you mention it . . ."

"He was a recommendation. It was a last-minute thing—" She broke off and clenched her teeth together. A muscle worked furiously in her jaw. "I said I didn't want to talk about it."

I waved her statement away. "Doesn't matter. It's over with. And why are you dressed like that?" I gestured at her pink fairy outfit. "Today is your day off. You don't usually wear that when you're not going in to work."

Liv grunted, before turning back to lock her front door.

Hmm. This wasn't going so well.

"Ever heard of free advertising? I'll be out and about all day. Might as well kill two birds with one stone," she announced while turning the deadbolt. "I have more things to do than I have time to get them done, so . . ." She turned back toward me, eyebrows lifted.

Her thinly veiled hint and stony expression had me at a loss for words. It was so un-Liv-like. "Uh, I h-had another dream," I stammered, trying to keep up with her as she hurried down the wooden stairs and over to where she kept her bike locked up. I watched her thumb and forefinger spin the dial of the combination lock on the cable. The lock popped open, she pulled the cable from around the bike's bar, and slung it over the fence post.

"So?"

Her attitude was starting to tick me off. "So! You were in it this time. The dog was coming after *you* with the knife in its mouth. I think you're in danger."

She paused briefly, opened her mouth to say something, and then snapped it shut. Turning, she swung her leg over the bar and settled her bottom on the seat, one foot resting on the pedal. "Thanks for letting me know," she replied without meeting my eyes.

Then she pedaled down the driveway, turned right, then left at the corner and was gone.

***

I fumed all the way to Jeb's shop. After placing my seafood order for the night's menu, I returned to my car and tried to calm down. I wanted to enjoy catching up with Noelle, and being in a tizzy over Liv would make that impossible. Besides, Liv and I would work it out. We always did. I couldn't remember ever having things be this tense between us before, but we'd been friends our whole lives. I refused to allow Barrett Clatrans to ruin our friendship.

I wheeled into an empty parking spot and hurried to the coffee shop. Noelle was already sitting in a booth. Her face lit when she saw me, and she waved me over. I leaned over and gave her an awkward one-armed hug and an air-kiss. "Sorry I'm late. I had to get tonight's seafood ordered."

She grinned at me. "No worries. How's the 'almost' bride this morning?"

I rolled my eyes. "Don't ask." I turned my mug up when a waitress approached the table, coffee pot in hand. "Good morning, Debbie. Yes, please. The sooner the better."

Noelle followed my lead. As soon as Debbie moved to the next table, she asked, "Okay. What's wrong?"

I waved her question away. "No. I want to hear about you. What happened with you and Francois? Did you guys have a fight?" I glanced at her left hand where her engagement ring was conspicuously absent.

Her smile was sad. "I guess you could call it a difference of opinion."

I frowned. "But, honey, *all* couples have those. You're two different people with different ideas. Of course you'll have differing opinions. That's part of marriage. You have to work through those."

She shook her head. "This one is a little more significant than which way to put the toilet paper on the roll or which end of the toothpaste to squeeze."

"But—"

"He thought he could have a girlfriend," she blurted in a furious whisper, her eyes glinting with unshed tears. "Or maybe I should say *keep* one. He'd been seeing her the whole time we were a couple."

"No!" I gasped.

"We were discussing our wedding vows. You know—what phrases were important, what ones we might want to add or leave off—that sort of thing. He had a problem with the 'forsaking all others' clause." She swallowed before continuing. "That was a deal-breaker for me."

I reached across the table and squeezed her hand. "Oh, Noelle. I'm so sorry."

She shrugged. "At least I found out before the wedding and not after. Saved myself a ton of money." Blinking away the tears that now spilled over, she drew a deep breath before letting it out slowly. "I needed to come back to the States anyway. I got a call from my sister, telling me that Dad is sick again."

"Oh, no." I knew her dad was a bit of a hypochondriac and had been for as long as I'd known her. "What is it this time?"

She looked heavenward, and shook her head. "His heart again. Merry says they're going to do some tests. I told her I'd drive up to Maggie Valley to see him as soon as you get back from your honeymoon. Let's change the subject. Shall we? So, when do I get the grand tour?"

The change was too abrupt. I gave her a blank stare.

"Black Pearl? If I'm going to be substitute chef for you while you're on your honeymoon, I'll need to know my way around your kitchen before I'm left manning it."

"Oh, yes. We'll head over there as soon as we leave here."

"Good. I want your honeymoon to be perfect. That means no worrying about anything at your restaurant. I want everything to go so flawlessly that your customers have no idea that you're gone."

I laughed. "Well, just don't cook better than me or they won't want me to come back."

"Right," she replied in a voice so dry she could've used it for kindling. "Like that'll happen. Now, what's going on with you?"

"Lots of stuff. Funny you should mention Francois having a girlfriend. Well, not funny, as in ha-ha, but funny, as in coincidence. I found out my dad had an affair while married to my mother that resulted in a baby. I have a half-brother out there somewhere. I had a dream about it and the next day is when I found out."

A crease appeared between her brows. "You still have those?"

"The dreams? Oh, yeah. And I've been having this creepy one about one of my Granddad's paintings—one I've never seen before—and there's this big scary dog and a knife, and last night Liv was in it. The dog was going after her. I went over to her house this morning to warn her, and she pretty much blew me off."

"What's going on with that? I thought you two were best friends."

"We are! Well, we *were*." I stared into my mug of coffee and sighed. "There's this guy in town—Barrett Clatrans. He's the curator of the art gallery where my Granddad's paintings are on display. He, well, let's just say something about him rubs me the wrong way, but Liv likes him. It's caused some tension between us."

"Did that have something to do with the bachelorette party?"

I groaned. "If I never hear those two words again, it would suit me just fine. She said someone recommended the guy, though I can't imagine him being recommended by anyone. Ever. I don't know what happened, but a goof of that magnitude—in front of the entire town—isn't her style. Not at all. She knew I wouldn't like it. I don't go for that sort of thing. But we'd just had another argument, and she was mad and—" I broke off and shook my head. "Anyway, it happened and that's another brick added to the wall between us. My wedding is day after tomorrow and my maid of honor won't speak to me. I don't know what to do."

She patted my hand. "It'll work out. You're too good of friends for it not to. But tell me about this dream. How do you dream about a painting you've never seen before?"

"I have no idea. I only dreamed that one once. The painting in the other two dreams was my favorite, *Delilah's Lilies*. Ford found out it had been stolen while I was in culinary school."

"Stolen?"

"Yeah. Someone broke in and cut it right out of its frame. It was that semester I came home and found all Granddad's paintings gone. Dad replaced them with his own ugly art. I didn't tell you about the painting being stolen because I didn't know about it until this week. But there's something else I didn't tell you."

"What?"

"Granddad's paintings were under Dad's."

"What do you mean?"

"I mean Dad stretched his hideous canvases right over the top of Granddad's."

"Why? To hide them? Did he think the thief would come back?"

I shrugged. "No way to know for sure, but I think, in his own twisted way, he was trying to protect his father's lifework." After taking a swallow of coffee, I continued. "I can't stop thinking about that new painting—the one I'd never seen before. I wish there was a master list of Granddad's paintings; you know, a way to be able to see them all."

"There probably is."

"Yeah, but where and how on earth would I find it?"

"Are you serious?" Noelle's eyes widened at my blank look, then she gave a little laugh and waved her cell phone in front of my face. "Hello. Twenty-first century calling. This device has access to a nifty little thing called the internet, and I just about guarantee you'll find exactly what you're looking for there. Here"—her thumbs were a blur of movement—"Let's type in *master list of famous artwork*,' and see what comes up." She pressed a button and scanned the screen before handing her phone to me. "Artlist.com looks promising. Take a look."

Artlist.com? I scanned the first few lines. "Twelve million + auction records from over 340,000 artists and 1,800 auction houses . . ." Hmm. Maybe.

Scrolling down, I saw headings for auctions, news, galleries, auction houses . . . ah, yes—Artists. I quickly typed in, "JD Campbell."

"Oh, wow! Listen to this—'JD Campbell started painting as a young boy, after his first encounter with Van Gogh's *Irises*. This marked the beginning of his appreciation for impressionism. By age twelve, he got a job after school painting murals. Here he learned techniques of acrylics on the grand scale of forty-foot canvases.

"He spent a year at the Savannah College of Art and Design where he immersed himself in landscape, using every medium until sticking with oils he mixed himself in the manner of the old masters. After repeatedly being told that no one could have a profitable career in art, he transferred to the University of West Florida, attaining a degree in bioengineering. After graduating, he surprised all the naysayers and entered the art trade as a professional, developing and originating Open Impressionism, the minimalist technique of impasto paint strokes without layering, which allowed him to create abstract mosaics of color and texture that lent a sculptural effect to his art.'"

I sat back, stunned. With a few taps on a screen, I just doubled everything I knew about Granddad *without* the sour grapes flavor my dad had always managed to add to any tidbits he deemed worthy of dropping. I knew you could find anything about anyone online, so why hadn't I thought to look? "I'm such an idiot," I murmured in a daze. "My brain must be short-circuited."

Noelle didn't agree, bless her, and sat there wearing a ridiculously pleased grin.

I scrolled some more, still in search of a list of his works.

"Wait!" My heart thumped excitedly. "Here's a whole page—two, no, *three—pages.* Look." I turned Noelle's phone around to face her. "Thumbprint versions of Granddad's portfolio! Including the title, the year it was completed, the current owner, and whether or not it's for sale." I turned it back around so I could see it. "Perfect. This is just what I need."

I scanned row after row of quarter-inch icons—clicked on a couple to get a better look—in search of the one I remembered from my dream. All of the ones Ford and I had discovered hidden under my dad's paintings were here—the ones I sold in order to buy my restaurant too. Those even listed the new owners' names. The list was extensive— almost as many that I *hadn't* seen as those I *had.*

My breath suddenly caught in my throat. "I found it!" I whispered "The painting from my dream. It's titled, *Amelia Sky*. Look." I handed the phone to her, watching her face as she studied it. She finally handed it back to me. I stared at the screen in amazement. Every shade of orange and crimson, purple and gold blazed like a banner flung across the canvas, casting iridescent reflections across the ocean's surface. Even on the phone's small screen, the water looked so real it seemed to move and shimmer in the light.

Though beyond beautiful, it caused a thrill of terror to snake up my spine. The sight of it made me hear the dog growl again, see the fear in Liv's blue eyes. My trembling finger tapped the screen for more information.

"Wait a minute. They have *Amelia Sky* listed as one from JD Campbell's 'private collection.' How can that be? I *own* his private collection. They're all on display at a gallery here in town that I told you about."

"Maybe there are others in that category."

I shook my head. "Maybe, but I wouldn't think so. His private collection would only be those that he personally kept—the ones from the beach house. *Amelia Sky* wasn't one of them." I chewed my bottom lip while puzzling over what I had just learned.

My eyes went back to the screen. I scrolled through a few more while puzzling over what I'd just learned and froze. "Hey, they included *Delilah's Lilies* on this list. That's the painting that was stolen from my house. Why would they include it? Seems kind of weird."

Then I scanned the line underneath it, and my mouth went dry. "No!" I could barely whisper. "They're saying some guy from Kyoto, Japan owns it. Fumitaka Wu!"

"What? Let me see."

"There's got to be some mistake." In a daze, I stared across the room.

"Uh," Noelle's voice sounded strange and I looked up. She looked like she'd seen a ghost. "It gets worse. Look." She handed the phone back to me.

My eyes went to the line where she was pointing. I read it. Then I read it again. There, in black and white, it listed the gallery that had handled the sale—Front and Centre Gallery, Fernandina Beach, Florida.

Noelle was talking. I could see her mouth moving, but I couldn't hear what she was saying over my confused thoughts.

Then one thought broke through, causing me to sit up straight—alert, heart pounding: Call Barrett Clatrans.

I nodded. In the words of Ricky Ricardo from the *I Love Lucy* show, he had some "'splaining to do."

CHAPTER TWENTY-TWO

Ford

I slipped out of the men's room and was dragging my feet on the way back to my table at the Fernandina Beach Golf Club restaurant where my "mandatory attendance" breakfast meeting was being held, when I overheard the excited jabber of a couple in the lobby. I caught six words: "emergency," "golf course," "overturned car," and "trapped." I grasped at the excuse they offered. Duty calls, I told myself. You're chief of police. You have a responsibility to help. The fact that it would get me out of the blasted breakfast that I never wanted to go to in the first place was just coincidental. Riiight.

I exited the clubhouse at a fast walk, intent on making my escape as quickly as possible without breaking out into an all-out run. I was afraid of being caught and dragged back. I knew when I took this job I'd have to hobnob with folks I might prefer to avoid, but I hadn't counted on the time it involved. Seemed like I was always in some meeting or another. It was all I could do to squeeze in a few minutes here and there to dig for information about Delilah Edmunton. So far I'd come up with a big, fat nothing. Even my man, Myron, hadn't been able to turn anything up. The woman had disappeared so completely, I was beginning to think that birth certificate Lacey found was some kind of hoax. I'd keep digging, though I wasn't sure anything would come of it.

I picked up my pace when I spotted my car, and my mind returned to the meeting I was bailing on. It wasn't that I had something against eating with the mayor and a bunch of big wheels. No, the food was good here, and the people weren't unpleasant to be around, but this time it was different. This time it was about *me*. They wanted to plan a fancy shindig where they'd present me with some kind of an award for my heroism in stopping the "Lullaby Murders" that had plagued the town a couple of months before. I should be proud. Lacey's words, not mine. She said it was an honor—a feather in my cap—that it would look good on a resumé. But the thing that no one seemed to understand was that stopping bad guys was my job. It didn't make me a hero. As far as I was concerned a dinner like that was a waste of time and money. Besides, the creep had been trying to kill Lacey. What else was I supposed to do?

I paused before pulling out onto the road. Which way? The conversation I'd overheard hadn't indicated where this emergency was, and I'd been too intent on my exit strategy to ask before leaving the clubhouse. This golf course wasn't small. With twenty-seven holes, it covered a good bit of real estate in both directions. I rolled the window down and listened. A siren whooped off in the distance to my left. Okay. Question answered. Left it was.

I soon joined the glut of other emergency vehicles and abandoned golf carts that were nearly blocking the road. Hmm. Must not be any crime happening anywhere else in town. I squeezed past not one, not two, but three fire engines and finally could see the crash site.

The vehicle—sadly a sporty, silver Audi R8—was upside down. All four tires jutted up in the air. Steam rose from the front of the car, scenting the heavy morning air with antifreeze.

"Keep that rubber-side down, now. You hear?" The words rang sharp and crystal clear in my head. Gruff, matter-of-fact— my Aunt Tilly's voice. I must've heard her say that a blue-million times. Her way of telling me that she loved me and to be careful. She and Uncle Ed had been unceremoniously thrust into the role of being my parents when my own were killed in a convenience store robbery gone bad. They were on a date. I was just a kid, so I was with a sitter when it happened, otherwise, I would've been with them. The whole horrible thing was simply a case of being in the wrong place at the wrong time.

Considering the fact that Uncle Ed and Aunt Tilly had been childless and considerably older than my parents when it happened, I think they did a good job. They'd instilled Christian values in me, had me in church every Sunday, and managed to steer me through the turbulent waters of adolescence and teen years without any significant problems. They deserved a medal for that. Both of them died while I was in college—Uncle Ed had a heart attack and Aunt Tilly followed him the next year. Tough as she was, I think she died of a broken heart. They'd been inseparable, taught me by example what marriage was supposed to look like. I hadn't thought about them in a while. I guess it was seeing those tires silhouetted against the blue sky that brought it all back.

After sidling through the crowd, I made my way to the perimeter of yellow police tape. A uniformed officer stood guard, his hand resting threateningly on his gun. He scowled his best bulldog imitation, but his almost comical scarecrow-thin frame made him look more like Barney Fife. He was Hollis Quinn, or "H" as he was known down at the station. Calling him that seemed a little too *CSI Miami* to me, though. I stuck to using his last name.

I still hadn't figured this guy out. He came across as the ultimate jerk to every other officer at the station, but with me, it was like he wanted to be best buddies or my righthand man. He was so over-the-top polite it was almost sickening. But just with me. With everyone else he was a royal pain. At first I worried he was bipolar; even checked his records. No mention of it.

His actions made no sense to me. By all rights, my job should've gone to him. He'd been next in line. So, if anything, he should have hated my guts, but that wasn't the case. I tolerated his sucking up simply because I wasn't sure how to stop it. I guessed it was better this way. If he spouted off to me like he did with the rest of the guys, I might have to punch him in the nose and that would only get me in trouble.

Approaching from the side, I lifted the police tape and started to step underneath.

Quinn whirled to face me, pulled his gun from its holster, pointing it at my chest and I froze.

"O-oh," he spluttered when he realized what he'd done. He fumbled his weapon; almost dropped it, which only increased my comparison between him and the fictional Mayberry deputy. Once he regained control, he jammed it back into his holster with a force that made him wince slightly. "Didn't realize it was you, Chief," he mumbled, obviously embarrassed.

I glanced around the area. There were few people gathered, most of them were emergency personnel. No crowds pushing or shoving, no one trying to get past the tape. A guard wasn't necessary, but I wasn't about to say anything. Instead I asked, "You okay, Quinn?"

"Sir?"

"You appeared to be in some sort of pain there." I motioned toward his hip area.

His face flushed. "It's nothing, sir."

"Maybe you should see the doctor, get it checked out."

His face turned even redder, and he ducked his head, readjusting all the accoutrements on his belt like it was of life-and-death importance. "The doctor is the problem," he muttered in a voice so low I almost didn't hear it. Then he looked up, tight-faced, and repeated. "It's *nothing*, sir."

"Hey, H," someone called. Dave Henderson, another one of my officers, approached us.

"What?" he snapped. One word and it somehow sounded rude.

"How are you doing on that lesson?"

Quinn's face went purple.

Dave elbowed me. "Ol' H here gave Dr. Mathis a citation last month. Guess he forgot he was scheduled for a colonoscopy." His eyes danced with suppressed amusement. "So when he woke from the thing yesterday, he could hardly walk. That's when he remembered rule number one." He glanced over at

Quinn, saw his puce-colored face and doubled over, howling with laughter. "Never give a ticket to your butt doctor."

It was all I could do to keep from doubling over myself. Quinn's face looked like a thundercloud ready to burst. I pressed my lips into a tight seam, fighting the urge to laugh.

A sudden wail split the morning air. Uh-oh. I gave the two men a distracted wave and hurried toward the action.

EMS workers had just smashed the back window and were wedging the jaws-of-life spreader into the buckled door. The air vibrated with the loud rattle of the gas generator powering it. The car door screeched and popped as metal gave way to the jaw's relentless hydraulic power. But even as loud as all that was, I could still hear the wails and moans of the car's occupant.

Another of my officers, Ed Owens, stood nearby. "What happened?" I shouted to be heard.

He glanced up, did a double-take. "Oh. Thought you had a meeting this morning, sir."

I waved away his question, mumbled, "Got out early."

Owens shrugged. "It's a case of car versus golf cart. The cart crossing is clearly marked, as is the twenty-five miles per hour speed limit. The car's driver—" he glanced at the slip of paper in his hand. "Mr. Elwood Burns, was going too fast and swerved to avoid collision. He missed the cart, but ended up rolling a couple of times."

"Sounds like he's hurt."

"Don't know yet, but from what EMS has been able to determine, he only has a few minor lacerations."

"But all that noise he's makin' . . . sounds like he's lost a limb or somethin'."

"That's because they're having to use the jaws-of-life on his brand-new car. The caterwauling is about them using a 'can opener' on his precious baby."

I winced. "I'd probably be cryin' too, if it were me. Shame. That's one sweet ride."

"Was," Owens corrected. "If it wasn't totaled before, there's no doubt now. They're having to cut the door off."

I groaned and shook my head in sympathy. "No other way to get him out?"

"'Fraid not, sir. You'll understand when you see him."

I frowned at the cryptic remark. What was that supposed to mean? Curiosity aroused, I moved in for a closer look.

At that moment the rescue workers dragged the door out of the way with a shout of triumph, and I got my first look at the driver. My eyebrows shot up in surprise.

The man weighed five hundred pounds if he weighed an ounce.

He reminded me of an overbloated tick, skin stretched so tightly it seemed he might pop at any given moment. Proportionately, his body seemed way too big for everything attached to it—short arms, short legs, tiny billiard ball-smooth head. The driver's seat, of necessity, had to be adjusted back as far as it would go to allow for his sizeable girth, but back that far, he needed gorilla arms to reach the steering wheel. Instead, his resembled those of a T-Rex. Ah, that was the problem. It was impossible to control a vehicle if one couldn't reach the steering wheel. Well, we'd cross that bridge later. The most pressing issue now wasn't how he'd wedged himself in or whether or not his arms were long enough, it was how to get him out of his car.

That thought seemed to have hit the rest of the rescue workers at about the same it hit me. I caught worried, uncertain looks passing between several of them. Removing your average adult male out of a vehicle was one thing. Getting someone his size out of an upside-down car that size would be like trying to pry a sea bass out of a sardine can.

"Bring me the ram," EMT Doug Byler shouted.

This was the third device of the Jaws of Life trio—commonly called JOL for short. The spreader was used for prying the door open; the cutter did just what its name implied, it cut right through the metal and enabled the rescuers to get the door peeled back out of the way. The ram was used when a victim's legs were trapped under the dashboard of a car. It could push the whole thing back, allowing enough space to pull the victim free. There wasn't going to be much more of this car than scrap metal left by the time they got Mr. Burns out.

I sniffed. In addition to the antifreeze I caught the ominous scent of something burning. A glance at the undercarriage of the car showed the hiss of steam escaping the radiator thickening with smoke. A jolt of adrenalin shot through my veins. "Gentlemen,"—I tried to sound calm while gesturing toward the front of the car—"time's up."

From his upside-down angle, Mr. Burns wasn't able to see the smoke, but we all knew when he caught a whiff of it. His moans and wails over the fate of his car turned to shrieks of terror. "Help! Get me out of here. Get me out! Now!"

The high-pitched screams reverberating in such a small space were too much for Doug. Red-faced, and with sweat dripping from his chin from manhandling the ram, he lost his cool. He tossed the ram aside, growling a string of curses before snapping, "Dude, screaming in my ear isn't making this go faster. Shut. Up!"

The look on Mr. Burns' face at Doug's outburst would've been comical in a different situation. Not so, now, but he did as he was told at the precise minute someone switched the generator off. For a long moment, the air rang with blessed quietness.

"Now." Doug snatched the harness off the waiting rescue litter basket. "Lean forward." He looped the nylon strap under the frightened man's arms, and pulled it tight.

"Ooof." I was close enough to hear the air whoosh from Mr. Burns' lungs, but he wisely kept any complaint to himself.

After fastening it securely, Doug tossed the rope ends to a flurry of waiting hands, then scrambled out of the way, muttering to himself as he took his place on the rope. Raising his voice, he shouted over his shoulder, "This isn't ideal, but we don't have time to come up with Plan B. Ready? Pull!"

Nothing happened.

Then there was a soft *poof* and I saw a small flame flicker from the bottom of the car.

Mr. Burns must've heard it too, because his whimpering started again. "Please, please, please . . ."

One of the firemen hurried forward with a fire extinguisher and blasted the flame, but another blaze whooshed upward, higher than the first one.

"Again! Pull!"

I found a place on the rope, braced my feet, leaned back, and pulled with all my strength. Its fibers dug into my palms. Every muscle in my body strained with the effort. Another flicker rose from the bottom of the car, necessitating another burst from the fire extinguisher. We were involved in a life-and-death tug-of-war, but slowly, slowly, our side was winning.

En masse, we took a small step back, then another, and another, larger this time. And finally, Mr. Burns flopped out on the grass, drenched with nervous sweat, but looking very happy to be free. Anxious hands rolled him to his side, slid the metal litter under his massive body, rolled him back, and then lifted/dragged him away from the mangled wreckage as quickly as possible, leaving deep ragged ruts in the manicured grass of the golf course. Once we were safely away, the firemen put some serious effort into controlling the flames and the fire was soon out. Disaster averted. We breathed a collective sigh of relief.

It took all of us, and a great deal of grunting and groaning, to get the overflowing basket loaded into the back of the ambulance. I wasn't a fortune-teller, but the way several of the men were walking, hands pressed to their lower backs, I believed I could predict two things: a rash of worker's comp claims and busy chiropractors for the next couple of days.

While the firemen did a final check and began the packing up process, the EMTs took care of Mr. Burns' vitals. My guys had their work cut out for them trying to clear out traffic so the ambulance would be able to get the patient to the hospital.

"Excuse me, sir?" a voice spoke behind me.

I turned. Mr. Burns was looking in my direction, beckoning me toward him. I looked over both shoulders. No one was there. "Me?" I pointed to my chest.

"Yes. I wanted to thank you."

"Oh, no sir, Mr. Burns. That's what we're here for."

"Name's Elwood. People call me Woody."

I grinned. "Nice to meet you, Woody. Sorry it's under these circumstances, but I'm glad you're okay."

"Yeah. Wish I could say the same thing about my car. I only had it a couple of weeks."

"Ugh," I winced. "That hurts."

He nodded his agreement. "At least I have good insurance."

"Right." I paused, waiting for him to continue. He clearly had something on his mind. After a couple of minutes of him saying nothing further, I decided I must've been mistaken. I turned to leave.

"You're Lacey Campbell's fiancé, aren't you?"

"I am," I answered, turning back to face him. "How'd you know?"

"I saw you on TV a couple of months back when that serial murder case was solved. I knew her grandfather, JD Campbell. He was a good friend of mine."

I eyed him with new interest. "You don't say."

"Yeah. That is until he took up with that little dark-haired girl a couple of years before he died. After he met her, he didn't have much time for anybody else."

"Dark-haired girl?" I felt my pulse speed up a bit.

"Yeah. Can't remember her name, but she was his shadow for two solid years. There were even rumors of an April-December romance."

"Interesting. And you don't remember her name?"

"Nah," he answered, his forehead wrinkled with effort. "Pretty sure it was a Bible name, though."

A Bible name? My heart beat even faster. I didn't want to jinx things by blurting out the name on the tip of my tongue. "Ruth? Naomi? Mary?" I began rattling off all the women's names I remembered from childhood Sunday school lessons. "Martha, Eve, Bathsheba?"

"No, no," he shook his head. "It was that story of the strong man with the long hair."

"You mean Samson?"

"Yeah, that's it. Samson and . . . and . . . *Delilah*. That was her name. Delilah."

My heart was pounding by this time. Before I could open my mouth to question him further, the EMT was at the back of the ambulance. "Chief? They've got a lane cleared so we can transport."

"Great." I turned back to Woody as the technician climbed in beside him. "I'll be wantin' to speak with you more later, Mr. Burns."

"Woody," he reminded me.

"Right. Woody. Hope you get a clean bill of health at the hospital." I closed the ambulance doors, banged them twice to let the driver know it was safe, and then stepped back.

So, Lacey's granddad had had a girlfriend named Delilah, and the woman her father had had an affair with . . . fathered a son with . . . was also named Delilah. Could it be a coincidence? Not a chance. The break I'd been looking for had just fallen in my lap. I didn't know how this woman was connected to both Lacey's granddad and her father, but I aimed to find out.

I checked my phone for messages once back in my car, afraid of a possible reprimand for skipping out of the breakfast meeting. Ah, a voice mail from Myron.

"Hey, Boss. Give me a call, would you?"

Finally, I thought, dialing his number. *Hope he has good news for me.*

"*Yell*-ow."

I didn't even roll my eyes this time. "Jamison, here. What ya got?"

"Sorry it took me so long to get back to you, but your girl has been hard to follow."

"How so?"

"Well, to start with, she's from Alaska."

"*Alaska?* How in the world did she end up here?"

"Don't know. All I got is a spotty timeline. I have early years up to teenager, then twenties until four years ago."

"Okay. Give me what you got."

"She didn't get Edmunton for a last name until later. That's why it took me a while to track her at the beginning. She's Yup´ik Indian. Last name, Chiklak."

"Can you spell those?" I asked, trying to scribble notes as Myron relayed them.

"I'll email all this to you. Just wanted to go through it in person in case you had any immediate questions."

"Great. I'll look for it. Okay, go on."

"She lived with her grandmother until the old lady died. Delilah was eight then. No other family. Mother had run off right after she was born. Father was an alcoholic. Nobody knows where he's at. Several sources said he probably drank himself into an early grave."

"Hard for a kid."

"Yeah. She bounced around the foster care system until she was sixteen. That's when they placed her with the Edmunton family. They actually started the adoption process on her, which was kind of unusual for a kid that age. From all appearances, it looked like things were finally turning around for the kid, but then right after the adoption was final, she ran away. Struck me as odd, so I dug a little deeper. Found a report of some kind of abuse, but it was never verified because she disappeared. I talked to a Mrs. Edmunton. She was pretty evasive at first, then downright hostile when I mentioned the report, so I'd bet money it was true. Lost your girl on her journey across country. It's hard to track a runaway who doesn't want to be found.

"She turned up again in Jacksonville when she was twenty. Worked full time at different jobs. Sometimes two at a time. Took one class per semester at Florida Career College—all of them were some kind of art class. Pretty impressive for a runaway. They usually end up turning tricks, getting hooked on drugs, or both."

"Unfortunately, you're right. Anything else?"

"Sometime when she was twenty-two she met JD Campbell. Don't know how, for sure, but his work was on display at the Museum of Modern Art that fall, so maybe there. Seems like it would fit."

"That goes along with what Woody Burns told me."

"Who's that?" Myron asked.

"Elwood Burns—the guy from the overturned car out at the Country Club this morning—used to be good buddies with JD. He told me JD and some young dark-haired girl were nearly inseparable for two years before he died."

"You think it was romantic?"

"Not sure. Woody said there were rumors to that effect, though."

"Hm. Well, she had a baby, but the timing wouldn't be right for it to be JD's. Unless I did my math wrong."

"You didn't," I replied, not wanting him to pursue that further. No one but Lacey and I knew her father was involved. I wanted to keep it that way. "What happened to the baby?"

"Died."

"*What?*"

"Yeah, apparently the girl was almost killed in a car accident. Baby boy sustained injuries too. Born alive, but died a couple of days later."

I was quiet while mulling over this information dump. "Anything else?" I finally asked.

"Only that she got a job with an insurance company. Worked with them until four years ago and then, for all I can tell, she fell off the face of the earth."

"Which company?"

"Wasserman and Fleischer. They specialize in insuring fine art. That's all I got, Boss. 'Nother call coming in. Gotta jet."

I leaned back in my seat after hanging up. "Well, well, well. Interestin'."

Delilah Edmunton had been involved with JD Campbell for two years, had an affair with his son, Dan, and worked for a company that insured fine art. During that time, the Campbell home had been burglarized with one of the Campbell paintings disappearing while forgeries of JD's work kept popping up in the same time frame.

I turned these pieces around and around in my mind first one way, then another, trying to make them fit.

They didn't. I was close. I could feel it, but I didn't think I had all the pieces yet.

What I needed was another run. All those endorphins pumping through my bloodstream was like a superpower enabling me to untangle even the most knotted up mess of clues. I glanced at my watch. Nope. No time now, but definitely later.

I sat forward abruptly, grabbing my phone. Time to check in with my FBI buddy, Greg Donovan. He'd said to keep him updated.

"Donovan. Ford Jamison. Got a minute? I wanted to touch base with you."

"Hey, man. I know you won't believe this, but I was fixing to call you. I'm in Jacksonville. Think you might be able to ride down later, meet me for a drink? I'd come up there, but my day is booked solid with meetings."

"Uh, yeah. I guess. Sure. What's up?"

"New info on the Campbell forgeries."

"Great. That's why I was calling. I have some news that I think pertains to that case too. I wanted to run it by you. What time should I be there? And where?"

"Let's shoot for four o'clock. I'll text you the address."

"Right. See you then."

CHAPTER TWENTY-THREE

Lacey

The day had been nothing but a blur from the moment I'd seen that *Delilah's Lilies* had been sold by Front and Centre Gallery. After I tried—and failed—to reach Ford in order to let him know the shocking news, I vaguely remembered taking Noelle to Black Pearl. I showed her around, introduced her to the staff, and went through all my procedures with her. It was sort of a crash course in the way I run my kitchen, but my head wasn't in the game, and Noelle finally ordered me to leave.

"What do you mean, *leave*?" I asked in a stupor.

"Just what I said," she answered as she turned me around and untied my apron. I watched her matter-of-factly tie it around her own waist. "Honey, you're as useless as the *t* in Pinot Grigio. I doubt you could even boil water tonight. Cooking something edible would be asking for a lawsuit—completely out of the question—and don't even get me started on the safety issue of you handling knives. Call Barrett. What time does the gallery close?"

"Six."

She glanced at her watch. "Perfect. It's almost that now. You have questions, which is understandable given the situation. He has answers. Go call him. I can handle things tonight. What better way to see how I'll do while you're on your honeymoon? Consider it a free test run."

"Are you sure?"

She gave me a little push toward the door. "Yes. Now go."

***

"Hello? Barrett?"

"Speaking." His sandpapery voice raised the hair on my arms.

"It's Lacey Campbell. I was wondering if it would be possible for me to come by after you close today. I have a few things I'd like to discuss with you." He laughed, but I could hear his uneasiness nonetheless.

"I hope it's not as ominous as your voice sounds."

"I hope not, too," I answered, refusing to elaborate over the phone.

There was a short silence before he continued. "Certainly. The door will be locked, but I'll listen for your knock."

"Good. I'll see you in a few minutes."

I texted Ford to let him know where I was going as soon as I hung up, then was on my way.

CHAPTER TWENTY-FOUR

Ford

A little after three o'clock I was on my way to Jacksonville to meet Greg, driving due west along Highway A1A between O'Neil and Yulee. It was a forty-five minute drive, but I'd allowed myself an hour hoping to counteract any possible delays. Commuters were forced to factor into their traveling time the practically permanent road construction along Florida highways. I hoped a fifteen-minute cushion was enough.

The drive allowed me time to sift through all the things cluttering up my mind. Usually, I was able to keep everything put away in nice, neat compartments, labeled so I'd know exactly where everything was. This allowed me to pull out exactly the drawer I wanted, then put it back when I was done. But lately, my fail-proof system wasn't living up to its name. It was as if the drawers containing data on Lacey's granddad, his paintings, forgeries, and Delilah Edmunton had all been pulled out at the same time, their contents dumped into a big pot, then stirred together into an inedible stew.

I was certain it was all linked. My job was to figure out how to digest the mess so things could get back in order. I hoped this meeting with Greg would help and not add more confusion.

"Drama," I muttered. "Always drama. Everywhere you go. Big-city or small-town America. You can't get away from it. It makes me wonder if I'm even doing any good." I sighed and pushed the thoughts away.

Mast-like long leaf pines crowded in close on either side of the highway, creating a bristling green wall that seemed to hedge in toward the road, giving me a claustrophobic feeling.

This was probably one of the top five most mind-numbing stretches of two-lane road in the state, but it was the shortest way to get to Jacksonville, so I endured it the best I could.

About a mile ahead, the sight of a set of emergency flashers over on the shoulder pulled me out of my coma. Uh-oh, I thought when I got a little closer and spotted the still form of a deer on the opposite shoulder. Better see if everyone is okay. I switched on my blue lights and pulled in behind the stopped car. Before opening my door, I sent Greg a quick text letting him know I might be a few minutes late.

I winced as I approached the older model Toyota hatchback. It always amazed me how much damage a deer could do to a car. With its hood folded and creased like an accordion and its entire front bumper pushed in, it had the pug-nosed underbite of a bulldog. It was totaled.

I tapped on the window, startling the woman inside. The glass powered down. "Everybody okay?" I asked, glancing at the middle-aged woman before scanning the interior of the car. No other occupant.

"Y-yes," she stammered, appearing dazed. "I never even saw it. It wasn't there, then suddenly it was, and *boom!*"

"Yes, ma'am. May I see your driver's license, registration, and proof of insurance, please?"

She fumbled for her wallet. Shaky fingers pulled the items from a plastic sleeve and handed them to me.

I read the name, paused, squeezed my eyes shut, then tried again. Naomi Moses? Could it be the same person? Had to be. Couldn't be two of them. I ducked my head a little so I could get a better look at her, comparing her to the Naomi Moses I remembered.

It was her all right, though she looked different—softer, somehow. The hard edge that I remembered was gone. Flecks of silver laced hair that was styled short and neat. "Hi," I said with an uncomfortable smile. "Remember me?"

The stare she gave me was blank at first, then recognition sparked and her face was suddenly buried in her hands, forehead pressed against the steering wheel. A deep red bloomed up her neck and her ears looked hot to the touch. "Oh, no!" she moaned over and over.

Naomi Moses. Of all people . . .

Though I hadn't heard her name since I'd been back in Fernandina Beach, she was well known at the station when I worked there before—had quite a reputation. In fact, I'd heard some of the guys joke that Johnny Lee's song, "Looking for Love," was about her. Divorced from husband number five, and not counting all the live-in boyfriends, she was the present-day version of the Bible's woman at the well. She was a barfly at a club named Confetti's on the outskirts of town, and had been brought in for drunk and disorderly so many times she had frequent flyer miles.

I'd just graduated from the police academy and was a rookie cop with the FBPD. It was my first Saturday night riding solo, third shift. I was out patrolling a stretch of road known for its drunk drivers when I saw a pair of headlights weaving toward me. Right before we passed each other, a bright flash lit up the other car's interior. A look in my rearview mirror showed the car swerving madly before it veered off onto the shoulder of the road and came to a bumping stop. Heart thumping, I switched on my blue lights, made a quick U-turn, and pulled in behind the disabled vehicle.

The aroma of cheap perfume mixed with something burning wafted out of the open window. I'd never forget that smell. I approached with caution.

The woman was probably in her forties, trying to look twenty years younger by filling in wrinkles and masking any hard edges with layers of makeup. Wisps of smoke still drifted from what used to be the hair surrounding her face. Whatever bangs she might've had were gone, as were her eyebrows, giving her a perpetually surprised expression. The rest of her hair was "big," curled and teased out '80s-style, like a lion's mane. But under the circumstances, her hair was the least of her worries. She was nude from the waist up.

That was my introduction to Naomi Moses, and nothing, I repeat, *nothing* I learned at the academy had prepared me for it. "Here." I shrugged out of my jacket without thinking and shoved it through her window. "Put this on."

It had taken a bit of doing—she was quite upset, which was understandable given the situation—but I'd finally gotten the story straight. She'd been at Confetti's where her latest boyfriend had gotten a little too friendly for her tastes. In the brief tussle that followed, she'd kneed him "where it hurt the most" and fled the scene. Everything would've been fine if he'd released his hold on her blouse, but instead, he'd clutched it tighter in his pain. Afraid of what he might do if she stuck around, she'd torn herself from his grasp and in so doing, left her blouse dangling in his hand. Once safely away, and in desperate need of a smoke to calm her nerves, she'd discovered that the flame on her lighter she kept in the pocket of her tight leather pants had gotten adjusted too high. When she tried to light her cigarette, the flame had ignited her hair. In the resulting *pwoof*, she found out the hard way that hairspray was highly flammable.

I drove her to the station and booked her, then turned her over to a matron who found her something to wear so I could have my jacket back. Word got out, of course. No way to keep something like *that* quiet. I bore the brunt of some jealous ribbing by the guys at the station until they finally got tired of it. She sort of fell off the radar after that, and I never heard from or saw Naomi Moses again. But I never forgot that name.

"Excuse me, ma'am?" I spoke loud enough for her to hear me over her wailing litany of *no's.* "I can see on your insurance card that you don't have collision, so if you're not hurt, I don't have to do a report, but we do need to call a wrecker. This car isn't goin' anywhere on its own. Do you have someone specific you'd like to use?"

Her face flamed bright-red with embarrassment when she finally looked at me. She swallowed once and shook her head.

"No? Okay, I'll take care of it." I stepped away and phoned the nearest towing service.

Once the wrecker was on its way, I returned to her car. She glanced up at me, not quite meeting my eyes. "I need to tell you something, Officer."

"What's that?"

"Thank you."

Thank me? "What for?" I asked, startled.

"Well, actually I was hoping I'd never have to see you again, after . . . well, you know." Her lashes lowered and fresh color washed over her face.

I was afraid anything I said would make things worse, so I kept my mouth shut.

"I even moved way out here, trying to get away from Fernandina so there'd be less of a chance that I'd run into you." She gave a wry smile, gestured toward the deer. "*That* didn't work very well, did it? But I think I know why. I think God wants me to let you know that your arresting me was the best thing that could've happened to me. I was on the wrong path—clubbing every weekend, drinking, and carousing. What happened that night woke me. Made me get my life straightened out. Got back into church and everything. That's actually where I was headed just now, to a ladies Bible study." She took a deep breath and finally met my eyes, smiled gratefully. "So, thank you."

I nodded once, returned the smile. "You're welcome."

She lifted her chin toward the deer across the road. "What do they do with deer when people hit them?"

"Well, County is supposed to dispose of the bodies, or occasionally the driver will want the meat."

Her expression brightened. "I was hoping you'd say that. You think that guy with the wrecker would load it up too, when he comes to get my car? I'd love me some venison in the freezer. Be a shame to waste it, it being dead and all."

I opened my mouth to speak, realized I didn't know what to say, and closed it. After a minute, I finally said, "We can probably arrange that. I'll get you a green slip."

I turned and strode back to my car to fill out the card that would give her permission to take the deer with her, shaking my head, laughing to myself at how wrong I'd been in thinking that small town law enforcement would be less exciting, more low-key than working for SBI. No, there was nothing boring about this job, nothing at all. And sometimes—like in the case of Naomi Moses—there was the added bonus of being able to make a difference.

***

I pushed through the doors of the hotel lobby where Greg was staying. Hmm. FBI sure didn't spoil its agents by putting them up in the lap of luxury. The shag carpet was matted and worn almost bare in places. Shades of burnt orange, antique gold, and avocado green were prevalent in the design color wheel. I knew the "retro" look had made a comeback and was now termed "mid-century modern," but from the looks of the décor here, this wasn't a comeback. The decorators responsible for this had long since retired. They were probably dead by now.

Greg hurried over to meet me. Not much blond hair left on top, but other than that he looked the same. "Classy, huh." He gestured around us. "Tax dollars at work, buddy." He gave a wry chuckle. "There's no bar, but believe it or not, the coffee is good. Over here." He directed me to the small breakfast area big enough for two of the four round tables they'd crammed into the space.

Greg poured himself a cup of coffee, added a generous stream of sugar before stirring it, and then shoved two of the tables against the wall to give us room to sit down. The resulting loud screech startled the woman napping behind the check-in desk. Her dark eyes scowled at us from under the vermillion bindi high on her forehead that marked her as a married Hindu woman. I poured my own cup of coffee and joined him.

"Sorry I'm late," I said as I took my seat. "Ran up on someone who'd just hit a deer. Waited until the wrecker got there."

"Goes with the territory, right? Thanks for driving down. I could've sent you what I had via email, but I hate typing and this gave me a chance to see you again." He gave me a tired smile. "Though I feel bad about having you make the drive since I just found out, literally ten minutes ago, that I'll be up to Fernandina Beach tomorrow."

"What?"

"Yeah, I thought about texting you and letting you know, but I figured you were almost here, so . . ."

"Why Fernandina?"

"I'll tell you in a minute. You first. You said you had information that might be pertinent to the Campbell case?"

I relayed what I'd learned from JD's friend, Woody, as well as what Myron had dug up on Delilah.

"So," Greg said after I'd finished, "you think this Delilah Edmunton is involved? That maybe she's the forger?"

I nodded. "Either that, or she has some connection *to* the forger. Unfortunately, she's gone ghost. My guy lost her trail and hasn't been able to pick it up again. We'll keep lookin', but I thought maybe the big guys might have avenues to information that I don't."

Greg grinned. "Maybe."

"Look, I know everythin' doesn't fit yet, but I wanted to let you know. Now, why are you drivin' up to Fernandina tomorrow?"

He sat forward, leaning closer to me. "The case isn't at a standstill anymore. Two identical paintings showed up at two different auctions—one somewhere in the Far East—Japan, I think it was—and one here in the States. But here's the clincher. When they tested them, *both* passed. The paint included the secret ingredient. Problem is, no one can tell if one of them is the real thing, or if both are fakes."

"Wow! How could that happen?"

"Someone who knows how to paint like JD Campbell has found out what the missing component is. I'm thinking it might be this Delilah Edmunton. Working at an insurance company like that, she could've connected with someone with that information."

"Okay. Makes sense. But what does that have to do with you coming to Fernandina Beach?"

"Well, we tracked one of those Campbell forgeries back to a gallery there."

"What?" My heart started racing and I knew what he was going to say before I asked. "Which one?

"Front and Centre."

Later, as I exited the hotel, I was filled with an odd anxiousness to get home. All this forgery stuff was getting to me. I checked my phone on my way to my car and smiled when I saw that Lacey had sent me a text. That smile faded as soon as I read her words.

Headed over to Front and Centre. Meeting with Barrett. Found out something very disturbing today. Please come to the gallery ASAP.

Oh no! I broke into a sprint.

CHAPTER TWENTY-FIVE

Lacey

Barrett's sleek, black Jaguar was parked in the reserved spot in front of the gallery. I couldn't help rolling my eyes. Good grief. Ostentatious much? He had a vanity plate too. And like so many I'd seen lately, it didn't make any sense. A "Support the Arts" insignia to the left and gibberish to the right: K10T. Huh? What could that mean? Kay, one, zero, tee? Kay, ten, tee? Neither one made sense. Why have a vanity plate if no one but the owner can decipher the meaning? Didn't that sort of defeat the purpose? What a waste of money.

I tapped on the gallery's door and waited. Shielding the glare with my hand, I peered through the glass and saw Barrett slip from a room to the right of the foyer. Feeling ill at ease, I watched him glide toward me, his movements more graceful than a man's ought to be. I tried to swallow my nervousness away, only half succeeding. The lock clicked and the door swung open.

"Welcome, Lacey," he gushed, all big smiles and effusive mannerisms. "Please come in."

I stepped inside and he paused to relock the door. The *click* sounded louder than it should, and for a moment I wished I'd waited until Ford could join me for this meeting. I shook the thought away.

"Now." He turned back to face me. "What was it that you wanted to talk to me about?"

I fought the urge to take a step back at his nearness. I couldn't breathe. The air between us felt suffocating, like someone had sucked all of the oxygen out of it, and the scar—the creepy, jagged scar—filled my vision. It was too close, crowding my personal space. My eyes couldn't stop staring at it. I felt like a rubbernecker at the scene of a car accident, unable to look away from the destruction. It took much more effort than it should to tear my attention away, my eyes desperate for another focal point. His scarf! The jaunty yellow print caught and held my gaze, something to cling to in the chaos. The colors danced unevenly while I drew deep breaths, attempting to gather my wits. Time to do what I came to do and get out of here.

Without answering, I reached into my purse, pulled out the sheet of paper I'd printed off from Artlist.com, and handed it to him. I watched his eyes scan back and forth over the page. When they rose to meet mine again, they seemed brittle, like dark glass ready to break.

"Can I offer you something? Tea? Coffee? No? Well, let's go to my office. I have nice chairs. We might as well be comfortable while we discuss this. Right this way."

CHAPTER TWENTY-SIX

Nick

Nick stared at the sign above the toy store's door with brooding eyes, fighting an inner battle. Driving back to Fernandina Beach after what happened the last time he was there should've kept him from coming back. Subjecting himself to the torture of seeing Liv again while knowing she was probably involved with someone else was nothing less than masochistic, and he was an idiot for putting himself through it. But he couldn't seem to help it.

So, here he was. He'd even gotten off work an hour early to do this to himself again. Now what? Should he go in? Introduce himself? Find out once and for all whether this was just wishful thinking on his part, or turn around and head back to Jacksonville and pretend it was all a bad dream? He knew himself well enough to know he couldn't do the latter. He had to know for sure. She was here. Her pink bike was right there, chained to the light pole in front of the shop. He drew a deep breath, straightened his shoulders, and lifted his chin in determination. This was it. He was ready, or as ready as he'd ever be.

Wind chimes tinkled when he pushed through the door, but he hardly heard them over the pounding of his heart. His eyes scanned the store from corner to corner.

No pink.

What? That was impossible! He glanced out the front window. There was her bike, plain as day. He hadn't imagined it. She had to be here somewhere.

He approached the girl standing behind the sales counter, trying to figure out how he was going to ask about Olivia without sounding like a stalker. Just as he opened his mouth, the curtain behind the counter swished open and there she was.

Blue eyes stared at him, then grew wide. "You!"

His mouth wouldn't form words.

"I remember you. You were at Eve Campbell's funeral."

He held his hand out to shake hers, felt a jolt of electricity *zing* up his arm when her fingers touched his. Every hair on his body stood at attention. He was afraid he might be glowing. Was this some kind of joke? Had she zapped him with one of those buzzers that kids sometimes used as a prank? He looked dumbly at his hand, then hers. No. Nothing there. He had to force himself to speak. His voice sounded rough with emotion. "Nick Bradford."

If possible, her eyes widened even more and she gasped, "You're the mystery man."

He laughed, feeling relief from some of his tension. "Mystery man?"

"You were the one the whole town was talking about. The man no one knew who slipped in late, then left early without speaking to anyone. You have no idea the range of descriptions your visit inspired. All the talk calmed down once Ford tracked down who you were, but up 'til then, the stories mushroomed."

"Ford?" His ears perked at the familiar name. "Jamison?"

At her nod he gave a dry laugh. "I had the pleasure of meeting Chief Jamison the last time I was here, though I'm not sure pleasure is the right word for it." At her questioning glance, he added, "He wanted to know if I'd gone to the funeral. Had me worrying that I was going to get a ticket for crashing the event."

"He's our new chief of police who's actually getting married Saturday." An expression he couldn't decipher flitted across her face, and she added, "To Lacey."

"Mrs. Campbell's daughter?"

Liv nodded again.

"You sat beside her at the funeral." At her curious look, he added, "She's a few years younger than me. She was in first grade my last year here. I never personally knew her, just that Mrs. Campbell had a daughter. So you and Lacey are what? Cousins?"

She gave him a puzzled frown. "No, we're not related."

It was his turn to look puzzled. "Oh, but I thought—" He broke off and shrugged. "You were sitting with the family."

"We're like sisters. Well, at least we *were*," she added so softly that he wasn't sure she meant for him to hear.

Hmm. It sounded like he might need to change the subject. He gestured around the shop. "You work here?"

"I guess so. I *own* it."

"I like it," he said with a grin. "It has character." He nodded and made a gesture from her head to feet. "Like you."

"Character . . ." she mused. "I ride around town on a pink bicycle wearing wings, halo, and a tutu." Then she giggled. "I think saying I have 'character' is being kind."

"Did I see a wand?"

"Oh, yes. Let's not forget the wand."

He threw back his head and laughed. "Any way you could sneak away for a cup of coffee?" He glanced at his watch. "Or maybe an early dinner?"

She gestured at her outfit. "You don't mind being seen in public with me dressed in this getup?"

His eyes performed a sweeping appraisal and he grinned. "Not in the least. In fact, I'd be honored."

"Well . . ." She gave him a considering look before nodding. "Lacey might not approve since you're technically a stranger, but you loved her mother and in my book, that makes you a good guy."

"Huh?" There must be a story behind that ramble, but he was clueless as to what it might be.

"Never mind." She waved her hand as if erasing what she'd just said. "What I meant to say was, since this is technically my day off, I guess I'm allowed an early dinner. C'mon." She motioned him to follow her. "You leave your truck parked where it is. I'll do the same with my bike. We can walk."

***

They were soon seated at a window seat in the Palace Saloon. Once the waitress had taken their orders, Liv gazed around the large room. "I love the history of this place. If the walls could talk. . ."

He glanced around the dining room, taking in the pressed tin ceilings, the forty-foot bar and the mural closest to them. The Shakespearean character Falstaff presided over the bar with a mug in one hand and a sly look on his face, causing Nick to grimace playfully. "Mmm. Not so sure I'd want to hear all they had to say. It *is* a bar as well as a restaurant, you know— the state's oldest, continually operating drinking establishment, if I remember the history correctly. But in spite of them trying to make it sound more refined by giving it the title 'gentlemen's establishment,' and hanging complimentary towels from the bar so patrons could wipe the beer foam from their mustaches, it's *still* a bar. Has been since the early 1900s."

"And the brass spittoons," she laughed. "Don't forget those."

"Heaven forbid we leave those out." His laughter joined hers. "That reminds me of a story I heard. A woman came up to the pastor after his sermon and said, 'Preacher, I'm sorry, but you can't tell me that something that tastes as good as snuff is a sin. I just know they'll have it in heaven.' And the pastor replied, 'I completely agree with you, Mrs. Smith.' His response surprised her. 'You do?' He said, 'Absolutely! They'll have snuff and chewing tobacco too.' Pleased with his answer, she started to walk away, but he stopped her. 'But Mrs. Smith, you'll have to go to hell to spit.'"

Her magical, trilling laugh was music to his ears, a sound he couldn't imagine ever getting tired of. In fact, he felt suddenly sure he wanted to put that to the test—*for as long as they both shall live*. The thought startled him. Don't be an idiot, Bradford, he ordered himself. You can't declare your undying love for her when you just met her. She'll think you're crazy. You'll send her running. She'll have you arrested.

"Thanks," she said, her eyes still sparkling with mirth. "I needed a good laugh. And for this, too." She gestured to their surroundings. "This is my favorite place to eat and I get lunch here every week—their famous Southwestern Dog, but, Lace—" A shadow passed over her face.

"What's wrong?"

"Lacey always picks it up and brings it to my store so we can eat together." Her voice cracked a bit on the last word.

He was unsure what to do. He didn't want to upset her any more than she obviously was already. Should he change the subject or let her talk about it? Feeling like he was tiptoeing precariously across a lake covered in thin ice, he asked, "I know you told me that you and Lacey were like sisters. Are things okay between you?"

Her big blue eyes suddenly welled with tears and the dam broke. "No," she whispered brokenly. "Things are not okay between us."

He fumbled with the napkin dispenser, pulling out a handful and thrusting them toward her. They would have to do. He didn't have a handkerchief. He watched helplessly as she pressed the wad of napkins to the tears streaming down her beautiful cheeks.

"Everything is all wrong," she wailed. "She's my best friend. She's getting married Saturday. I'm supposed to be her maid of honor. I'm supposed to help her take care of things, give her a fun bachelorette party, but I ruined it. I should've never trusted that ridiculous note. Exotic dancer, my eye."

His eyebrows shot up. Exotic dancer? This should be good. He leaned back in his chair and waited.

"I knew better," she continued, sopping at her tears. Her words became harder to understand as her sobbing grew more intense. "Why w-would I trust a recommendation from s-someone who won't even sign his n-name? I should've checked it out first. It's my f-fault. I embarrassed her in front of everybody. The *whole town* knows because *I* invited them—

like an idiot. I w-wanted everyone to h-help us celebrate Lacey's happy da-aay."

Nick sat forward, pulled out another handful of napkins to replace the damp ones. "Thank you," she managed to gulp before another wave of tears welled up.

People were starting to stare. There were a couple of guys standing together beside a nearby pool table, heads close together as they whispered angrily to each other. He could tell by their body language that they were trying to decide whether they needed to intervene. Waves of hostility rolled in his direction. Accusatory eyes drilled into his back. He could feel them, but he didn't blame them for reacting like that. He'd do the same in their shoes. A gorgeous woman dressed in a pink fairy costume bawling her eyes out in a bar? Of course they'd think the guy she's with was to blame. But it was okay. He was tough. He could take it, as long as no one called the cops, or worse—took matters into their own hands. He didn't relish the thought of dodging a pool stick. He was a librarian, not a tough guy.

"Everything was fine until he showed up and started being nice to me," Liv continued, ". . . giving me little gifts . . ."

Wait. What? He must've missed something. *Who* was giving her gifts? Being nice to her? Some guy trying to make a move on her? "Who are you talking about?" he dared to interrupt.

She lifted tear-filled eyes to meet his. "Barrett, of course."

Barrett! He couldn't think the name without mentally sneering it. "Is that his first or last name?" he asked through stiff lips.

"First," she sniffed. "His last name is Clatrans." She swallowed miserably, then whispered, "How could I have let a guy come between me and my best friend? I feel terrible. No! Worse than terrible. I feel like a dog—a low-down, good-for-nothing dog."

Nick couldn't stop his short laugh.

Liv looked up, startled.

He shook his head. "Sorry. Please forgive me. Sometimes my sense of humor can be ill-timed."

"Sense of humor?"

"Yeah. You saying that you feel like a dog and his name and all . . ."

"I still don't—" She broke off, shaking her head in confusion.

"Clatrans?" he said, watching her closely. "C. latrans?" he added hopefully. She still looked confused, but there was a hint of anger creeping into her eyes. "Please, please don't think I'm a geek. Well, I kind of am, but I'm a librarian, so it goes with the territory. I read a lot—especially nonfiction, and I happen to know that Canis latrans or C. latrans is the Latin word for coyote, which is basically a wild dog. So if anyone should feel like a low-down dog, it should be this Clatrans guy. Not you."

Liv stared at him with wide eyes. He could tell she was processing what he'd said. He could almost see the wheels turning in her head. Suddenly, her mouth dropped open and she snatched up her purse. After a moment of scrambling, she pulled out her phone, pressed a button, and waited impatiently. "C'mon, Lacey. Pick up. Pick. Up!"

He surmised that her wince meant the call went to voice mail. She hung up and bit her lip, uncertainty written across her face.

"Liv?" He reached over and touched her hand, startling her. "Hey, is everything okay?"

She shook her head. "No, things are definitely not okay. Clatrans means coyote. Coyotes are dogs. Lacey's dreams have all had a dog in them. She's been warning me. I should've listened. Ford. I need to call Ford."

Picking up her phone again, she pressed another button, repeating the impatient waiting process. "Ford! Thank God I got you. Listen,"

Nick felt as if he were watching a foreign drama unfold on stage without the benefit of knowing the language. Liv repeated the same gibberish she'd just told him, but amazingly Ford must've been able to make sense of it. She listened to his reply and gasped. "No! Where are you?" She frowned and added, "You're a cop. Use your lights and siren. Just hurry. I'm on my way."

She raised stricken eyes to Nick. "Do you have a pen?"

He retrieved one from his pocket and handed it to her wordlessly.

She scribbled something onto a napkin and handed both back to him. "Here's my number. I'm sorry we can't have our dinner," she said, shoving her phone in her purse and rising to her feet. "I know you don't understand anything that's going on right now, but I don't have time to explain. Lacey is in danger. I've got to go. Please call me."

"Wait. What?" He jumped to his feet as well. "You just said it was dangerous. What kind of a guy do you think I am? I'm not going to let you go—*alone*—into something like that. I'm coming with you."

"No, you're not, and I don't have time to argue about it."

"Then stop arguing and let's go."

"You aren't involved in this."

"I am now." He pulled out his wallet, threw some bills on the table for their drinks. "You ready?"

She bit her lip, blue eyes troubled, uncertainty outlining her entire body. Finally, she drew a determined breath and turned to one of the men who still watched them from the pool table. "Chip?"

Alerted by his name, one of the muscle-bound goons, sporting two days' beard, sauntered over, right hand still gripping his pool stick. "What's up, Liv?"

"I'd like to introduce you to my new friend." She gestured at Nick. "This is Nick Bradford. Nick, this is Chip Carson. Chip and I have been friends since first grade."

Nick could tell by the way Chip glowered at him that he took the "friend" job seriously. In fact, unless he misread things, he was sure Chip would be more than willing to take their relationship to the next level if Liv would allow it. That information made him glower right back at Mr. Carson. Why was she wasting time with this anyway? She said she was in a hurry.

As if in answer to that question, she continued sweetly, "Chip, I have an errand I need to do, and I need to do it *alone*. Would you be so kind as to make sure Nick doesn't follow me?"

Nick's jaw dropped. Why, that little brat!

"Liv, no!" he exclaimed, but it was drowned out by Chip's hearty, "Be glad to, honey." The look on Chip's face was all the warning he needed.

With a resigned sigh, he sat back down at the table, crossing his arms over his chest.

She had the grace to look apologetic. "Call me?"

He gave her a grudging smile. He had to hand it to her. She'd just pulled one slick move. "Go on. Get going!"

She flashed him a smile before turning.

"Hey," he called as she hurried to the door, "should I call the police?"

"Ford *is* the police!"

The swinging doors flapped behind her and she was gone.

CHAPTER TWENTY-SEVEN

Lacey

I started to turn in at the door I'd seen Barrett come out of. It had a brass plate beside it that read "Barrett Clatrans - Curator." He stopped me with a motion to follow him. "I have something special I want to show you before we talk. It won't take long."

The hair on the back of my neck rose, my fingertips tingled a warning. "Ford will be joining us in a minute. Shouldn't we wait for him?"

"He's welcome to join us when he gets here, but I know you'll want to see this. It's one of your grandfather's missing paintings."

"What?" I gasped. His words were a game changer, which I'm sure he knew, but even realizing that, I could no more have stopped myself from following him downstairs than I could sprout wings and soar to the moon. I pushed aside my body's inner warning system and hurried after him. "Which painting?" I asked, breathless with excitement. "Can you give me a hint? And how did you get it?"

He chuckled. "Not very patient, now, are we? But I have good news." We stopped in front of a solid metal door, then he turned and gave me a bright smile. Maybe a little *too* bright? "Your wait is over. We're here. Just let me unlock the door."

The door swung open, pulling the scent of linseed oil out of the dark room and into the hallway. The unmistakable smell of an art studio. It brought back memories of my dad scraping globs of overmixed, muddy-colored oil paint across a canvas with a palette knife. I never enjoyed watching him at work. He'd always looked so angry, his face dark as a storm cloud. I guessed standing in my granddad's shadow for most of his life wedged a permanent chip onto his shoulder.

The light flicked on, confirming my assessment. A round-topped, wooden barstool sat beside a small, square table. The surface of the table was covered with tubes of paint, a palette, and a ceramic crock filled with paintbrushes. The rest of the room was dark.

My mouth went dry. This room was disturbingly similar to the one from my dreams. The tingling feeling was back. My fingertips were nearly vibrating with it. I turned to Barrett in confusion. "Where—"

He made a motion with his head toward the darkness beyond the easel.

I turned back, tried to swallow, but my mouth was too dry.

With a *click*, the darkness was illuminated and there was— *Amelia Sky.*

But it was different from my dream. There were three canvases instead of one. The center one was the one from my dream, though the colors seemed brighter than I remembered them. They were more breathtaking in real life. An exquisite banner flung across the sky presenting every shade of orange, crimson, purple, and gold in glorious splendor. Each color mirrored back from the ocean below, shimmering and alive. The other two canvases were only roughed in versions of *Amelia Sky*. My brain felt sluggish, on overload, unable to assimilate the data my eyes were receiving.

That's when I caught a glimmer from the corner of my eye. I turned to see what might have caused it and gasped. It was *Delilah's Lilies*—the one stolen from my home, and the one I'd just seen listed as belonging to some Japanese guy on the other side of the world. It was impossible for it to be in two places at the same time. Yet, here it was!

I stopped breathing. The room seemed void of oxygen. It was a long time before I was able to pull in a ragged breath. That action broke the spell. It was time for some answers.

But before I could face Barrett, something hard and painful crashed into the back of my head, making the explosive colors in Granddad's painting dull in comparison. A kaleidoscope of stars and spangles shot like fireworks, swirling behind my eyelids, then slowly fading to black.

***

I awoke to a headache that throbbed with every beat of my heart, and the sound of Barrett's gravelly voice raised in a full-fledged, grade A rant. My wrists and ankles were secured with something, rendering me unable to move. Some sixth sense told me to keep my eyes closed. My ears, however, were fully tuned in, listening hard.

"Argh. Everything's imploding and it's all Dan's fault," he snarled. "All of it."

"Not JD's death." The voice changed slightly. Still Barrett's, but different somehow. Not so low and raspy. "I can't pin that on him. I take the blame for that."

Then the snarl was back. "Fine! But everything else is all on Dan. He's responsible. If it weren't for him and his stupid choice, none of this would be happening."

Dan? Was he talking about my dad? That Dan? No, that couldn't be right. Barrett had just moved here and Dad was dead. He had been for years. It must be some other Dan. Their having the same name was just a coincidence.

"My baby," the less raspy voice wailed in misery, and the sound of it raised the hair on my arms. "Why did my baby have to die and hers live? Why? My precious baby boy," he sobbed. "It's not fair. If he'd chosen me, my son would be alive. He should've chosen me. Why didn't he choose me?"

A chill colder than the subzero freezer at Black Pearl wrapped around my heart. I swallowed hard and took a chance, peeking through my lashes at the crazed man pacing back and forth in the studio. His slight frame was silhouetted against the light at the end of the room. His hair tie and jaunty scarf were both missing, and their absence only seemed to emphasize his effeminate mannerisms. I'd never seen him like this. He was completely disheveled, a stranger; the dark, shoulder-length hair swung around his face like a curtain, nothing like the Barrett I knew. He almost looked like a—

No!

But the germ of an idea was there now, planted in my mind. Part of my brain tried to piece his words together with what I was seeing, part of it flatly refused.

Then the curtain of his hair swung back, allowing me a clear profile, the long graceful neck rising from his collar with no camouflaging scarf to hide the telltale absence of an Adam's apple.

"Who are you?" I asked in a voice that sounded almost as gravelly as his, or should I say *hers?*

Barrett, or whoever it was, threw back his head and gave a laugh that would rival that of the wicked witch from *The Wizard of Oz*. Goose bumps sprouted all up and down my arms. "I'm surprised you hadn't guessed, my dear. Or maybe I'm *not* surprised. You seemed to have inherited your father's lack of intelligence." I received a long stare from narrowed, dark eyes that were full of poisonous venom. "My name is Delilah Edmunton." Then she gave a mirthless laugh. "No, this is the end. I should use my real name—my Yup´ik name—as a tribute to my family heritage." She pushed her sleeve back, revealing a tattoo I'd never noticed before. She touched it almost reverently. "The eye and the hole. It symbolizes the movement between the spiritual and the physical worlds. Now is the time. It's only right. My name is Delilah Chiklak."

Her words triggered a confusing flash of memory. Barrett's personalized license tag. I tried to shake the thought away, but it wouldn't budge. I could see it as clearly as I had when I'd walked by it earlier: K10T.

Now? Really? I'm dealing with a crazy woman who hates me for a reason that's not fully clear yet—who, up until a minute ago I thought was a man? Sure. Why not? It's not any crazier than the rest of this situation.

K10T. K-10-T.

No. That was a mistake. The one and zero didn't make ten.

The one was the letter *i,* the zero an *o.*

K-I-O-T. Coyote.

The dog from my dreams.

I suddenly felt sick and swallowed hard, trying not to throw up. I didn't know what she had planned for me, but it couldn't be good if she was the coyote. But Ford was on his way. I clung to that thought like a drowning victim. If I could keep her talking until he got there, I might make it to my wedding on Saturday after all.

"Why coyote?" I asked in the loudest voice I could muster, which wasn't much more than a whisper. It was the first thing I could think of, and I really wanted to know.

Delilah had been reaching toward the ceramic crock on her worktable, but my question made her pause. A frown flitted between her brows, then cleared. "You figured out my license plate. Very good. It's my familial animal, or totem. The coyote or brush wolf's strength is its adaptability, the ability to adjust to difficult circumstances. I've depended on it to survive."

Think of something else, I told myself. Keep her talking. "So, one way you 'adapted' was by pretending to be a man? What was that about?"

Her features hardened. "Barrett was the name I gave my son before he . . . died." The last word was a ragged whisper.

Dead? My half-brother was dead? He wouldn't be trying to stake a claim on my inheritance? I sagged with relief, then felt guilty for it. Black Pearl was safe. I could stop worrying about losing my restaurant and start worrying about living through this encounter with a crazy woman.

The look on Delilah's face urged me to change the subject. "Uh, how did you meet my granddad?" I blurted in desperation.

Her dark, staring eyes turned sad and wistful. "He was my idol. I practically worshipped him for years. The first day I got to see him in person was one of the best days of my life. A dream come true."

Good. I mentally urged. Keep going. "Where did it happen?"

"At MOCA . . ." She glanced at me, must've seen my confusion and elaborated, "The Museum of Contemporary Art in Jacksonville. They were exhibiting his paintings. He was there to kick it off. We bumped into each other after the program. *Literally.* He nearly knocked me down and ended up walking me to my car. We talked the whole way. I told him I was a painter and he asked to see my work. After he saw it, he offered to apprentice me. Sounds unbelievable, I know, but that's how it happened."

"You loved him," I said softly.

Tear-glazed eyes met mine. "Yes," she choked out.

It was the only word she could manage. Her face sort of crumpled, then I watched her make an almost superhuman attempt to gather the unraveled ends of her emotions together and tie them into a knot. It took several minutes for her to regain her composure, then she whispered, "He had a fatal heart attack the night I told him I loved him. I blame myself for his death. I've lived with that blame for twenty-six years."

What do you say after something like that? I had nothing, and the silence that followed her confession almost proved to be my undoing.

Delilah sighed, then reached into the ceramic crock that held her brushes, pulling out a long ivory-colored knife. The thing was massive, the size of a small machete. About ten inches long, it had a wide, flat blade, decorated with ornate carvings.

The sight of it jolted my heart into hyperdrive, sending it hammering so loudly I could hardly hear what she said next.

"My story knife." She held it up so I could see it better. "I've had it since I was four. It's sharper now." She ran her thumb over the blade and blood instantly welled from a thin line. "I'm going to kill you," she said as she strolled toward me, twirling the knife in her fingers like a baton.

The menacing words were spoken in the same tone of voice and with the same inflections as if she were telling me her favorite color or that she liked chocolate ice cream better than vanilla. They didn't go together, like mismatched socks.

"I mean—" Her voice was crushed velvet. "Not immediately. First, we'll have some fun. I want us to match." She gestured toward the disfigured side of her face. "Though he won't see it, we'll consider it my gift to your dad. Retribution for him choosing you and your mother over me and his son. Too bad your mother is already dead. " She almost crooned the words. "I would've loved to carve her up too." Then she smiled, and it was the smile of a crazy person.

Anger boiled up inside me at her words. It overpowered the fear that was nearly choking me. How dare she talk about my mother like that!

She knelt down beside me, pressed the flat edge of the blade against my cheek, just under my left eye, a triumphant smile on her face. I lifted my chin in defiance. I refused to beg. Go ahead, my eyes dared her. After giving her one final glare, I squeezed my eyes shut and waited.

That's when I heard it—the desperate rapping on the glass door upstairs.

I opened my eyes. Delilah's head was cocked. She heard it too.

It got louder. Whoever it was went from using their hands to something harder than their knuckles. A shoe? A rock? Glass wasn't made to withstand that kind of abuse.

It couldn't take it for long.

Delilah must have come to the same conclusion. She hoisted herself to her feet, muttering curses under her breath as she stalked to the metal door, heaved it open, then slammed it shut behind her.

As soon as I heard her pounding up the stairs, I sat up and managed to lurch to my feet. It wasn't as easy as it might sound, especially with duct tape binding my wrists and ankles so tightly that blood was having a hard time circulating in them. I was in a panic, panting like a dog, and my arms and legs had the strength and consistency of Jell-O.

I managed to hop over to Delilah's work table, looking frantically for the knife. Where was it? Had she taken it with her? I tried to remember if she'd had it in her hand when she left, but couldn't. Focusing was difficult and the worry that I might have a concussion from the blow to my head only made things worse. Okay, I thought finally. You can't find that knife. Think of a Plan B.

In my haste, my clumsy taped-together hands knocked the crock over with a crash and I froze, fearful that the noise would bring Delilah rushing back downstairs to finish what she'd started. When that didn't happen, I continued picking through the heap of brushes. I figured out that using only the pointer fingers of both hands—folding the rest of them together, out of the way—gave me more control. It made me look like a one-armed sloth, awkward and slower than I would've liked, but it was the best I could do under the circumstances.

There! Hallelujah! A utility knife. That would work. I snagged the knife out of the tangle with my sloth-fingers, sat down on the stool, then, swiveling it so the blade faced downward, I wedged it between my knees, sawing my taped wrists clumsily back and forth against the blade, praying I wouldn't slash a wrist in the process. My heart was nearly thumping out of my chest and I was light-headed from all the panting.

I gasped when my hands were free but had no time to congratulate myself. Feet next. Bending over, I frantically set to work on the many layers of tape that formed a hard shell, as tough as the hide of a rhinoceros.

A shrill scream echoed down the stairwell and my heart nearly stopped.

I knew that sound. There was no one on earth who could scream like Olivia Hale.

I sawed harder, desperately pulling my feet apart at the same time.

There! My feet broke apart and the knife clattered to the floor.

"Get your hands off me!" Liv shrieked, closer this time. They were coming down the stairs. Delilah snarled something in reply, but it was too low for me to make out. Whatever it was made Liv whimper.

Okay, Jack Bauer, now what? Use the knife or find something to knock Delilah in the head with when she comes through the door? I had a split-second to make my decision. Snatching up the wooden barstool, I rushed to stand behind the door. I figured I'd have better luck with it. The blade on the utility knife was short, too short to go up against Delilah's knife. That ten-inch blade would allow her too much of a reach.

I waited. Shaky arms held the barstool over my head while I tried—without measurable success—to get my breathing under control.

When the door burst open, I jumped and almost dropped my "weapon." Delilah dragged a sobbing Liv into the room, her fist wrapped tightly in Liv's curls. The instant they cleared the door, I kicked it shut behind them. The resulting *slam* sounded extra loud. Startled, Delilah whirled around, losing her grip on Liv's hair. I brought the barstool down on her head with a solid *thunk,* actually splintering one of the rungs. She dropped to the floor like a sack of cement. The long ivory blade clattered to the floor beside her.

My legs were shaking so badly they could hardly hold me up. I held my arms out to the ashen-faced Liv, but she looked from Delilah and then back to me, back and forth, like she was a spectator at a life-and-death tennis match.

I finally grabbed her arm and pulled her to me. She was shaking like a leaf, but I felt her arms go around me. She squeezed me so hard it was difficult to draw a breath, but I didn't have the heart to tell her.

"It's okay. We're okay," I soothed. The words were for me too. I needed the reassurance as much as she did. "It's over. Everything's okay."

Then I heard an angel shouting my name. "Lacey!"

Ford.

"Down here," I screeched. "Down in the basement."

Footsteps thundered down the wooden stairs and the door exploded open. The doorway framed him for the millisecond it took for him to take in and assess the entire room. Then he had his arms wrapped around both Liv and me. "Thank God you're safe," I heard him rasp, his voice rough with emotion. "Thank God you're both safe."

I was faintly aware of him kicking the knife away from Delilah's limp hand before I lost it.

All of the pent-up emotions—the fear, worry about wedding stuff, the brother I didn't know I had, the nightmares, Granddad's paintings, paying for my restaurant, Barrett and the rift between me and Liv—all of it hit me at once. Shoot! My crazy psyche even pulled my mother's death and the Lullaby Murders into the mix. I thought I'd put that behind me. I hadn't realized it was all there, lurking just below the surface, until the dam broke. Wave upon wave—tsunamis of it—pounded and battered me with an intensity I wouldn't have thought possible. I wept until I started to wonder if a person could get dehydrated from crying.

When the storm finally abated I drew a shuddering breath and lifted my head. I was in Ford's lap, cradled like a baby in his arms. I stared around with dull eyes. We weren't in the art studio anymore. How could he have moved me without me realizing it? "Where are we?" I croaked.

"Barrett's office," he answered, smoothing back my hair.

I reached a finger out and touched the soft leather arm of the chair we were in, noting the other one to our right. "Mmm. He does have nice chairs."

"What?"

"Never mind." I shook my head and laid it back against his chest. "It's something he said earlier."

He didn't respond except to kiss the top of my head, his warm hand gently stroking my arm. I listened to the steady beat of his heart.

"You mean Delilah's," I countered after a quiet minute.

"Huh?"

"This is Delilah's office. Apparently Barrett and Delilah are one and the same." Before he could respond, I changed the subject. I wasn't sure I was ready to talk about what happened downstairs quite yet. "Where's Liv?"

"She left. Said somethin' about needin' to rescue someone else."

I frowned at his words. Liv and I still needed to talk.

"Are you all right?" He tipped my chin up, studying my face. "I was starting to get worried. All those tears . . ." He shook his head, touched the corner of my eye. "I was beginnin' to think your tear ducts had somehow gotten hooked up to the ocean—it's the only way to explain all that salt water—and was afraid you were goin' to cry the Atlantic dry."

I smiled tiredly. "Maybe I helped. You know, all that 'global warming' talk of ice caps melting, rising ocean levels. Maybe I was able to bring it down some."

"I'm sure the eastern seaboard thanks you," he laughed, and I heard relief in it. "But you don't have to do it all on your own." He sobered, and a frown etched between his brows. "And on that note, I want you to know you almost gave me a heart attack when I saw your text. If I weren't so thankful that you're okay, I'd shake you until your teeth rattled. Why would you do something like that?"

I stiffened, got awkwardly to my feet, and then turned to face him. I couldn't put it off. "I found evidence that the painting from my dream, *Amelia Sky*, was sold to a man in Kyoto, Japan. Front and Centre—this gallery—handled the sale. I had some questions about that and Barrett was the only one with the answers. How is he, by the way?" I shook my head and corrected myself. "Uh, I mean *she*."

"They transported her to the hospital. Pretty sure she has a concussion. You gave her a pretty good wallop."

I rubbed the goose egg on back of my head. "I know the feeling."

"Yeah, I'll be takin' you to the hospital so they can check you out too." He rose to stand in front of me, placed his hands on my shoulders, and bent his knees so his eyes were level with mine. "Next time, wait for me, please. Your life has been in danger twice in two months. That's two times too many in my book. My heart can't take it."

I nodded.

"I know you have questions. So do I, but I'll get the answers. As soon as the doctor gives me the green light, I'm goin' to interrogate Delilah. I think she just might be the centerpiece of a puzzle that's bigger than we realized. There's a bunch of other pieces waitin' in line to take their position on the table. I believe, if I can get her—what she knows—then all the rest will fall into place."

I opened my mouth to speak, but he stopped me with a kiss. "I'll tell you when I get the whole picture. I promise." He kissed me again, more seriously this time. He knew exactly how to sidetrack me. I molded myself to fit him perfectly, my fingers twining in his baby-soft hair. My pulse rioted, skyrocketing as his arms slid around me, drawing me even closer. Time melted away.

When he lifted his head, my muscles felt like mush and I would've fallen if his strong arms weren't supporting me. "Ready?"

"Mmm. Yes."

"Can you walk, or do you need me to carry you?"

Walk? Carry me? "Where?"

"To the hospital. So the doctor can check out this hard head of yours." He touched an index finger to my forehead. "We have a wedding rehearsal tomorrow. I want to make sure you're okay. Wait." He arched a brow at me. "What did you mean, *yes*?"

"That I was ready to go," I answered, though I couldn't meet his eyes and my cheeks flamed.

He laughed and gave me another quick kiss. "That fever-colored face of yours is tellin' a different story, sweetheart."

Scowling, I muttered, "Traitor. Whose side is it on, anyway?"

"Mine," he grinned. "Always mine. And don't worry. It won't be long now."

CHAPTER TWENTY-EIGHT

Ford

I stepped off of the elevator of Baptist Medical Hospital and turned right. Thank goodness Delilah wasn't in ICU. I had no desire for another run-in with Gestapo nurse Greenley. I'd had the unfortunate experience of encountering her two months ago when the Lullaby killer had left Raine Fairbanks for dead. Nurse Greenley wasn't one to bend the rules, no matter how dire the need.

Dr. Hawkins was at the nurses' station. "Chief Jamison," he greeted me. I hadn't met him in person before. We'd only spoken on the telephone. He had Santa Claus-white hair, wispy and fine, like dryer lint stuck to his head. His eyebrows could have used a trim, and his girth was roughly the same as his height. Overall, though, he reminded me of an ancient teddy bear.

"Dr. Hawkins." I reached out to shake his hand. His grip was firmer than I expected it to be. Maybe I needed to reassess his teddy bear status. One corner of his mouth quirked up. His shrewd hazel eyes missed nothing. "Thanks for your call. I'm on my way to talk to Miss Edmunton."

He nodded. "Glad I caught you, then." He scanned the area, and then with a muttered walls-have-ears explanation, he motioned me over to a quieter, more private part of the hallway. "I agreed to let you talk to my patient," he began, once we were in what he deemed a safe zone. "But don't push it. Physically, she'll recover. She has a concussion—a significant one. Someone beaned the heck out of her, but that's not what I'm worried about. No, the real problem is her mental state."

I glanced over my shoulder, then lowered my voice. "Dr. Hawkins, are you supposed to be telling me this?"

He impatiently waved my question away. "Son, I used to enjoy being a doctor, but I'm ready to retire and I'm old school, which is code for 'I've got common sense.' Sometimes information needs to be shared. This, I believe, is one of those times. I've had it up to here"—he slashed the air above his head with his hand—"with all the ridiculous regulations they keep piling on us. It's taken all the joy out of practicing medicine. Now, I've given you the go-ahead, you keep what I say under your hat, and we'll call it even. I've requested a psych evaluation. They'll no doubt want to run a bunch of tests. I'll let you know what they conclude."

"Thank you, Doctor." I grinned as I watched him walk away, lab coat flapping in the breeze. I liked the old coot. He reminded me of Miss Lily, the formerly homeless woman who'd been maid of honor in my college buddy, Jonas's, wedding. She had the same kind of tell-it-like-it-is philosophy as the doctor, only hers came out in crazy sayings and famous quotes. Too bad they were a dying breed.

Officer Dwayne Hembree stood ramrod-stiff outside Delilah's room. Hembree was the baby-faced officer I'd reprimanded while working the Lullaby Murder case when I was still with the SBI. He'd been a little overenthusiastic in his questioning of an innocent bystander. I still had a hard time believing this guy was old enough to have a job that required him to carry a gun. He looked about fourteen.

"At ease, Hembree. This isn't the army."

If anything, his posture stiffened. "Sir."

I rolled my eyes and entered the room. The curtains were drawn. The only light came from the bathroom whose door was about half open. The metal handcuff attaching her wrist to the bed gleamed in the dim light.

Delilah's eyes were closed, but opened as soon I sat down. "Chief Jamison. Figured you'd show up," she rasped.

"Miss Edmunton." I flipped open a notebook, pulled a pen from my shirt pocket, and started jotting down the date and time at the top of the page. "You're looking better than the last time I saw you."

She scoffed. "You mean after your fiancée brained me?"

I stopped writing and gave her a look. "I saw the knife. Yours were the only prints on it. Her actions were self-defense and you know it. There's a witness to corroborate that."

"Fine." Delilah closed her eyes, dismissing me.

"I have a few questions for you. Your doctor said it was okay."

Her eyes opened again and she fixed me with a stare before asking, "Did he tell you I was crazy?"

"Do *you* think you're crazy?"

Her eyebrows rose, the corners of her mouth turned down, and she nodded. "Impressive. Answering a question with a question. You'd make a good shrink." Drawing a deep breath, she exhaled slowly, staring at the ceiling. "I'd say that a woman who pretends to be her dead *son* is certifiable."

I cocked my head at her, considering my words before replying. "Tell you what, you let me ask you a few questions, then if you want to talk about that, I'll be glad to listen."

After a minute, she nodded. "Might as well. I doubt they'll be unlocking me this time."

I sat up, alert. "This time?"

"I spent time in a psychiatric hospital before. I'm familiar with the process. If I'm not thrown in jail, I'm sure they'll throw away the key once they have me back in the nuthouse."

I didn't answer, but scribbled the words "Dr. Hawkins" and "records" as a reminder to myself. "Were you responsible for the Campbell forgeries?"

There was a long pause. Would she answer? I decided to wait. "Only the best ones."

I nodded, trying to keep my face expressionless while scrawling her reply in my notebook. "Were you aware that

Campbell added a secret ingredient to his paints to keep people from copying his work?"

"Not until the night he died," she answered, her voice flat and emotionless. "He told me he added something. He just didn't have time to tell me what it was."

"But you still tried passing off forgeries."

She sighed. "I've spent my life trying to paint like JD Campbell. I added every substance you could possibly think of, hoping each time that I'd finally found the right one. Occasionally, I hit on something I thought came close. It would *look* right. Those were the paintings I put out there. I called them his 'personal collection.'" She gave a short, mirthless laugh. "The art world ate them up. Then they'd test it for that stupid ingredient and I'd realize it wasn't right yet—that I hadn't found it after all."

"You worked for an insurance company. Wasserman Fleischer. Their specialty was insuring invaluable art pieces."

"Not a question."

I gave her a narrowed look.

"Okay, I'll let you slide this time. Yes. That's how I learned all the tricks of the trade, how to get around all the tests. And essentially, it's how I finally learned JD's secret."

"Care to enlighten me?"

"I had a date with a forensic art expert I met through the job. He knew what the elusive ingredient was."

"And he just *told* you."

The corner of her mouth turned up. "Well, he was how I found out."

"As much as I'd love to hear the story behind that, we'll save it for another day," I answered wryly. "So now that you know the secret ingredient, any chance you'll tell me what it is?"

"Maybe." She shrugged. "Maybe not. It looks like I won't be painting any time soon." Her cuffed hand pulled against its restraint, making a harsh metallic sound. "Maybe I'll take it to my grave so no one else can copy his work. Seems fitting."

Her eyes closed. She looked tired. I needed to wrap this up.

"You took *Delilah's Lilies* from the Campbell home about five years ago."

She sighed, "Another nonquestion."

"Okay, why?"

"I intended on taking all of them. I had a plan to paint two copies of each one, sell them as originals at auction houses on opposite sides of the world—with all the necessary documentation, of course—and keep the originals for myself. I was the only one who truly appreciated JD's work, after all. Dan certainly didn't deserve them. Taking *Delilah's Lilies* was a test to see if I could get away with it. I came back for the rest of them. Did you know that?" She gave a sly smile when I looked up. "No, I didn't think so. Dan had already gotten rid of them, and I was furious. Not because it ruined my plan. I didn't like it, but that wasn't it. No, it was because I believed he'd destroyed them out of sheer spite. The thought of JD's work being destroyed was unforgivable." Her jaw hardened as she clenched her teeth. "But I believed that's what had happened until about two months ago. With my interests, I make it a point to keep up with who has sold what to whom in the art world. So when I saw that two of JD's missing paintings were owned by the one and only Lacey Campbell and had been sold through a gallery in Fernandina Beach that just *happened* to be searching for a new curator, I knew it was fate, and I knew what I had to do. Once I got the job, I did a little digging and found out what Dan had done. Ingenious little snot. Hiding them in plain sight. He was smarter than I gave him credit for."

"You obviously harbor no love for the man, yet you had a child with him."

Her dark eyes shot up to meet mine. She seemed shocked that I knew. I shrugged. "Lacey found the birth certificate."

She scoffed. "I should've never given him a copy. And to answer your unasked question, Dan reminded me of JD." Her mouth twisted as if tasting something bitter. "Only in looks, though. He was nothing like his father."

I could feel the weight of her dark gaze as I finished up my notes. I had one more question, but I wasn't sure she was up to it. By the time I looked up, she'd closed her eyes again. Now she looked exhausted. The jagged scar stood out, stark against her ashen skin.

"Ask it. Go ahead. I know you're dying to."

I couldn't help it. I had to know. "Why Lacey? Why did you want to hurt her?"

There was a flash of sadness in her eyes, so raw and deep I almost felt the pain myself, but then, while I watched, something changed in their depths. A maniacal laugh began bubbling up from somewhere deep, deep inside her and right before my eyes I saw her last tie to sanity sever.

"Because," she said with a smile so crazed and evil that an involuntary shudder traveled up the length of my spine and I was glad she was handcuffed to her bed. "She lived. My son didn't."

CHAPTER TWENTY-NINE

Nick

"It's okay, Chip. I got this now."

At the sound of Liv's voice, Nick stopped in his tracks. He was in the process of being escorted to his vehicle by her guard dog, after an excruciatingly long evening at the Palace Saloon where they'd waited, and waited, and waited some more for her to return from her "errand." The only reason they weren't still sitting at that blasted table was because the restaurant management had run them out. It seemed they wanted to close up and go home. Chip, no doubt, planned to follow him out of town. The goon wasn't about to take the chance that he might double-back and bother Liv. He was angry and tired and so incredibly ticked off at himself for having this harebrained idea in the first place, all he wanted to do was get home, grab a beer, and put this whole nightmarish thing behind him. Bachelor life, he determined, had its merits. He'd just keep right on living his life the way he'd been living it, and try to forget he ever set his eyes on one Ms. Olivia Hale.

"You sure 'bout that, Liv?" Chip asked. Nick ground his teeth at the solicitous tone of voice.

"Yes, I'm sure. Thanks."

"Anytime. Glad to help."

He heard Chip shuffle off, but refused to turn around. He stood rigidly, shoulders taut, fists clenched. Tension radiated from his entire body like a force field. Heaven help anyone who got too close to him at that moment, they'd be vaporized. He drew a deep breath, let it out, and then continued marching to his car in long, ground-eating strides.

He heard a surprised yelp behind him and then the sound of hurried footsteps. She was soon jogging along beside him.

"I'm back," she said, a little out of breath from trying to keep up with him.

He stared straight ahead, trying to ignore her. It wasn't easy. She exuded a soft, sweet floral scent. It surrounded her like an aura. He considered breathing through his mouth so he wouldn't be able to smell it, but was afraid that might be worse; he'd *taste* it. Besides, the smell was delicious. He might as well enjoy it while he had the chance. He shortened his stride ever so slightly.

"I don't blame you for being mad at me," she continued, panting. "I would be too . . . if I were you . . . but if you'd give me . . . a chance to explain . . ." The effort to keep up with him was taking its toll. It was hard to talk and run at the same time.

Finally she stopped. "Nick Bradford. Stop walking this instant and turn and look at me!"

Her tone demanded obedience. He stopped and slowly turned around.

"Oh!" she said in surprise, and her eyes widened in wonder. "That worked better than I thought it would."

He bit the inside of his lip to keep from grinning and tried to recapture his anger from a moment before, but it was no use. How could one stay mad at a woman who was dressed up like a pink fairy?

She approached him the same way she would a wounded creature—slow and timid—as if unsure of his reaction. He watched her without speaking. Her pink wings quivered in a sudden breeze. The sequins on them glittered in the streetlight.

She stood in front of him, twisting her fingers, her head bowed in contrition. "I'd like to apologize for the way I handled things earlier. It was wrong of me to do that to you. I didn't want you to follow me, but I should've thought of a different way. In my defense, I didn't realize Chip would be quite so diligent. I thought he'd let you go after I got safely away. Anyway, I hope you can forgive me."

He let her suffer in silence for a long minute, then another. It was only fair after the way she sicced Chip on him. When she began fidgeting, he pressed his lips tightly together in an effort to keep from smiling, but gave up all pretenses of anger when he saw her peeking up at him through her lashes. "Okay, okay. You're forgiven," he said, helplessly shaking his head. "But never"—he pointed a finger at her and tried to look stern— "and I mean *never* do that again. Got it?"

She nodded once, beaming at him.

"Good. Now come on. Let's go get your bike. I'll drive you home. And on the way you can tell me about what happened while Chip was holding me prisoner."

***

When they turned onto Second Street, Nick immediately checked to make sure Liv's bike was still chained to the light pole in front of her shop. Good. It was there, but so was something else. There was a dark spot in front of the shop's door. A misplaced shadow in a place where there shouldn't be one because of the streetlight. Then, as he watched, it moved, elongating until it was the size and shape of a person.

"Hey," he shouted, breaking into a run when the shadow moved away from the building out onto the sidewalk. At the sound of his voice, it turned and fled down the street.

"What is it, Nick?" Liv shouted in alarm.

"Someone messing around in front of your shop," he yelled back. "Stay there."

Whoever it was, was pretty fast, but so was he. The runner tried to cut across the lawn of a house on the corner and he dove at them, managing a spectacular football tackle that he was sure he would regret the next day.

"Get off me, you idiot. You're crushing me," the voice shrieked. Though muffled in the grass, it sounded furious. And feminine. A woman? Uh-oh. He rolled off, panting from the chase, and waited.

Liv jogged up, just as the dark-clothed figure sprawled in the grass rolled over and sat up. He heard Liv gasp, "Raine! What on earth? Why are you dressed like a cat burglar?" Then her eyes narrowed in suspicion. "What were you doing lurking around in front of my store at this time of night?"

"Last I heard," Raine snapped, "the town's sidewalks are public property."

"That may be, but someone has been slipping anonymous notes under my door, and I'm thinking that someone might be you. Let's all go back to my shop and see if the culprit has indeed struck again."

"Why do you think I would go anywhere with you?" Raine's voice was sullen.

"Because if you don't," Liv said in a voice that was saccharine sweet, "I'll report you to the police for sending threatening messages."

Raine scoffed. "Good luck. There was nothing threatening about those—" She broke off when she realized what had just happened.

"And people think I'm just a dumb blonde." Liv winked at Nick before turning a stern look on Raine. "My shop. Now."

Raine got to her feet, looking anything but happy.

***

When Liv unlocked her door, there was, indeed, another envelope lying on the hardwood floor just like she'd suggested there might be. She gave it a long look before bending to pick it up. Without opening it, she turned to Raine. "I think it's time you and I had a little talk. Join me in my office."

Nick followed, though he hadn't been invited. He had a feeling this was going to be good.

"Who are you and don't you have someplace else you need to be?" Raine snapped.

Liv answered before he could. "This is Nick Bradford. He's a friend and he's exactly where he's supposed to be right now.

Sit," Liv ordered, pointing at the chair across from her desk as she seated herself in her own. Nick leaned against a storage shelf just inside the door. He didn't want to get in the way, but he didn't want to miss anything either. He sent Raine a smug smile that widened when he saw her jaw harden.

Raine sat down, though it was clear that she didn't want to.

Liv slid her finger under the flap and opened the newest letter and read, "She's only pretending to be your friend." She folded the paper, inserted it back into the envelope, and stared at it for a long moment. Finally, she looked up at Raine, and one of her eyebrows arched. "Another Lacey dig?" Opening her drawer, she withdrew a stack of envelopes, added the one in her hand and fanned them out across her desk like a deck of cards, then she looked up at Raine. "I'll start. I suspect, if these were dusted for fingerprints, yours would be all over them," she said, giving a pointed look at Raine's gloveless hands. "I'm sure you'd prefer not to get the police involved with this, as would I. So, I'm going to ask you some questions, and you're going to answer them. *Capeesh?*"

"Capeesh?" Raine snorted. "What are you, the Fernandina Beach mafia?"

"No," Liv snapped. If she'd had the power of laser vision, Nick firmly believed Raine would resemble crispy bacon. "I am a woman whom you've made a laughingstock, not just in front of the entire town, and not just me, either. You included Lacey in the mess because the party was in celebration of her. You humiliated us both with your anonymous recommendation."

"I didn't think you'd actually hire the guy without checking him out first," Raine said with a laugh.

Nick winced. Ooh. Was this woman an idiot or just blind? Didn't she see the death rays?

"Well, I did. I was mad at Lacey at the time and it seemed like a good way to get back at her. That was my mistake. What I want to know, though, is why you did it?" Liv's reply was much calmer than he expected. Too calm. A storm was brewing and he was afraid it would be of catastrophic proportions when it hit.

"A friend suggested it. I thought it was a good idea. I owed Lacey. She knew I was going to buy Black Pearl, so did everybody. I'd even planned a new owner party, ordered food for the menu, and invited the whole town. Can you imagine how embarrassing that was? How many times I had to explain what happened? This was fate, paying Lacey back, plain and simple. She embarrassed me; I embarrassed her. You know, the ol' what-goes-around-comes-around adage."

"Why do you hate her so much? And I'm not talking about just this. You've had a . . . a . . . *thing* against her for as long as I've known you."

"I don't *hate* her."

Liv spluttered in disbelief, unable to think of a suitable reply.

Raine shrugged. "If she were on fire and I had water, I'd probably drink it, but I don't hate her."

Liv opened her mouth to reply, shut it —twice. Finally she said in a voice that dripped sarcasm, "Well, at least you don't hate her, but let's get back to the issue, shall we? I want to know about the notes about my dad, the suggestion that Lacey knew something about him that she was keeping from me. What was the purpose of that? Other than to cause a rift between us?"

"That was it."

"What?"

"To cause a rift between you. That was for my friend too."

"Who is this 'friend' you keep mentioning?"

"Barrett."

Liv stilled. Hearing that name clearly bothered her.

Raine continued with a sly smile. "You thought he liked you, didn't you? That was a ploy. He just used you to find out stuff about Lacey. He has some sort of a beef against her. Never told me what it was, but it doesn't really matter. He knew what you guys meant to each other, that you're her maid of honor. He thought if we could break you guys apart, it would mess up the wedding. Maybe keep it from happening. Anything to hurt her."

"And you went along with it."

"Well, why should she have everything?" she snapped. "She's got Ford, she's got the restaurant, and she's got all the money she's going to get from her grandfather's paintings. Well, minus Barrett's commission, of course." She smiled like the proverbial cat who ate the cream.

Liv's brows rose. "Barrett's commission?"

"You know, for the sale of those paintings. He's the broker. And that job doesn't come cheap. He'll be getting a very nice commission when all is said and done. And he promised that he'd make it worth my while for helping him."

Liv nodded. "And just so I have this straight, Barrett was behind both the exotic dancer and the notes. But how'd he find out about my dad?"

Nicks brows rose. Wait a minute. Again with the exotic dancer? *That* was the recommendation they were talking about. Oh, he hated he'd missed that.

Raine looked slightly abashed. "Well, I might've mentioned him. You know, the way he'd disappeared. Barrett was the one who came up with the idea to frame Lacey."

Liv pressed her lips into an inflexible straight line. Nick wouldn't have thought that things as soft and full and, well, *kissable* as her lips could look so hard. Same thing with her beautiful, peaches-and-cream face. In fact, he would have bet his life savings—not that there was that much of it—that such a thing was physically impossible. But her appearance seemed suddenly chiseled out of stone. She drew a deep, deep breath, let it out slowly. When she finally spoke, her voice sounded brittle.

"It's late. I haven't had anything to eat since breakfast this morning. I've been threatened. I've been yanked down a set of stairs by a friend I thought was a man, but who turned out to be a crazy woman. By the way, I'm talking about Barrett, in case you didn't know." She paused her tirade at Raine's horrified expression. "Surprise, surprise! That's right. Barrett is a *woman* and she—not he—yanked me downstairs by my hair. Let me repeat that. I was dragged down stairs. By. My. Hair!

"I've been questioned by the police," she continued, her voice rising. "And I saw my best friend smash someone's head with a barstool. Frankly, I don't have the stomach to deal with you right now. But I do want to give you something to chew on. You think you have a whole list of reasons to hate Lacey Campbell, but allow me to let you in on a little secret. *She* is the reason you're still alive. That's right. Lacey." Nick could practically see icy sparks shooting from her eyes. "Lacey is the one who told the police where to find you that night in the cemetery. That's why they were able to get to you in time. If it weren't for her, you'd just be another name on a list of dead girls. You need to think about that. Now, if you don't mind, I'd like you to leave."

Raine looked shell-shocked. Nick watched her get up, looking dazed, and stumble through the curtain. There was the tinkling music from the wind chimes over the front door, then silence.

Liv's head drooped forward into her hands.

He approached her more cautiously than he would if he were walking across a field of land mines. As if sensing his presence, she tilted her head, peering up at him through her fingers, before sagging down again. "You know—" She paused and sighed. "I think I need to spend some quality time with Ben and Jerry. I'm convinced they're the only men to be trusted."

He bit back a smile, but didn't speak for a long moment, just stared down at her bowed head. "You're tougher than you look," he announced in an awed voice. "Remind me never to get on your bad side."

She made a sound somewhere between a laugh and a sob.

He held out his hand. "C'mon. Let's load your bike in the back of my truck. We'll stop and get some ice cream, and I'll drive you home."

CHAPTER THIRTY

Lacey

A finger of sunlight snuck through my bedroom curtains and poked me awake. I sat up so quickly it gave me a head rush. I carefully touched the back of my head, wincing as I did so. The lump was still there. What happened in the basement of the art gallery hadn't been a dream. The knot wasn't as big as it had been the previous night—which was good. It was still tender, but at least the throbbing had stopped.

I clambered out of bed, went to the window, and pulled the curtain back. The sky was a dictionary definition of it how it should look in June, brilliant and without a single cloud to interrupt its blueness. It would be perfect for that evening's rehearsal, and the next day's forecast was calling for more of the same. Beach wedding it would be! I hugged myself, smiling at the thought. We wouldn't be forced to use Plan B, after all.

First things first. I picked up my phone, dialing Liv's number. I still hadn't been able to talk to her. She hadn't answered the night before. Maybe I could get her this morning.

I sighed when the fourth ring ended and her voice mail picked up. *You've reached Olivia's mailbox. Leave a message, please.*

I hung up and quickly texted her. "Liv, where are you? Why haven't you called me back? I need to talk to you. Call as soon as you get this."

How many messages was that now? Three? Four? I frowned, worry gnawing away at my stomach, giving me a hollow feeling. My hope that everything would go smoothly seemed increasingly fragile. The wedding was the next day and my maid of honor/wedding planner was missing in action right when I needed her most. I tried to tell myself that it was just Liv being Liv. She'd always been known for being a little scatterbrained, but over the years she'd developed her own method of compensating for that. Whenever anything really important came up—like my wedding—she focused on it to the exclusion of everything else so she wouldn't get sidetracked. For her to go dark like this, right before my big day . . . well, maybe I'd been wrong. Maybe she was angrier about my interference in her relationships than I'd thought. Did I need a pinch hitter? Should I let Noelle know? Give her a warning?

No. Not yet. There was still time. Liv would come through and everything would be fine. "To quote the title of a country song," I muttered, "that's my story and I'm sticking to it."

I turned and headed to the kitchen. I needed coffee.

***

I set my mug on the wide arm of the Adirondack chair and stared out at the water. The morning light rippling across its surface made it look as if God had sprinkled gold and silver glitter all over it. The spangles made me squint. Seagrass pitched wildly in the ocean breeze. The fronds of the palmetto trees next door clattered like light sabers against the steady pound and crash of the waves and the laughter of the seagulls. As early as it was, the beach was mostly deserted, with only a handful of runners and the occasional beachcomber searching for treasures left by the previous night's high tide. My pen sat poised against a pad of paper in my lap. I was making a checklist of all the things I needed to get done that day.

I'd be on my own. Ford had gone to the station early. In addition to any last-minute groom stuff he needed to get done, there were all the things at work that had to be done so that hopefully everything would run like clockwork in his absence.

My mind drifted back to the conversation we'd had following his disturbing interview with Delilah at the hospital. I finally knew why there'd been three canvases set up in the basement studio. Delilah had been in the process of copying *Amelia Sky* the same way she had *Delilah's Lilies*; making two copies to sell, keeping the original.

Mystery solved. And after the authorities finished their investigation, I would finally get my favorite painting back. Best of all, there wouldn't be any more nightmares. At least for a while. I hoped.

I had no trouble visualizing the crazed look Ford described Delilah having at the end when her final tie to sanity snapped. I'd seen more than enough of that look while trapped in the gallery's basement with her. The whole thing left me feeling conflicted. While I was glad she was locked up, I couldn't help feeling sorry for her. She'd loved Granddad. There was nothing wrong with that other than incredibly bad timing. No, the wrong came later, when she met my dad. He was married, and she knew it. She'd wanted him to leave Mama, to choose *her* instead. That was hard to swallow. But then she'd been in the accident and lost her baby, the half-brother I never knew. I couldn't imagine the anguish she went through after that. No wonder she hated me. I represented everything she lost. Every time she looked at me it must've been like throwing another log on the fire of hate in her heart.

I didn't know how to feel. While I was thankful so many of my questions now had answers, my emotions were a mess. A kaleidoscope spinning one way and a merry-go-round spinning the other and I was stuck in the middle.

I tried to turn my attention back to the task at hand. Black Pearl would be closed the next night since everyone associated with the restaurant would be at the wedding. Also, it would be all decorated for the reception we'd have there afterward. But, that evening it would be open despite the fact that neither Noelle nor I would be there. My sous-chef, Mia, and the rest of the crew would be running the kitchen, which was why we'd booked a room at St. Elmo's for the rehearsal dinner that night. Yes, St. Elmo's was where the great bachelorette party debacle had occurred, and the thought of showing my face there again after that fiasco made me a little queasy, but it wasn't like the whole town would be there this time. Our group was small, so I thought it would be okay. I didn't want to risk overloading Mia. She was good and I trusted her, but this was her first time solo. I didn't want to press my luck.

I still needed to run by Jeb's to place my order for that night's menu. Noelle was going to meet me there so I could introduce the two of them, and I was a little nervous about that. I worked well with Jeb, but I knew his looks as well as his manner could be a little off-putting with some people. I hoped he would be on his best behavior that morning. I wanted Noelle to hit it off with him, for him to make a good impression on her. They would need to get along since they would be working together for the week Ford and I would be gone on our honeymoon.

Our honeymoon. The words brought a thrill of excitement. We'd be flying to Maine, staying in a sweet little cottage in Camden—population 4,823. It was a small harbor town dubbed "the jewel of the coast," according to its website. It was located on Penobscot Bay "where the mountains reach down to the sea." Neither of us had ever been to New England before, and we were looking forward to trying out the restaurants and exploring the shops and sights of several nearby towns together. I could hardly wait, and *not* just for the sightseeing, either. Our flight didn't leave until the morning following the wedding, so we'd be spending our wedding night at the beach house. I'd been so worried about the money situation—the possibility of having to share my granddad's fortune with a half-brother—I hadn't felt we could afford paying for someplace else. Now that that was no longer a worry, it was too late. Every place I called was booked.

No time to dwell on that, I thought, scribbling "florist" and "bakery" on my to-do list. I needed to run by both of them one last time to ensure there'd be no surprises the next day. "Decorations" came next, not that there were a lot of them; white folding chairs, lanterns to hang from tall hooks pushed into the sand, a rustic arbor wrapped in twinkly lights for the pastor, Ford, and me to stand under. That's all. I wanted it simple.

My dress was simple too. I'd chosen an A-line in cream-colored silk with layers of airy chiffon that belled out at my waist. It reached just to my ankles with no train. Hopefully that would keep me from tripping in the sand. The only ornamentation it had was tiny seed pearls and crystal beads trimming the deep V-neck and spaghetti straps. My flowers were peach-colored roses—to coordinate with the coral color of the bridesmaids' dresses—and gardenias. I quickly added "Tricia" to the list. She'd offered to come out to my house to do my hair rather than me having to go into town the next day. I needed to double-check on that. I wasn't wearing a veil and planned to wear my hair up, with peach rosebuds and baby's breath woven in like a crown. My mother's string of pearls and her blue sapphire combs would be the final touch.

Mama. My eyes misted at the thought, and a wave of longing for her presence washed over me. Oh, how I missed her! I never imagined my wedding without Mama being there. I knew she'd be watching from Heaven, but she wouldn't be there in person, and that made me sad. "I love you, Mama," I whispered aloud. "And I'll be proud to wear your pearls and combs—symbols of your love for me."

Thinking of those combs brought a sigh. Liv was the one who suggested I wear them and I was counting on her to be there to put them in place. My heart gave a little squeeze at the thought that not only would my mother not be there, but my best friend might not share my most important day, either. She still hadn't called.

"She will." I spoke the words out loud as I grabbed my keys and headed for the door. "I know she'll be there." But without meaning to, my voice had gone up at the end of the sentence, making it sound not so much like a statement as a question.

***

"Thanks, Jo. The cake looks fabulous. See you tomorrow."
I stopped at the door before exiting Meaux Jeaux's, pressing
my list against the window so I could draw a line through the
word "bakery" before leaving. I sighed with relief. This had
been the second attempt at producing my wedding cake. Jo
hadn't meant to tell me about it, but had let it slip, now that
she was sure everything was under control. Apparently the new
assistant had flubbed the first one, producing another one of
her "duds." Jo had taken over, donning her superhero apron
and producing spectacular results. The cake looked perfect and
would be delivered to Black Pearl the next day right before the
wedding. Everything was right on schedule, no thanks to the
assistant. Being in the food industry myself, I didn't like to be
too hard on others in that field, but this girl probably ought to
think about finding another line of work. She didn't seem to be
a good fit for a bakery.

I folded my list, pushed it back into my purse, reached for
the door handle, and looked up. There, on the other side of the
glass, was Raine on her way in.

I gave a loud groan, which caused a couple seated at a
tiny table near the door to glance at me in surprise. "Great," I
muttered. "Sorry about that." I tossed my apology to the startled
couple, then pulled the door open and held it for my nemesis.
"C'mon in," I called, trying to be polite. "I was just leaving."

She stayed where she was. "I thought I might find you
here," she said.

Oh boy, I thought. Here we go. "You mean you were
looking for me?" I asked, stepping out onto the sidewalk.

She nodded once. "We need to talk."

"Ohh-kay," I replied, more than a little puzzled. What could
she possibly need to talk to me about? "But can we walk while
we talk? I'm on my way to check on the flowers for tomorrow."

Without a word, she fell into step beside me.

She didn't say anything for almost a block, which was
unusual in itself. Raine always had plenty to say. Most of the
time it wasn't something I wanted to hear, but that wasn't the

point. She said she wanted to talk to me, but she wasn't. I didn't know whether I should try to break the ice or leave it alone. I decided on the latter, opting for an imaginary conversation with her instead.

Imaginary Raine: Well, tomorrow is the big day. Are you ready?

Me: I think so. Just have a few last-minute things to do.

Raine: Need any help with anything? (I said it was imaginary, right?)

Me: Oh, how sweet. Thank you for asking, but no, I think I've got it covered.

Raine: Well, if you change your mind, the offer stands.

Me: Thanks! You're a peach.

Raine: And I wish nothing but the best to you and Ford. You guys deserve it.

(I know. Even for make-believe, that's a little over-the-top.)

Before I could come up with my perfect fantasy reply, she finally spoke. "Liv told me what you did."

"Liv?" The mention of my best friend's name jerked me back to reality. "You talked to her? When?"

"Last night."

"Last night?" My heart sank at the words. Liv wouldn't return my call, but she talked to Raine? "So what, pray tell, did I do?" The words came out sharper than I intended, but I was upset.

"Saved my life."

What? I came to a dead stop in the middle of the sidewalk, turned, and faced her, dumbfounded. Who was this girl? Raine certainly never looked like this. Was that gratefulness I saw in her expression? A hint of *humility*? Seeing those two emotions, so utterly foreign where Raine was concerned, seemed to short-circuit the connection from my brain to my mouth. I was speechless.

"I didn't want to believe it at first," she continued, looking down at the sidewalk. "But I went down to the police station to fact-check. They backed her up. They said you're the only reason they got there in time. They wouldn't tell me how, but I'm assuming it was one of your dreams." She gave a short laugh and shook her head. "When I think about all the grief I've given you about that through the years, the irony of it isn't lost on me." She pressed her lips together, then finally looked up. "So, three things. One, I want to apologize for all the crap I've put you through. Two, I want to thank you for what you did, *however* you did it. And three, I know you and Ford don't fly out until Sunday morning, so I'd like to gift you guys my best room at Fairbanks House for your wedding night."

I closed my mouth once I realized it was hanging open. I had no idea how long it had been like that, but I imagined it had been a while. "I . . . I . . ." I tried to shake off my surprise and gave it another try. "I'm sorry, I don't know what to say, except one—" I mimicked the way she counted off, holding up a finger for each point—"I forgive you. Two, you're welcome, and three" —I felt a huge smile spread across my face because this was even better than my imaginary conversation—"that would be wonderful. Thank you!"

A real smile touched her lips. "Good. I'm not sure we'll ever really be friends, but I think now we won't be enemies." Then she held out her right hand and I took it, gave it an enthusiastic shake, then impulsively leaned forward and hugged her.

"See you tomorrow at the wedding?" I asked.

It was Raine's turn to be stunned. I reached forward, placing a finger under her chin and pushing up. "Careful," I warned with a grin. "Don't want anything to fly in. So? Will I see you there?"

"I wouldn't miss it for the world."

They were the same words she'd spoken at my bachelorette party, but this time they made me smile.

***

The rest of the day was a whirlwind of activity. Ford had told me not to worry, that Liv would show up, but I hadn't told him

I'd stopped by Par-a-dux hoping to catch her, and she hadn't been there. Nor had I told him that I'd stopped by her house, and though her bicycle was chained to the fence like normal, she hadn't been there either. No one I asked had seen or talked to her, and I tried calling her again. In fact, I called several more times, but it always went to her voice mail. It was as if she'd disappeared.

Now, it was almost five o'clock, the time we'd set for the rehearsal, and I was well past the stage of worrying whether Liv would be my maid of honor. I was afraid I'd see something about her on the evening news. The only thing that kept me from falling completely apart was the fact that I hadn't had a dream about her the previous night.

Noelle didn't know yet. I kept hoping for a miracle, but it looked like I was going to have to tell her. Maybe Ford's best man, Jonas, whom I'd yet to meet, could convince his wife to be my other bridesmaid. Ford had told me that Cleo was four months pregnant—barely showing, past morning sickness, and not to the uncomfortable stage yet. Maybe she'd step in.

I stepped out on the porch and looked out toward the beach. Ford was already out there, talking to Pastor Brooks. Sergeant Craig had just arrived. I could see his distinctive bald, pink head bobbing along above the sea grass as he made his way out to our designated spot. Three others were just starting down the path—Noelle and a couple I'd never seen. That must be Ford's best man, Jonas, and his wife, Cleo. A safe assumption, since they looked exactly like Ford had described them. I saw no sign of Liv's blonde curls, though, and felt tears sting my eyes.

She wasn't coming. I couldn't believe it. My best friend wasn't coming to my wedding. We'd met in kindergarten and had been closest friends ever since. How could I get married without her here? We'd pinky promised! In my mind's eye, I could still see the two skinny little girls we'd been, standing out there at the edge of the water, facing each other, our hands linked by our hooked little fingers while froth-edged wavelets tickled our ankles. I could still feel the wind whipping my hair around my head—see the way it tousled hers. The words we'd said came back like it was yesterday.

I solemnly swear I'll be there.

By your side when you become a bride.

Always in my heart. Even when we're apart.

Best friends forever.

Then we'd sealed it by pressing our thumbs together while our pinkies were still linked. In some countries this was just as binding as a signed and notarized contract. Pinky promise. I'd looked it up once. The custom had been around at least since the 1840s, originating in Japan, I think. A place where they were dead serious about such things. If I remember correctly, they cut off the pinky of any promiser who went back on their word. Though I had no desire to take things that far, I meant it when I made that promise years before. I *still* meant it. I thought Liv had too, but she wasn't here.

Ford turned toward the house, shielding his eyes against the sun hanging low in the western sky. I saw a flash of a smile, heard him shout, then he waved his arm to get my attention. I waved back with as much enthusiasm as I could muster. It was time. I needed to join the others on the beach.

"Lacey, how many times have I told you to keep your front door locked?"

I gasped, whirling to face the person I most wanted to see. My hand went to my mouth and tears filled my eyes. In an instant, we were holding each other in a bone-crushing bear hug. "I was afraid you weren't going to come," I wailed.

"Don't be silly. I had to be here. I'm your maid of honor. Not to mention I'm the one responsible for putting those combs in your wedding hair tomorrow. Where else would I be?"

"That's exactly what I'd like to know," I replied, stepping back and wiping my eyes. The relief of seeing her there, safe and sound, allowed all the worry from a moment before to suddenly morph into anger. "Where have you been?" I demanded. "And why didn't you return my calls or texts?"

Before she could answer, I caught movement out of the corner of my eye. Turning my head, I saw a tall, dark-haired, exceptionally handsome young man hovering in the doorway. My eyebrows shot up. "Oh, I see, now. You've been off gallivanting around with a guy while I've been sitting here worried sick."

Liv ignored my temper, smiled, and held her hand out to the man. He hurried over to join her. "Lacey, I'd like you to meet Nick Bradford. Nick is the mystery man from your mom's funeral."

"Nice to meet you, Nick," I replied in staccato syllables, giving him a curt nod before turning my attention back to Liv. "If you think that bringing a gorgeous man home with you will make all this be okay, then think again, sister. I was worried about you. I was afraid I was going to dream about seeing your body show up somewhere."

Nick looked startled and opened his mouth to ask Liv a question. She gave him a quick shake of her head. "Not now, sweetie. I'll tell you about that later." Then to me, "If you'll let me explain, we can get out there to your rehearsal. Ford's probably wondering if you changed your mind."

I crossed my arms, stony-faced. "I'm waiting."

"Nick's good with computers. He's a librarian. He knows how to look things up. So, when I told him about my father's disappearance, he offered to do a search." She sent him an adoring glance, before looking back at me. Her eyes suddenly filled with tears. "He found him, Lacey. He found my dad. I got to *talk* to Dad. We drove down to St. Augustine to see him."

My anger evaporated. "St. Augustine? I thought you said your mother hired a private investigator and that he'd searched for months and couldn't find him. St. Augustine isn't that far away. How could he not find him?"

"Mother lied to me," she answered, her blue eyes flashing fire. "Not only that, she gave me other false information. Remember? Right after that detective gave her his report, I asked for Daddy's social security number? I wanted to do my own search. I don't know, maybe subconsciously, I didn't trust her. But I found out she gave me the wrong number. I've kept that number in my wallet ever since Mother gave it to me. I think it's because it helped me feel close to him. I showed it to Dad. It wasn't like it was just one digit off. The whole number was different. It wasn't even *close*."

"Why would she do that?"

"She ordered him to leave and threatened to have him arrested if he tried to have anything to do with me."

"Arrested? What are you talking about?"

"Daddy got addicted to prescription pain medication. He was in a minor car accident that I didn't even remember him having, but it messed up his back. Mom caught him using her prescription pad. He was writing his own prescriptions and forging her name. He's clean now. He attends a support group and started going to a chiropractor who was able to get his back straightened out so he's not in constant pain. But even after all that, Mother wouldn't change her mind."

"And he's been in St. Augustine all this time?"

She nodded. "He's snuck back several times. He told me he would sit in the parking lot at school and watch me on the playground."

"I understand the sentiment, but that sounds a little creepy. I'm surprised someone didn't call the police."

"Yeah, me too," she laughed. "But Lacey, he was so happy to see me, and now that I know where he is, we're going to stay in touch." Her jaw hardened. "Whether Mother likes it or not. He might not be able to come here—Mother might carry through with her threat if he did—but I can go there to visit him."

"Good for you. I'm happy you found him." I glanced up at Nick. "Thank you."

"Hey, you guys." Ford stuck his head through the doorway. "We're missin' a couple of key figures at this rehearsal gig out here. You wanna come join us?"

"Coming, sweetheart," I replied with a thousand-kilowatt smile, then linked my arm through Liv's. Nick hurried to catch up with Ford. I watched them shake hands and saunter down the trail to the beach. I squeezed her arm. "So, I take it this means you're still going to be my maid of honor?"

"Yes," she whispered, her face glowing with a happiness I hadn't seen before as her eyes followed the dark-haired man in front of us. "If you'll be mine."

THE END

From the Recipe File of Black Pearl Bistro:

PRAWN PASTA WITH BISQUE SAUCE

1 onion, roughly chopped
1 large carrot, roughly chopped
1 stick of celery, roughly chopped
45 ml olive oil plus another 30 ml to fry the prawns
3 cloves garlic, sliced
12 large prawns
100 ml cream
salt to taste
chopped parsley for garnish
100 to 150 grams fresh pasta per person

- In a large pan, heat the olive oil and add the onion, carrot, and celery. Cook until the onions are translucent, around 5 minutes, then add the garlic cloves. Season with salt.

- Peel and devein the prawns. Chop the meat into large pieces and set aside for use later. Place the prawn heads and peel with the vegetables and sauté for around 5 more minutes. Add 750 ml of water and allow to simmer until the liquid halves, around 50 minutes to 1 hour.

- When the sauce has reduced, strain the sauce and add the cream, continue to simmer until the sauce thickens. Taste and season as required.

- Heat the 30 ml of oil in another pan and fry the prawns until cooked, around 3 minutes. Add this to the bisque/cream sauce.

- Meanwhile, heat a large pot of water until boiling. Salt the water once it reaches a boil and add the fresh pasta. Cook until al dente. Drain the pasta and add to the bisque sauce.

- Place in serving bowls and sprinkle with parsley.

CHEESY PARMESAN SHRIMP AND GRITS
Grits:
1 cup quick grits
½ tsp salt and ¼ tsp black pepper
2 T butter
2 T heavy cream (optional)
1 cup grated Parmesan cheese

Shrimp and Sauce:
4 T unsalted butter
1 ¼ lb extra-large shrimp (peeled, deveined with the tails removed)
2 cloves garlic, minced
pinch cayenne pepper
¼ cup fresh lemon juice
2 T fresh parsley, chopped

- Bring 5 cups of water to boil over high heat. Once the water is boiling, whisk in 1 cup of grits, ½ tsp salt, and ¼ tsp pepper. Reduce heat to low and continue cooking, whisking frequently to prevent lumps. Cook for about 5-7 minutes. Stir in 2 T butter and 2 T cream and mix well. Add the Parmesan cheese and mix well again. Remove from heat and cover to keep warm.

- Season the shrimp with salt and pepper. Add 4 T of butter to a large skillet. Add the minced garlic, shrimp, and cayenne pepper, and cook, stirring frequently until the shrimp are pink, about 3-4 minutes. Add chopped parsley, lemon juice, and 4 T water and mix well to coat the shrimp.

- Divide the grits into four bowls and top with the shrimp mixture. Sprinkle with extra parsley if desired.

SOUTH CAROLINA SHE-CRAB SOUP

5 T butter
1 small white onion, grated
1 stalk celery, grated
2 cloves garlic, minced
salt and pepper to taste
2 quarts half-and-half cream
1 pint heavy cream
2 cups chicken broth
1 tsp hot pepper sauce
2 tsp Worcestershire sauce
1 lb lump crabmeat
2 T chopped fresh chives
½ cup sherry wine

- Melt butter in a large stockpot over medium heat. Stir in flour to make a smooth paste and cook for about 3 minutes, stirring constantly. Mix in the onion, celery, and garlic; season with salt and pepper. Continue to cook and stir for about 4 minutes.

- Gradually whisk in the half-and-half cream so that no lumps form. Stir in the chicken broth and heavy cream. Bring to a simmer, and pour in half of the sherry. Season with Worcestershire sauce, and hot sauce. Cover and simmer for about 30 minutes, until soup has reduced by 1/3. Add crabmeat and simmer for another 10 minutes.

- Ladle soup into bowls and top off with a splash of the remaining sherry and a sprinkle of chives.

Dear Readers,

I must be honest. I never intended to write this novel. In my mind, *Hush* (Book One in this series) was supposed to be a stand-alone story. But my publisher encouraged me to consider writing a sequel to it, and that started me thinking about Lacey's granddad's paintings, flirting with the idea of forgery, something I knew little to nothing about. Since I needed to know about it before I could write about it, I started digging. That's my favorite part about writing a book—the research part. I consider it a sort of continuing education experience without having to pay for college credit.

One of the first things I had to do was find the perfect artist to pattern JD Campbell after. I'm a very visual person, so I needed to be able to see the work while writing. The minute I saw my first Erin Hanson painting, I knew I'd found exactly what I was looking for. Her *Lilies on the Lake* (https://www. erinhanson.com/p/lilies_on_the_lake) was the inspiration for *Delilah's Lilies*, Lacey's granddad's missing painting in the book. I absolutely love her open impressionism style.

The next thing I learned was how much I needed to learn about forgeries. The process of both creating forgeries and catching forgers is a lot more involved than I ever realized. Doing the research is what really spawned this story. I hope you enjoy the results.

But now my brain is bursting with ideas for Lacey and Ford and their friends, and Book Three is already in the works. Stay tuned for more Amelia Island adventures.

Blessings,
Leanna